IT DIDN
TO ROUS

Slowly, he pulled Abby to him, and for a time they lay tasting the night sweetness of their lips, languidly enjoying the sensations, purring together like contented felines.

"But we can't do this every night."

"Why not? The kids are asleep..."

Abby sighed. "I was thinking about work. I'll be exhausted."

"I'll bet you're thinking about your bank account right now, aren't you?"

"What if I am? Money...or let's call it security...means a great deal to me."

"No kidding." Ty's voice was sarcastic and scratchy.

Oh no, thought Abby. *Here we go again.*

"If I had—" Abby paused "—if I had enough security, I wouldn't feel so afraid, and then you and I could—"

Ty swung his legs over the side of the bed and came to his feet. "You know," he said, while pulling up his trousers with hurried, irate jerks, "all that glitters, Abigail McAlister, is not your damned gold!"

ABOUT THE AUTHOR

Regular Harlequin readers will need no introduction to Lynn Erickson. The team of Carla Peltonen and Molly Swanton are mainstays of the Superromance line, and *Fool's Gold* marks their eighth collaboration on a Superromance. Fans of their wonderfully evocative settings will be pleased to learn that Molly and Carla have designs on Sante Fe, New Mexico, and Cozumel, Mexico, as possible locales in upcoming stories.

Books by Lynn Erickson

HARLEQUIN SUPERROMANCE

132–SNOWBIRD
157–THE FACES OF DAWN
184–A CHANCE WORTH TAKING
199–STORMSWEPT
231–A DANGEROUS SENTIMENT
255–TANGLED DREAMS
276–A PERFECT GEM

HARLEQUIN INTRIGUE

42–ARENA OF FEAR

Lynn Erickson

FOOL'S GOLD

Harlequin Books

TORONTO • NEW YORK • LONDON
AMSTERDAM • PARIS • SYDNEY • HAMBURG
STOCKHOLM • ATHENS • TOKYO • MILAN

Published March 1988

First printing January 1988

ISBN 0-373-70298-1

Printed in U.S.A.

This book is dedicated to Bea Hoverstock,
whose grandmother lived in Cripple Creek,
and who gave me the story of Mike Mann,
which is in essence true;
to the miner Don Grimme,
who answered dozens of questions;
to Sheriff John, who answered dozens more;
and to Stephan Albouey, a miner himself.

Goin' up to Cripple Creek,
Goin' on the run.
Goin' up to Cripple Creek
To have a little fun.

Old Anonymous Jingle

CHAPTER ONE

"YOU MANIAC!" cried Abigail McAlister, staring furiously after the motorcyclist who had almost run her down. For goodness sake, she'd been practically waving her yellow sign in the driver's face. "The sign says slow," she muttered into the dust cloud left by the souped-up Honda and its inconsiderate driver. "Can't you read?"

It was a warm day in Newark, New Jersey, one of those unseasonably muggy April days. Abby adjusted her hard hat, wiping at the dampness under the forehead band. At least she had seen the last of the raw cold days of winter that made her job as a flag girl miserable: cold feet, cold hands, dripping nose.

Abby wondered sometimes just what she looked like standing there in the cold or rain. Bundled up, she knew she appeared chubby. She needed to lose ten pounds. Eating was one of her stress relievers and she couldn't seem to stop. She hadn't always bulged in the middle so much; it was only since her husband, Steve, had left. Once she had only carried one hundred and twenty pounds on her five-foot-five-inch frame, and Steve had thought she was so pretty. He'd admired her dark, wavy hair and especially her eyes, which were an unusual golden brown.

These days, however, Abby pulled her pretty hair back in a lank ponytail, wore loose tops over too-tight pants and tried not to fret about what she looked like or the fact that her makeup was always hastily put on.

The cold weather had fled for the time being. The salt-marsh flats of New Jersey were turning from monotone gray-brown to pale green. But with her job, Abby barely noticed the scenery. She heard the crackle of her radio and pressed the button. It was her supervisor, telling her to stop traffic until the convoy from the opposite direction went by. She could practically do the job without thinking by now—her mind, as if set in free-fall, could be otherwise occupied with imagining, wondering, hoping, planning. And worrying, too often worrying.

The flag-girl job for Elam Paving paid surprisingly well. The hours were good, too, from seven to three, so that she could make it home by the time her twin boys, Sean and Benny, got off the school bus at the corner of their street. First grade. Her baby boys were already in first grade. She could hardly believe it, just as she could hardly believe she was thirty-one years old. Why, Benny and Sean read road signs to her now when they drove to the supermarket.

"Utica Street," Sean would say.

"Fifty-seven Avenue," Benny chimed in. "Nonny's Furs."

"Stop!" yelled Sean at the corner. "Furnel Home."

"What's a furnel home, Mommy?"

"*Funeral* home, honey," Abby would correct, smothering a laugh.

A long line of cars and trucks swept past Abby in the far lane. She hardly smelled the gas fumes; automatically, she pulled a bandanna up over her nose to keep out the dust. She shifted her feet and let her arm drop for a minute—the yellow stop-slow sign was darned heavy. Her radio crackled again. While she tried to listen to it, the driver of the first vehicle in line, a battered pickup truck, leaned out of his window and hollered belligerently to her, "How long ya keepin' us here, lady?"

"Fifteen minutes," she called back.

"Great!" he growled, disgruntled.

You want a new highway? Abby almost snapped back at him. *Then you wait fifteen minutes!* Abby's head was always filled with retorts and answers, explanations and clever repartees. Most of them were either R-rated or too smart-alecky to ever speak out loud. She often wondered if other people manufactured mental conversations as she did. What fun it would be to compare notes with someone whose head was filled with irreverent remarks like hers!

Steve's head had never buzzed with commentary, Abby knew that for certain. She had been married to Steve for eight years, and until their recent divorce, she had tried to tell him about the funny things that came into her mind at odd times, but he really hadn't been interested.

Steve McAlister. Abby turned her sign from "stop" to "slow" and absently waved the line of cars on. He certainly had been handsome when they'd met at N.Y.U. Young and intense and so full of himself that Abby had been swept off her feet. She'd loved him through the early years. She'd had faith in his endless get-rich-quick schemes. She'd borne him the twins, a fact that had made him prouder than punch and adoring—for a while.

A year ago Steve had left. Abby had known it was coming and had felt almost relieved as she had watched him move out. Oh, she'd been miserable and scared.

Terrified, to tell the truth. But when it came right down to it, Steve had not contributed very much to the family larder as one after another of his schemes fell through—due to someone else's fault, of course. Abby had always worked a few nights a week at the Newark Holiday Inn, so she had just asked for more time there, got her flag-girl job with Elam and made do.

Her radio crackled. She answered automatically, still waving people on. It was nearly three. Patty would relieve her then and she could get one of the lead vehicles to give her a ride back to her old Dodge station wagon. She hoped the traffic wouldn't be bad that afternoon and Patty would be on time.

Abby's biggest problem was time—no time to herself, no time to relax, no time with her kids. She hated to see them grow up without their father. Would it harm them? Would they be well-adjusted adults? She read all the opinions on how destructive divorce was to children and she worried about her boys a lot.

She often felt at the end of her tether, stressed out, working too hard and getting nowhere. Spinning her wheels. She kept telling herself that things would turn out all right, that she'd manage, that her life would become easier one day. Then she'd count her blessings: her boys, her health, determination and intelligence, her house.

Thank goodness she had the house. Her parents had helped Steve and her substantially with the down payment, and the mortgage was very small. Steve had signed it over to her when he left. It had been generous of him, but then meanness had never been one of his traits. Steve, in fact, had been overgenerous with his time, his money and himself. With his body, that was, anyway.

Patty arrived in one of the foremen's pickup trucks. "Hi, how's it going?"

Abby handed her the sign and the radio, pulled off her hard hat and wiped her forehead with the back of her wrist. "The usual. You know." Picking up her thermos and lunch box, she climbed into the truck that had delivered her replacement, and then leaned out the window. "Watch the motorcycles, Patty!" she called as her driver spun his tires on the gravel and took off for the mobile office.

Abby punched out, walked to where her dusty green car was parked and slid in. She kept glancing at her wristwatch as she drove through the traffic. Would she make it home before the boys? They had instructions to go to Mrs. Howell's if she wasn't home, but even sweet, patient Mrs. Howell could have enough of two six-year-old demons. Darling, precious, smart boys, but demons nevertheless, whose favorite stunt was to trade clothes in secret so that even Abby confused them at first glance.

Sometimes she wished desperately that their father was around to discipline them. Maybe she'd spoiled the twins dreadfully, ruined them forever. But Steve was not even living in Newark anymore. The only link Abby had to him was a post office box number in California, where he'd gone to start a new business of some sort.

"I promise I'll send you two hundred dollars a month for the boys," he'd said in his intense, utterly sincere way. But the money had never been forthcoming and Abby had finally given up writing to the box number. There had been one Christmas card from Steve, and then nothing.

She turned the corner to her street a little too quickly and an empty soda-pop can tumbled across the floor to wedge under the gas pedal of the car. Reaching down to push it away, Abby reminded herself to clean the car out. But *when*? When on earth would she have time?

The school bus was stopping at the other end of the street. Good, she'd made it. She hated the boys to come home to an empty house. Abby herself had never once had to do so, not even in high school. Things were different nowadays, it seemed. Of course, Sean and Benny didn't complain. They were happy-go-lucky, as they'd always been, seemingly untouched by their parents' bizarre behavior. But Abby wondered. Maybe they were subconsciously suffering, and problems would appear when they were older, hidden scars left by their father's desertion. She'd read about those sorts of things. And she worried.

"Hi, Mom!" yelled Benny, running up to her car. "Mrs. Bluestein gave me a gold star today!"

"Wonderful. Did you read your story extra specially well?"

"I sat still during story time!" he announced proudly.

He'd gotten a gold star for sitting still. Holy cow! Poor Mrs. Bluestein. "That's great, Ben."

"I sat in the corner," said Sean defiantly.

"Oh, dear. Why?"

"I *wanted* to," he replied decisively. Sean's dark brows were drawn together angrily. The expression was Steve's, but the face was very much a mirror of Abby's.

The boys gobbled chocolate-chip cookies and orange juice, then ran out to play down the street. Shouldn't she do something with them, spend some "quality" time with her boys? But wouldn't they much rather go outside on this warm spring day and play with their friends? Guilty relief settled on Abby's tired shoulders.

She took a long hot shower and shaved her legs. She might wear a skirt to work tonight since it was so warm. She had a denim skirt with an elastic waist that would still fit. Denny would, no doubt, make a remark. He pursued her relentlessly, four nights a week, while she was bent over the adding machine or entering figures into the computer.

Denny was the night auditor at the Holiday Inn, ruler of his small domain, a short, dapper man with crooked teeth, a benign smile and lovely long eyelashes. He'd asked her out on an average of once a night for a year now, seemingly undeterred by Abby's repeated refusals. It was kind of flattering, she admitted to herself, but the last thing in the world Abby was interested in was a man. There was absolutely no room in her life for a man, not even a dusty corner.

Abby turned the shower off and toweled her hair dry, avoiding her reflection in the steamed-up mirror. She really wanted to crawl into her bed and take a nap or read a book. But there was dinner to fix, laundry to do and some bills to pay. Then work until eleven-thirty, to bed and up at six, work at seven. An endless round that went nowhere. She asked herself often when her life would change, *if* it would change, *how* it would change. Oh, boy, if there was a way out, she was going to grab it!

"Mommy!" she heard through the bedroom door. "Benny hit me!"

"He took my ball! It wasn't his turn!"

Abby sighed. How serious was this altercation? If it was serious she'd have to mediate; if not she could ignore and change the subject. She put on her terry-cloth bathrobe and opened the door, smiling brightly. "Chicken or hamburgers tonight?" she asked.

"He *hit* me," Sean repeated, glowering.

It was serious.

Mrs. Howell arrived promptly at seven-thirty, as usual, with the half-finished afghan she had been crocheting for a year. "How are my boys?" she asked pertly.

"In the bath. Make sure they don't eat any of the chocolate ice cream, Mrs. Howell. They get hyper and won't sleep."

"We'll be fine." Mrs. Howell always said that. Then she went ahead and stuffed the boys with ice cream. Oh, well, they loved her. And Mrs. Howell was a blessing. A widow, she lived right next door, and appreciated some extra money. She forgot to remind the twins to brush their teeth and flush toilets, but she was trustworthy and always available. Once in a while Sean and Benny even did what she asked them to.

Abby yawned as she waited at a stoplight. Her skirt was tight and her hair was pinned back unflatteringly with clips. She'd love to get a perm and a manicure and a pedicure, she thought. She'd love to have time to do a little shopping. A new dress, maybe. Oh, well, one of these days she would.

Abby's mother always laughed when Abby said, "One of these days." The day never came, as her mother pointed out only too often.

"You need a vacation. We'll take the kids," her mother had offered time after time.

"One of these days I will."

But now her mother and father were moving to Tampa, Florida, because her dad was finally retiring, and there went the free baby-sitter. Her folks had been wonderful during the awful mess with Steve—supportive, accepting, loving. And now they were leaving her, abandoning her. They had every right in the world to their long-awaited retirement, but it made Abby sad. And the boys would miss their grandparents; Abby's father was the only man they had to relate to.

Her parents had asked her to join them in Florida. But the employment opportunities in Tampa didn't impress Abby. She couldn't go for long without two lucrative jobs or she'd lose everything. And then what would happen to her boys? Who would feed them and clothe them and keep them in Babe Ruth baseball mitts? Who would put them through college?

By the time she paid Mrs. Howell that night and dropped into bed, her eyes burned with fatigue. Denny had cornered her in the office and asked her to his nephew's bar mitzvah. She had declined politely. It wasn't that she disliked Denny or even bar mitzvahs, it was just that there was no time. Nor, she admitted to herself, had she anything to wear that wasn't too tight.

The next night Abby attended her group therapy session at the neighborhood community center. She needed it. The weekly meeting cost only ten dollars and was run by a lovely lady psychologist named Joann. Abby blurted out her worries to the group. They had, of course, heard them all before.

"And now even my parents are moving away. Everyone's leaving me. And I don't know how to get Denny to stop asking me out!"

"Now, Abby," said Joann, "you do realize that you're being irrational. Your parents are moving away physically, not emotionally."

"I know, but..."

Then one of the others in the group started in on her unfulfilling sex life and Abby's brain clicked into overdrive: *Sex life! I don't even have an unsatisfactory sex life. I hardly remember what sex is!*

When the woman was finished, Abby held up her hand. "I'm sorry to interrupt, Joann, but I really need to scream tonight."

"Well, group, what do you say? Shall we all join in?"

"I could use a good holler," put in a burly man.

The group agreed to scream. It was a great way to release tension. Joann had set up the rules and they stuck by them: permission had to be granted, no one could scream alone, words could not be articulated. The participants all drew in deep breaths of air and then the room filled with howling, inarticulate, ragged sounds. Some people screamed with closed eyes or waving arms, some with heads buried in hands, some in a falsetto, some in a deep bass. Voices cracked and shrieked and roared. Then, seemingly in unison, the noise stopped.

"That was wonderful, group." Joann beamed at them. "You're all getting better, much more unrestrained. Now, how do you feel?" She turned to Abby. "You first, Abby."

"Better. My throat hurts."

"Of course it does! You screamed beautifully. Your throat will be fine tomorrow and your tension will be reduced for days. What a good idea that was, Abby."

"Thank you, Joann." And she *did* feel better. Things didn't look so bad. Her body felt light and loose and relaxed. A good scream could do it every time.

Saturday was Abby's one free day, if one could call grocery shopping, housecleaning and running errands "free." She left her chores that particular Saturday morning, though, because she'd promised her mother to help with their garage sale. It was a cool, sunny day, perfect for the sale, but the boys didn't want to wear their windbreakers. Abby finally got them into the car with the jackets tied around their waists.

Her parents, Ed and Lily Walton, were trying to get rid of an attic, a basement and a garage full of accumulated treasures. Ed called the stuff junk, but Lily had trouble parting with so much as a pair of faded old curtains. She even had Abby's senior prom dress packed away somewhere.

The Walton house was a comfortable bungalow with a deep front porch, a walk along the side to the kitchen door and a narrow driveway leading to the garage. The yard was already crowded and Lily was taking money from people as fast as she could stuff it into her deep apron pockets.

"Grandma!" Sean and Benny yelled. "Is there cake? Can we have spaghetti for lunch?"

"Darlings!" said Lily. "Grandpa will take care of you. He's inside." She rolled her eyes at Abby. "He's hiding, I think." To a neighbor, she continued, "One dollar, Mrs. Marcus, that's a perfectly good doormat." Then she turned to Abby. "Abby, honey, help me. I'm so afraid people are just walking off with the mementos of my life."

"Sure, Mom. How much do I charge?"

"As much as the traffic will bear. Don't give these valuable things away."

Abby wanted to laugh. Can openers and boxes of rusty nails and dresses from 1941. Treasures. Her mother was still slim and spry and full of energy and as opinionated as ever. There was no way anyone was going to convince Lily that her accumulation of items from the last half century was worthless.

Most of the stragglers were gone by noon, but the Waltons' front yard was still littered with cluttered tables, boxes and clotheslines hung with garments of all descriptions.

"I'll have to hold another sale next week," said Lily decisively.

"Come on, Mom, no one will buy this old stuff. Call the Goodwill and ask them to pick it up. Maybe they'll give it to some people who can use it."

"Old stuff, indeed! Abby, you never appreciate anything from the past. Why, our past is fascinating and important."

"Sorry, Mom, I didn't mean to put down your collections, but really, you can't move everything to Florida. Your condominium won't hold it all."

"*Someone* will want it. Now, call your father, Abigail, and we'll carry these boxes back into the garage."

Sean and Benny helped carry a few things, too. Abby stayed in the garage and tried to make space for all the paraphernalia. It was when she was lugging a split cardboard box of old books out of the way that the mildewed leather volume fell out.

"What's this?" she asked her mother idly, noticing the tiny lock on the cover. There had been gold script on the front, but it was rubbed off and Abby couldn't make out a title.

Lily snatched it. "My Lord! I didn't mean to sell *that*! Thank goodness no one bought it!"

"It's your diary, isn't it, Mom, from when you were a teenager?" Abby teased.

"It is *not*. It's your great-grandmother Nola Jane's diary."

"Let me see it."

"It's very precious, Abby."

"Is there a key?" Abby turned the book over in her hands.

"You'll have to pry it open. I used to have a key but Lord knows where it is now. Probably sold the blasted thing."

"Can I take it home and look at it?"

"Of course. It's a fascinating story. Your great-grandmother was some woman. I told you all about her."

"I forget. She lived out West or something..."

"Cripple Creek, Colorado. The biggest, most famous gold camp in history."

"Grandma, we're hungry!" piped up the twins, dropping their boxes and leaving the contents scattered on the garage floor.

"I guess it's lunchtime. Come on, you two eating machines," said Lily. Then she turned to Abby's father. "Ed, now don't you carry too many heavy things."

Ed Walton grinned at Abby. "She thinks I'm going to pop off, and then who would put up with her sassy mouth?" he said. "Go on, now, and feed those boys."

Abby trailed after her mother into the house, still holding the diary. Its old leather felt warm and smooth in her hand.

While her mother heated up spaghetti for Sean and Benny, she opened a drawer and found a knife to pry apart the rusty lock on the diary. It popped open immediately; the mechanism was evidently meant more for show than strength. The pages were yellow; they smelled musty and some were stuck together. The first had neatly ruled lines on it and spidery, faded, old-fashioned script that said: The Diary of Nola Jane Randall.

She turned a few brittle pages, saw the writing covering them, and noticed the dates go by—November

1891, May 1892. On the page dated July 4, 1893, Abby's eyes stopped and she began to read.

> Dear Diary, Today, at the Fourth of July parade, Mike Mann asked me to marry him. And I am going to! I had to tell somebody, Dear Diary, and I am quite positive Mama and Papa will not be keen about the idea. Yes, Mike is much older than I am, I know, but we are so much in love!

There was more to read, but just then her father came in with a cut finger and Lily had to find a Band-Aid. The spaghetti sauce was boiling, the boys were still demanding lunch and she just had to put the book down.

"Mommy! Not *that* juice. Grandma has fruit punch!"

"Oh, sorry, Ben." But her mind was back at the Fourth of July parade in Cripple Creek, where a much older man had asked her great-grandmother to marry him. Had Nola Jane married Mr. Mann?

Fourth of July in 1893. Nola Jane had carried a parasol, she decided, and worn a bustled skirt and high button shoes. What did she look like? What did Mike Mann look like? What did Cripple Creek, Colorado, look like?

"Mommy! There's chocolate cake, Mommy!" Abby's mind ceased its meandering and emerged into her mother's neat-as-a-pin kitchen.

"There, Ed," Lily was saying, "it'll stop bleeding now."

"You'd think my arm had been cut off," muttered Abby's father.

Sean's chocolate cake slid off his plate and onto the floor, frosting-side down. While his grandmother cut him another, Abby cleaned up the mess.

"I'm sorry, Mom," she said, pushing herself up from the floor.

"What're grandmas for?" asked Lily. "I see you got the diary open."

"It looks really interesting. What was Nola Jane's married name, Mom? On the first page I read, she'd just been asked by Mike Mann to marry him."

"Oh, yes, that bounder. Mike was her *first* husband. She was eighteen."

"Eighteen! So she married him, then. Well, where did my great-grandfather come from?"

Lily narrowed her eyes and put her hands on her hips. "I've told you all that, for goodness sake, a million times."

"I didn't pay attention, I guess," admitted Abby, shamefaced.

Lily shot her one of her looks. "All right, I'll give you the background. I don't remember all the details, but *I* listened when *my* mother told me things." She leaned back against the sink, gooey plates of chocolate cake crumbs in her hand. "Nola Jane's family moved to Cripple Creek in 1892, just when the town was booming like crazy with all the gold they found. There was this drunken old cowboy, see, named Bob Womack, who'd been cattle ranching right there before there was a town, and he'd always been convinced there was gold in the old volcanic bowl. Well, he was right, but it took him years to convince anyone else.

"There I go, off on a tangent. Anyway, Nola Jane's father opened a grocery store in Cripple Creek and did very well. People had to eat. But my grandmother was somewhat headstrong, at least in those days she was thought to be.

"So she met Mike Mann, a gambler, a womanizer, a no good so-and-so. But he was flashy and, well, I guess he had sex appeal, although in those days no one spoke of such things. Nola upped and married him against her parents' wishes and, let me tell you, she rued the day.

"No sooner had they stepped outside the church than six women brought paternity suits against Mr. Mann."

"Six!" gasped Abby.

"And he had to pay them off, too. Well, good old Mike went and got himself shot to death in a barroom brawl over some floozie not a year later, much to my great-grandmother's relief, I'm sure, and left her a young and lovely widow."

"Holy Toledo."

"*But*—" Lily dumped the plates in the sink and held up a finger "—he left her with not a penny, nothing but a gold mine he'd named after her—the Nola Jane Mine."

"What'd she do?"

"Well, eventually she remarried. She was tough and smart and daring."

"Did she make it big? Was there gold in the mine?"

A terrible scream came from outside, shattering the moment. Sean came dashing in, banging open the screen door, holding his hands over his mouth as blood dripped from between his fingers.

"Oh, my Lord," said Lily, "his teeth!"

It turned out to be only a split lip, but Abby decided she'd better run him over to the hospital to get some stitches. "It would have to be on a weekend," she muttered to Lily. "Kids never get sick or hurt on weekdays when you can get some stitches at the doctor's office for, say, thirty or forty dollars. No, it has to be on a weekend when you have to go to the hospital emergency room and it ends up costing at least a hundred and fifty!"

That evening Abby called her mother to explain the outcome of Sean's trip to the hospital. Lily still got very upset when one of the boys injured himself but, to tell the truth, Abby was getting used to it. One of them did something minor at least once a month.

"So, Mom, tell me more about Nola Jane. We didn't finish. Did she strike it rich?" she pressed.

"She did all right, that is, until the First World War, when all the mines shut down."

"Why? Was the gold gone?"

"I really don't know, hon. Let me see." Lily paused in thought. "I think it was lack of miners. All the men were in the army, you know. And I seem to remember something about a gold embargo. Everything went to the war effort in those days, and I guess there wasn't any mining equipment either."

"What happened to the mine?" asked Abby.

"Oh, it's still there. They all are—the mines, I mean. The town just sort of faded away to almost a ghost town."

"The mine's still there?"

"Oh, hon, I've told you a million times. Nola Jane left that mine to my mother and she left it to me, the mine and her folks' old house in Cripple Creek."

"Mom, *you own a gold mine*?"

Lily laughed. "I pay forty-two dollars a year in taxes to Teller County and I own a hole in the ground and a house that's been rented out twice, maybe three times, in the last ten or fifteen years. Darned if I can remember. It's probably fallen in."

"And you've never gone out to see any of it?"

"Owning a gold mine in Cripple Creek is about as interesting as owning a piece of Florida swampland. I bet lots of people own defunct mines out West."

"Why did they leave, Mom? I mean your grandparents."

"The mines shut down and everyone left. My grandmother had to sell the house on Cascade Avenue in Colorado Springs. They moved to New York and my grandfather worked as an engineer for the tunnels they were building under the Hudson River."

"How sad."

"We didn't think so. They were happy people. They loved New York, too."

"They never went back?" asked Abby.

"Nothing to go back to. It's a dead town. Why, they couldn't even sell the house in Cripple Creek then, and I'm sure it's worse now. Nobody mines gold there anymore, hon. It's all done in South Africa now."

"But the price of gold's been rising lately. Wouldn't it be worth it to open an old mine and see if there was gold in it? I mean..."

"Oh, Abby, what do I know? I don't follow the price of gold. You'd have to be an expert."

"Then why haven't you quit paying taxes on the mine, Mom?"

"That's a sort of trust, don't you think? Every female member of my family leaves it to her eldest daughter. I've always been disappointed you didn't have a girl. But I'm sure, hon, a pretty girl like you, you'll find another man and get married again. And then you'll have a daughter."

"Mother, I am never marrying again, I've told you!"

"Oh, that's right, I forgot," replied Lily mildly.

Abby read herself to sleep that night. It didn't take long because her eyes started closing shortly after she began skimming the yellowed, closely written pages. It would take forever to read the whole thing, she thought in dismay, and she never had time. But Nola Jane wrote with such feeling of everything that happened to her that Abby was entranced. Nola Jane's spidery handwriting with its precise curlicues, her quaint phrases, her descriptions, her feelings, touched her great-granddaughter.

Abby read bits and pieces, turned pages, read more pages here and there. She read the end carefully, however. Oh, yes, Nola Jane had done very well. She wrote about her mansion on Cascade Avenue in Colorado Springs, the city about forty miles from Cripple Creek where all the mine owners moved to flaunt their wealth. And Nola wrote about Randy, the man she fell in love with and married in the formal parlor of the beautiful house.

Abby woke up with a start at 3:30 a.m. Her bedside light was still on, the diary lay open on her covers, and Sean was whimpering in his room. She got up to check on him, found him merely tangled in the blankets, stumbled back to bed and lay there wondering just how a person could get some information about gold mining.

BY MAY, ABBY WAS FLAGGING CARS in her old jeans and a T-shirt and her nose was peeling from too much sun. Her mind strayed more and more, even as she answered the radio, waved cars on, ate lunch by the side of the tarry-smelling resurfaced road. Cripple Creek, Nola Jane. Gold.

She kept a close eye on the price of gold. It was inching steadily toward five hundred dollars an ounce, higher than it had been in years. What if it *was* worth mining gold again?

You're nuts, she told herself. *You don't know anything about mining. You're broke. How do you think you'd open a gold mine?*

She could sell the house. It was worth a lot on today's market. What if...? But suppose the mine wasn't even there anymore, suppose there was no gold? How could she find out?

One night at her group Abby broached the subject.

"Well, group, would somebody like to comment?" Joann broke into the uncomfortable silence.

"Lady, you really *do* need a shrink," was the kindest remark.

But the diary wouldn't release her from its spell. She read it as often as she could, but it was slow going, and she kept falling asleep in the middle of sentences.

All day long she kept thinking, *What if, what if?* What if there was gold in the mine? She saw herself in Cripple Creek with a pick and a shovel. No, with a jackhammer. What *did* a person mine with these days? She walked with Nola Jane down damp, dripping tunnels, a miner's lamp on her head. No, they were never called tunnels. Miners called them winzes or drifts or crosscuts, she recalled.

The mining terminology seeped into her dreams. She stood at a dark-mouthed hole in one dream and there was a sign over it that read "The Nola Jane Mine." Inside, a treasure of gold coins spilled from a cornucopia.

She pictured Cripple Creek in her head, but the image was hazy around the edges. The main street was

Bennett Avenue and, since it ran along the side of a hill, one lane was fifteen feet lower than the other.

"Mike told me the joke currently going around," wrote Nola. "It concerns the town drunk, who fell off Bennett Avenue and broke his neck. I didn't think it amusing."

And there was Myers Avenue, notorious street of the brothels—the Parisian, Laura Belle's, the Bon Ton. More than fifty thousand people lived in Cripple Creek in its heyday, and three railroads serviced the city. People descended upon the remote valley from all over the world. It was an exciting, raw, wide-open town, and Nola Jane had loved it.

What was Cripple Creek like nowadays? Abby wondered. She'd looked it up on a map. It was forty-four miles from Colorado Springs, a tiny dot on the broad face of the state of Colorado. Its altitude was ten thousand feet. That was almost two miles high!

She wondered if the swank hotels were still there, the National, the Imperial, the Independence. She would picture handsome, swaggering Mike Mann in a vest and waistcoat with a big gold chain across his belly. Boy, she sure could empathize with Nola Jane. Steve had been more subtle than Mike but just as dedicated a womanizer. It hurt like the devil.

Lily and Ed moved to Florida. Abby cried when they were gone. When would she ever have time to go to Florida to see them? She felt alone, so very alone, and scared of going on that way forever. But every morning she woke up, realized that it was a new day and anything was possible, squared her shoulders and went to work.

And still, Nola Jane's diary stayed with her, growing larger in her imagination each day, until sometimes she was not sure of the line between the present and the past. She'd look around herself at work and wonder what Nola Jane would say about her radio or the computer at the Holiday Inn. She wondered if she were going crazy but she was afraid to bring up her preoccupation at the group therapy sessions. They just didn't understand.

Her mother called every week on Saturday morning. "We went to the beach yesterday, hon. I wish you could bring the boys down when school's out. They'd love it so. What if we send you the fare?"

"I can't get off work." Abby sighed.

"Bah! That's an excuse."

"Mom, do you think the house in Cripple Creek has really fallen down? I was thinking we could go out there and stay... I mean, sort of camp out..."

Lily sighed. "You won't let go of that, will you? In the movies they call it gold fever."

"Don't be silly. It's just that it's part of our past. You're always telling me..."

"Sure, but you never listened before until you heard the word gold."

"Okay, so I'm curious," Abby admitted.

"Honey, if you really want to visit Cripple Creek, I think you should. Take a week off. You deserve it. You know, your father and I worry, you work so hard."

"But there're my jobs—and the boys. It's just impossible."

"I'll send you money for the tickets. It's next year's Christmas present, how's that?" offered Lily.

"Oh, Mom..."

"And you know Mrs. Howell will take care of the boys. Heck, she practically does anyway!"

"Mother!"

"Sorry. Now, you've got vacation time coming. Do it, call your travel agent. Let me know how much the tickets are. Do it, Abigail!"

On May sixteenth, while sitting in the airplane, Abby read in the newspaper that gold hit five hundred dollars an ounce on the world market, an event much celebrated in some circles. She turned to the small window next to her and saw the flat expanse of mile-high Denver, Colorado, below. To the west stood the jagged, glistening peaks of the Rockies, partially obscured by the silver wing of the airplane as it banked to land at Stapleton Airport. And then the gear thumped down onto the tarmac and Abby's heart pounded furiously. What in God's name was she doing in Colorado? Had she gone nuts, spending her precious vacation time on some crazy whim, some silly desire to see a depressing old ghost town?

Abigail McAlister, you've really lost it now.

CHAPTER TWO

ABBY STOPPED IN FRONT of the Hertz counter at the airport and gasped. Forty-two ninety-five a day! Plus insurance! For a week that would add up to... wow, were these cars made of gold?

The girl behind the counter sized up Abby. "You can get a heap at a place down the highway," she suggested. "Fifteen or twenty a day plus gas. Free mileage, though."

"Great," said Abby. "Where do I pick up the van to take me there?"

"Van?"

It must have been a mile walk to Rent-A-Wreck but it was worth it once Abby had signed the papers and was seated in her '72 Ford Galaxy, bent over the road map. It was early in Colorado—two hours earlier than in Newark—only eleven in the morning. She moved her finger along the lines of the map southward down Interstate 25 to Colorado Springs, then west into the mountains to find the tiny dot labeled Cripple Creek. It couldn't be that far, a couple of hours' drive, maybe three if she stopped for a bite at a fast-food joint along the highway.

She turned the ignition key. *Sputter.* Abby tried again. *Umph, sputter.* Amazingly, the engine turned over. A black cloud of exhaust puffed from the tailpipe. The engine choked and hacked and complained but finally settled down to a bumpy idle. She put it into reverse, began to back out, then had to go forward again. The old Ford was the size of a boat, for Pete's sake, a twenty-two footer!

Sputter, screech, lurch.

"Say," said Abby to the attendant at the gate, "is this thing going to make it?"

"Where you headed?"

"Cripple Creek."

He only grinned.

A cloud of smoke, a "Heigh-ho, Silver," and she was off. Sort of.

The traffic in Denver was heavy but not nearly as congested as around New York City. And once she was lurching along in her wreck, it seemed a whole lot cooler out than she'd thought at first. Of course, the lack of humidity in the arid Colorado air dried the perspiration on her skin as fast as it formed.

Interstate 25 followed the smooth rolling foothills south. To her right, Abby could see the white-capped peaks of the Rockies jutting up out of the earth, rank upon rank. On her left, the wide expanse of prairie land rolled away to the horizon. It was fertile now in the spring, endless and pale green. There sure weren't any wide open spaces like this in Newark!

"Oh yes," said Abby aloud, "it looks just like the pictures." She had spotted the Air Force Academy, nestled proudly against the foothills, its modern silvery spires gleaming in the midday sun.

It didn't take Abby long to recognize much-photographed Pike's Peak, a dark massive hump rising like a giant out of the earth, dwarfing the surrounding foothills.

What had Nola Jane thought of this impressive hunk of rock? Surely, in that rickety old wagon her great-grandmother had described, the mountain had seemed intimidating. Of course, now there was a road to the top. Why, with a tune-up, even this old buggy could climb it!

She gassed up in Colorado Springs, then followed the rising ribbon of highway west into the foothills toward a place called Manitou Springs. From an Indian name, she supposed. Were there Indians there still? *Wild Indians? Come off it, Abigail, this isn't 1892.*

In Manitou Springs, Abby stopped for a hamburger, but could find no fast-food spots in the quaint, Western-style town. Painted Victorians mingled with rustic, false-fronted buildings, signs boasted of mineral water spas, and men wore tall riding boots and real sweat-stained cowboy hats. There was a look about these Western men in their jean jackets and healthy, weathered tans, a look she really liked. And they moved differently from the men she knew; these cowboy types loped along with a free, swinging, self-assured stride.

Her skirt again snug around the waist, Abby made for the main highway once more. The road climbed and curved and climbed. Then it climbed some more.

The car seemed to rattle the steeper the highway became. It kept choking, threatening to stall out. Then it would belch out a cloud of black smoke and run smoothly for a mile or so before beginning the hacking process all over again.

This wreck is never going to make it.

As she climbed, she gaped at the unusual terrain, the low, red rising hills dotted with stunted, windblown ponderosa pine and the table rocks—clay red—that rose up from treacherously steep gulches. A sign read Cave of the Winds, and another warned: In Case of Flood Park and Climb to Safety.

"Wow," said Abby, craning her neck to glance apprehensively up at the spiraling mountains.

Her ears popped several times as she climbed, the Ford chugging for its life now, and still the road rose steadily until finally, she broke out of the twisted canyon and into high-country meadowland.

The car kept rocking along but Abby was paying no attention to it now; if it broke down, then it broke down—she'd worry about it then. Instead, her head was in the clouds—*no, above them*—as she steered and stared and tried to imagine what this magnificent country had looked like to Nola Jane when she'd first seen it.

Her great-grandmother had written of her journey into the wilderness of the Rockies:

> My heart is pounding with the beauty and wonder of this climb and I am frightened. What if our wagon should break down? Are there wolves and savage Indians ahead? What lies beyond that curious rock formation?

What a brave woman, Abby thought, her very own great-grandmother, a dyed-in-the-wool pioneer.

When Abby turned onto the road that led to Cripple Creek, the terrain altered once again. Now the meadowland climbed sharply and gave way to low gray hills that seemed to march away in files, until beyond them there were sharp-pointed peaks devoid of trees. She thought she must be nearing the mining country, where a hundred years ago men had cut all the trees for shoring in the tunnels, for firewood and cabins.

Suddenly Abby slammed her foot on the brake and lurched forward. "Holy Toledo!" she cried, her car nearly crashing into the side of a mountain when the road abruptly and unaccountably ended. But no, she saw as she caught her wind, there was a tunnel that bored into the rock, a narrow pitch-black hole. Was she supposed to drive into *that*?

Eventually a car emerged, coming from the opposite direction, and the driver waved at Abby, who was still sitting there unmoving, undecided.

"Well, here goes," she muttered. "I just hope it comes out somewhere." The single lane twisted through the mountain, unpaved. The tunnel walls were held together by rotting old timber, and Abby drove too quickly for the conditions, afraid *this* might be the day the mountain decided to cave in. It was a darn good thing the twins weren't with her.

Daylight. The Ford lurched, jettisoning her out into the brilliant Colorado sunshine. Then the road immediately proceeded to drop away, following the sweeping contours of an ancient, bare volcanic bowl; the highway dipped and twisted down, down, along denuded ridges and past an occasional mountain cabin that had long ago been abandoned. It wound by low grassy hills, utterly treeless, spotted with tan, gray, purple and orange mine dumps and weathered gallows frames that rose above clusters of unpainted mine-shaft buildings. The scene seemed like one from the distant past, as if Abby had somehow gone through a time warp and come out of the tunnel into an earlier era.

Another curve swept her down into the smooth-sided, grass-covered caldron, where not a tree could be seen. How odd after the miles of Alpine forests she'd passed on the way up there!

And then, finally, there was the town. From her vantage point, it looked to Abby like a toy village, as if the buildings had been placed carefully by an unseen hand in the gut of the volcanic bowl. Beyond Cripple Creek, in the distance, the long line of the Collegiate Peaks pierced the blue sky, like an army marching along in snow-capped helmets, as if that godlike hand had set them there, too.

The town itself was tiny and quaint. The brick and wood buildings sat askew on the steep side of the bowl, giving the impression they'd slid partway downhill and then gotten caught there in a cozy jumble.

And, yes, there was even a tiny creek running downhill! Her heart beat with excitement. She was there. She'd made it to Cripple Creek, to that odd, half-forgotten, out-of-the-way relic of a bygone time.

Approaching the outskirts of the town, Abby saw the sign that advertised the Molly Kathleen gold mine. "Visitors welcome. Guided tours." So there was at least *one* mine open then. The road curved around, heading toward the center of town, and Abby craned her neck, staring, gaping, eager to see everything.

The description of Cripple Creek her great-grandmother had written was stamped into Abby's brain. She remembered every word.

> The town is growing so I hardly recognize it from one day to the next. Houses and stores and fancy hotels have sprung up like mushrooms after a spring rain. Why, there must be over fifty thousand folk here now and on last count seventy-three saloons. How can so many newcomers hope to strike it rich? Nevertheless, father's store is doing marvelously with all the new prospectors pouring

into town in an unending flood. It's too bad, Mama says, we can't grow vegetables to sell in the store, but the altitude prohibits it.

Ten thousand feet, thought Abby, clearing her head, trying to keep a grip on the here and now. She was at ten thousand feet and amazingly still breathing. And yet nothing seemed quite real to her; Cripple Creek was truly stranded in its past. It really could have been a hundred years ago, Abby decided, as she drove past an adorable green and yellow narrow-gauge train that sat puffing gray smoke next to a minidepot. And the buildings! Some were rough, wooden false-front structures, others were Victorian and painted in pastel colors. The shops and hotels were evidently all on the one main street, which was only four or five blocks long—the same singular Bennett Avenue that was built on two levels, the street that the drunk fell off and broke his neck. *It's still exactly the same, Nola Jane,* Abby thought, exulting.

Finally she pulled up—very steeply *up*—a side street, following a sign for a hotel, and stepped out, breathing in the thin, pristine air and stretching her legs. She'd get a room and then explore the town. She'd find her house, certainly, or at least see if it was still standing.

The sign said the Imperial Hotel and it looked funky-elegant, as if recently remodeled. The climb to its entrance from Bennett Avenue left Abby panting. Wasn't anything in Cripple Creek level?

Inside was a quaint lobby and bar decorated in charming Victorian profusion. It seemed warm and inviting, and the young female desk clerk greeted Abby as if she were a frequent guest, taking the edge off Abby's apprehension: would she be welcome in Cripple Creek or treated as an outsider?

Another steep climb up the curiously tilted staircase and Abby was on the second floor, more sure than ever that the building was sliding downhill, and panting from the combination of altitude and exertion. Up to the third floor and into her room. It was authentic, gold-camp Victorian. A brass bed, an Oriental rug, an oak dresser, a washstand and chair. No bathroom, no phone and no TV. The bathrooms, Abby soon learned, were down the hall, and Victorian as well, with those big standing enamel tubs on clawed feet. Abby absolutely, one hundred percent, adored the place.

The urge to explore overcame her need for a rest, and Abby was soon snatching up her purse and heading back down the peculiarly tilted staircase. Paper in hand on which she'd written down the address of her house—mining shack, she corrected herself—she sought the help of the clerk.

"Do you know where Myers Avenue is?" asked Abby.

"You mean the street where all the cribs used to be?"

"Cribs?"

"You know," began the girl. Then she giggled and Abby looked up to the ceiling, feeling dumb.

"Oh, I knew that," she said finally, laughing at herself and thinking: so her house was somewhere in the old red-light district. "Actually," she continued, "I'm looking for Myers Avenue and B Street, it says here." She turned the paper for the girl to see.

"Oh. Well that would be up on the hill then, at the other end of Myers. You know, past the sheriff's department 'bout a block."

Abby didn't know but pretended she did; she'd displayed enough ignorance for one day. She was hoisting her purse strap back over her shoulder, passing by the door of the hotel's bar, when some unseen force made her pause. It was, of course, simple curiosity; nevertheless, she couldn't resist peeking into the saloon. It was awfully dark inside, considering the bright sunny day outside. And her nose twitched with the smell of cigar smoke—a real man's domain. Along one long wall stood a polished mahogany bar; behind it the barkeep, who wore a gold-flecked, black satin vest and a bow tie, was wiping glasses. He even had a handlebar mustache! Against another wall was an upright piano, and several tables filled the center of the dim room.

There were two men in the bar but only one caught her eye, and held Abby rooted to the spot. He was seated, his back to her, talking to the other person, who was wearing a Stetson. Her guy, though, had on an orange baseball cap and a Western shirt. Jeans, she thought, and tall boots. But his face was hidden to her and all Abby gleaned was the impression of height and leanness, a nice set of shoulders, a relaxed manner and a pleasing way of holding himself.

She caught herself suddenly, realizing that she must look foolish standing there, peeking in like a timid little thing. But then, surely all tourists were curious about the old Western saloons.

Abby glanced around once more, and noticed that the stranger in the orange cap had shifted, affording her a glimpse of a very nice, masculine profile. Then she readjusted her purse on her shoulder and headed for the front door. *I wish he'd turned around,* she thought idly for a moment. Then she rolled her eyes upward. *You really don't have time for that, Abigail.*

The car chugged along Myers Avenue, which wasn't too hard to find, as there were only two main streets in Cripple Creek. Then she proceeded up the hill past the sheriff's department, which was not too hard to spot, either, and onto B Street, where it intersected Myers Avenue.

She recognized the house instantly because of the wagon wheels that were attached to the fence. In the diary, Nola Jane had written about them.

> Today Papa nailed up old wagon wheels around our newly painted fence. Mama was near to having the vapors and neighbor Garret laughed so that Papa said he was going to punch him square in the jaw if he didn't stop snickering. Mr. Garret stopped his chortling. I'm partial to the wheels myself.

So this was Nola Jane's house. She stopped the car, parked in the dirt street, and then climbed out and surveyed the grounds. It was a nice corner lot, though badly overgrown and rough. Still.... And the house. Not too long ago it had been painted—by someone, a renter, or a squatter?—barn red and white with lavender trim. The paint on the one-story, elongated building was peeling and chipping and nails had popped out all over. Still.... The windows were all small but there were plenty of them. Of course, several were broken and all were filthy. Still.... There were trees in this treeless land. A few squat spruces nestled up against the long porch, and that must have been an aspen tree pushing the kitchen steps aside. Still....

She wiped accumulated grime off a window and looked in. The rooms were dirty and empty, depressing looking. There was an old white range and a refrigerator with its door hanging open in the kitchen, an old tub in the bathroom. No toilet. There was a black potbellied stove in the living room. That was it.

Abby circled the place, then circled again. It had possibilities, but then—what was she thinking? This was merely a vacation, a time away from kids and housework and her two jobs. The fact that she'd read in the newspaper on the plane that the price of gold was on a steady rise meant absolutely nothing to Abby, or, by the looks of Cripple Creek, to anyone else. South Africa, that's where it mattered, didn't it?

The sun was beginning to set beyond the town, sliding behind a pyramid-shaped mountain until only a lone ray of long golden light touched Abby's cheek and quickly faded. She turned up the collar on her heavy cardigan sweater, circled the place once more, then headed back down the steep, unpaved hill toward the hotel. Her house, she thought as she parked, was truly in need of a lot of work, and that meant money. But honestly, it *had* possibilities.

Abby dined by herself at the hotel. She felt nervous and out of place, and she hated to eat alone, especially in public in a strange place. But there was a nice, older couple sitting next to her and they graciously included Abby in their conversation.

"It's a great old town," the man was telling Abby. "Lucy and I have been coming here for years. We're from Denver."

"So sad, though," put in Lucy, "to see a once prosperous town go by the wayside like this. Still, they have a decent summer tourist season and I suppose that helps."

"What about the gold?" ventured Abby.

"Too expensive to mine anymore," said Dick.

"Well, I read in the *Denver Post* just the other day," said Lucy, "that there's a Canadian fella down here reopening a mine right now. The price of gold is soaring, Dick. You know that."

"Sure. And you can get it out of the ground, all right, but then processing it eats up all the profits, Luce."

"So you're telling me," said Abby, "that there's only one working mine here right now?"

"Well, I wouldn't know that for sure," finished Dick.

Abby lay beneath the patchwork quilt that night and couldn't stop her brain from buzzing. She saw Cripple Creek as Nola Jane had described it a hundred years ago, booming, the streets swarming with mule skinners, ministers, drillers, hoisters, railroad men and gamblers in sharp shoes; with unshaven prospectors, sporting women, ladies in Paris gowns, pimps, politicians, brokers, mine owners. Donkeys brayed, dogs fought, streetcars whined on the curves, trains clanged, mine whistles blew.

And she saw it as it was now. Quaint but tiny, dormant, with great gaps like missing teeth along the main streets, where buildings had fallen down and never been rebuilt. It was as if Cripple Creek were waiting, suspended in time, for the return of all those hearty souls.

At dinner Dick had shaken his head. "World War One ended everything. They just couldn't make the mines pay after that."

Lucy had added: "And the town sits at ten thousand feet, so farming is out. And industry... well, it's so isolated up here. Of course, the tourists do love to chase the burros around the streets and everyone rides the narrow-gauge railroad. And, then, during the summer, they stage those wonderful old-fashioned melodramas every night here in the Imperial."

Abby fell asleep finally, her dreams filled with technicolor images of smooth green hills, wild burros roaming dusty streets and brightly painted trains puffing up the sides of mountains.

Snow, carried by strong gusts of wind, tapped at Abby's window the next morning. She sure hadn't counted on this! She rummaged through her suitcase but found nothing warmer than a pair of slacks and nylon panty hose. So slacks and cardigan it was. She looked down at her feet and her neat flats, and then shrugged.

Using the pay phones off the lobby area, Abby got Mrs. Howell and the twins. The boys were on one extension, Mrs. Howell on another. It was quite a conversation.

"They're fine, Mrs. McAlister, really."

"Benny took my bike and crashed it!"

"Sean bit my finger first!"

"We'll go to that matinee at the movies on Saturday if it's all right with you. . . ."

"Sure," yelled Abby, holding the phone away from her ear.

"Aren't you going to punish Sean, too?" Wailing commenced. Two thousand miles away from their mother and neither boy had even said he missed her.

"I love you, boys," said Abby. "And I want you to be good and we'll settle all the battles when I get home. Okay?"

"Okay, Mom!" Was that Sean or Benny?

Abby finally hung up and leaned back against the booth. Wouldn't it be nice if she could raise the boys in a clean atmosphere like Cripple Creek, where they could grow up close to nature? Where the school was only three blocks away and kids only carried knives to whittle with? Where there was no traffic, no smog, no crime? Wouldn't it be nice if...

Pipe dreams. She was playing with half a deck, thinking too much about rising gold prices and deep dark tunnels twisting into mountainsides. This was a vacation and nothing more.

Abby met Karen Lockley quite by accident. She'd been exploring the town on foot, her cardigan pulled tightly around her against the biting, snow-laced wind, when she saw a sign: Karen's Secondhand Store. Maybe a parka? Some old boots? How much could it cost compared to a doctor's bill?

"Guess nobody told you about springtime in the Rockies," said the store owner, who stood bent over a box brimming with sweaters and socks.

"They certainly didn't," agreed Abby. "In Newark, where I come from, it's probably sweltering."

"Newark? New Jersey?"

It didn't take long for a friendly conversation to bud. Karen was a big-boned woman, tall and broad-shouldered and buxom. She was strong looking, with large features, great high cheekbones, blue eyes and beautiful fine, straight, golden brown hair that fell in a soft, shimmering curtain to below her shoulders. She was as welcoming to Abby as everyone else in Cripple Creek had been. Obviously these folks were friendly, warm and honest, cheerful and capable, even if times were hard. Abby found herself enthralled, so unused to the welcoming atmosphere that at moments she had to admonish herself for being suspicious.

"I know what you mean," Karen was saying. "Kids can drive you nuts when there's no man around to yell at them once in awhile."

"Sean and Benny, those are my twins, always seem to be getting into mischief. Trouble follows those two around like a lovesick puppy." Then, as Karen helped her into an old, patched navy-blue parka, Abby exclaimed, "Good God! I look like the Pillsbury doughboy!"

Karen laughed. "Everyone does in these things. And up here, we practically live in them. Winters are what we call *long*. But look on the bright side, Abby. The parka's only eight dollars and it beats the hell out of freezing to death."

"You've got that right. I'll take it."

While Abby rummaged through the used boots—boy, did she hate the idea of putting her feet into someone else's discarded shoes—Karen worked and chatted. "You know, I've seen you before, Abby," she said offhandedly, her fine brown hair swinging into her face as she leaned over.

"Where? I mean, I just got here yesterday afternoon." God, were those boots gross!

"Looking into the old Randall place, next door to my house. My daughter, Janet, was ready to call the sheriff. You should have heard her." Karen mimicked her fifteen-year-old. "Mom, there's this weird lady walking around next door and looking into the windows. Geez, I think she's a kook or something. Think we should call the cops? Mom."

"That's *my* house, Karen. I mean, actually, it's my mother's. She inherited it from my great-grandmother, Nola Jane Randall."

"Well, I'll be."

"What a coincidence," said Abby, while she wiggled her nose at an odoriferous pair of climbing boots. "I mean, your living next door."

"Nothing is coincidental in a place this size, kiddo. We *all* live practically next door to one another." Karen tossed her hair back and stood straight, stretching her back. "You planning on fixing up the house or something?"

"Well...not really. What would I do with it if I did?"

"Rent it out. Live in it." She shrugged.

"Maybe rent it . . ." Her mother had said it had been rented out a few times over the years. But who would rent it in the condition it was in now?

"About four years ago, I think, this old geezer was living in it. I remember because he just appeared one day out in our yard and asked if I had any old paintbrushes he could borrow. He said he'd rented the place but I never believed him."

"The nerve of the guy!" gasped Abby.

"Well, yes, but around here there're lots of abandoned homes. It's not unusual for an old-timer to have some hard luck and move into a place for a while. This guy was okay. He painted the place and fixed a few windows. You know."

"What happened to him?"

"He disappeared. Probably moved on to another mining town, looking for work."

"That's sad."

"For these old miners around here life *can* be very sad, Abby. But they manage. We all do. It's safe for our kids and it's clean and it's home, I guess. My husband, my ex, that is, brought me here twelve years ago from Wyoming and then one day he just up and split on us. The creep hasn't even called in nine years now!"

"I know just what you mean," said Abby darkly.

"So we make do. And the people here look out for one another."

Abby decided on a pair of shoes finally—her own, that were on her feet already. "I guess just the parka, Karen. The shoes are okay but . . ."

"Yeah, I hate the smelly old things, too," put in Karen. Then, while she rang up the eight dollars for the parka, she asked, "Nola Jane. . .that's a mine, isn't it?"

Abby nodded. "It's part of my inheritance, too."

"You wouldn't be considering reopening it? I mean, there are a lot of men out of work here and . . ."

"No way." Abby laughed. "I came for a vacation, Karen, that's all."

"But the price of gold is right up there now."

"I know. Problem is, I'm broke. That is, I work two jobs to make ends meet as it is."

Karen shrugged those broad, womanly shoulders. "You ought to go up and see the mine, anyway. The places are fascinating, Abby. And you ought to at least check at the courthouse and make sure it's still in your name. I mean, there're mines reopening right now and you never know."

"Maybe I *shouldn't* check on it. I might get gold fever and be hooked."

"You might. On the other hand, your house isn't bad. It would hardly cost you a thing to make it livable. And there's this big Canadian company, Wayne Consolidated, buying up mineral rights around here like crazy. You could get some ore samples from the Nola Jane and have them assayed. You never know—this Wayne fella might make you an offer. Or. . . you could think about reopening the mine yourself."

"Hold on!" Abby laughed. "I don't know from beans about mining. Honest. And besides, I live in Newark. I have two kids and two jobs."

"And here I thought you were a woman of vision, Abby McAlister," joshed Karen good-naturedly.

Abby left, grateful for the warmth of the parka, her head swimming with new information that she tried desperately to dismiss. Sure, Karen, she thought, easy for you to say—fix up the house, reopen the mine. All pipe dreams! She couldn't leave Newark, move the kids out West and risk everything.

Her thoughts flip-flopped. Risk what? Risk losing two lousy jobs and selling the tract home? Big deal. What did she really have, anyway? Years and years of struggling ahead of her, that's what. Some great future.

A woman of vision, Karen had said. Like Nola Jane? Fat chance of that!

Still, it wouldn't hurt to follow Karen Lockley's advice and check on the courthouse documentation, to make sure the mine was really in her mother's name. A woman of vision could do that much, at least.

Abby trudged up the uneven, rippling pavement of Bennett Avenue toward the sheriff's department and the courthouse, blinking her eyes while dust kicked up off the street and the gusty wind buffeted her. Winters sure would be long in Cripple Creek, no getting away from that. But summer and autumn in the mountains were supposed to be breathtakingly lovely. A trade-off. And at least the air here was pollution-free.

Why was she thinking these things? What difference could it make to her? She lived in Newark, New Jersey, and she'd *always* live there.

Darn, thought Abby as she pushed open the door to the courthouse, *fantasies sure are a nuisance.*

Like everything else Abby had seen of Cripple Creek, the courthouse lived up to her expectations; it was old and venerable and solid. It had been there for nearly a century and promised to last another one. She stood for a minute in the entrance, caught her breath from the steep uphill climb, and then made her way to the Teller County clerk and recorder's office.

The clerk was an elderly man who must have been in his mid-seventies, and he'd been clerk, he told her, for the last fifty-two years! Now there was job security. He was cute, too, with his baggy wool trousers, old wool striped vest over his white shirt, visor and bifocals. He hunched over the big black ledger book on the oak counter and mumbled, "Um . . . um . . . aha . . . um," as he flipped over each handwritten page slowly and methodically. "Here we are," he said finally, pushing his glasses up his nose with a finger and eyeing Abby.

"Is the mine still in my mother's name?" she asked.

"Certainly is, young lady. And all the taxes are up-to-date."

"Oh, good."

"You got plans for the old gal?"

"You mean the mine?" Abby made a rueful face: if only he understood the quandary she was in. "I don't think so. I don't know the first thing about mining or gold or anything."

"Neither did the first settlers here, young lady. Didn't stop them, though." He made a rumbling noise in his throat. "Course the gamble is, gold's rising good now but that don't mean it's gonna keep goin' up. Just as easy for it to fall."

"And the mine's probably played out anyway," put in Abby matter-of-factly.

His chin jutted forward. "Now there's a flatlander talkin' if I ever heard one! Played out, indeed. No, sir.

There's enough gold in these hills here to fill up the Vatican and Fort Knox and whatever else you please!"

"Really?" asked Abby, trying to keep the lid on her renewed excitement.

"You bet. What's more, gold is rising and I'm thinkin' it'll hit six, maybe seven hundred before it levels off. You'll see more than one old mine reopening. You can count on it. Yes, indeedy."

"A minute ago," said Abby teasingly, "you said the price could just as easily fall as go up."

"That was before I knew you. I don't go tellin' everybody what I know."

"Well, thank you." She hid a smile. "So, say gold kept rising and a person wanted to reopen a mine.... You understand," Abby was quick to interject, "this is just a hypothetical question, but anyway, say all the equipment the person needed was ready. And, of course, there was a crew hired, what else would a person need? I mean, surely there are licenses and what not."

"Guts, ma'am," came an enticingly deep voice from over Abby's shoulder. "And a whole lot of luck."

She whirled around, surprised by the interruption. And then she had to look up, way up. He must have been six foot two and, oh, my goodness, he was a fine-looking man.

"Didn't mean to barge in like that, ma'am," he said then in his Western drawl. He proceeded to tip the brim of his orange baseball cap—a Denver Broncos football hat—and Abby remembered him immediately from the bar that morning at the hotel. Sure it was him! He wore the same red and black wool plaid shirt and underneath it, she could see the top of his white long underwear at his throat. And there were those long, slim jeans and the same boots . . .

She mumbled something like, "No problem. I was just asking some questions." Or maybe she really said, "I've never met a man as tall and lean and spine-tinglingly handsome as you. I've never seen such beautiful eyes, so dark and sparkling with humor. I've never seen such strong arms or neck and those long lean legs . . ."

"You're talkin' about the Nola Jane mine, ma'am?" Oh, that smile! That wide, lazily curved mouth!

"Ah, yes," replied Abby, "the Nola Jane."

"Well, like I said, hope I'm not stickin' my nose in . . ."

"Oh, you're not," she said too quickly; she was leaping on every word out of his lovely mouth. *Calm down, McAlister.*

"Anyway, name's Ty, ma'am, Ty Hollinger." He smiled readily, a broad, youthful smile, and in those dancing dark eyes she thought she could read a message: he was telling her that he acknowledged her interest in him and that it was okay.

"Abby," she managed to say, and then remembered to put her hand out. There, that showed she was in control, didn't it?

"Abby," he said. "Just Abby?"

"Oh. Abigail McAlister."

He took her hand in his with deliberate care, and his strong, capable fingers closed over hers warmly. She noticed then how light his hair was in places, a sun-streaked chestnut brown. It was shiny, boyishly long in back, sticking up a little where he'd removed his cap and run an artfully careless hand through it.

It took all of Abby's strength to round up her thoughts as she stood there, her hand still in his. She forced herself to remember that she'd washed her hands of men and that she couldn't go around ogling every handsome man she saw.

On the other side of the coin, she was aware of the fact that her knees were buckling and that she was staring at him a dreadfully long time and cultivating very wicked thoughts. Could that really be her, standing there only a breath away from the most delicious man she'd seen in years? Could it be plump-as-a-chicken, straitlaced Abby, mother of two, could it really be her?

"Pleased to meet you, Mister, ah, Hollinger," she finally managed to say through the disconcerting thoughts that were jumbling her brain into scrambled eggs.

CHAPTER THREE

"LIKEWISE," TY SAID, releasing her fingers reluctantly. What a nice, soft hand she had. "You know, I wouldn't butt in like this except that I'm familiar with the Nola Jane and I'd sure hate to see a pretty gal get her hopes up."

Abby McAlister cocked her head to one side. "Do you mean there's something wrong with the Nola Jane mine?"

"Heck, no, nothing's exactly *wrong* with any of the old mines 'round here, ma'am. Nothing that money and lots of it wouldn't set straight."

"Mr. Hollinger, just how do you know so much about these mines?" She had big round eyes that were a curious color—like aspen leaves in autumn or old, burnished gold—and right now they were turning from open and friendly to the slightest bit suspicious.

"I'm a mining engineer, born and raised in Colorado. Leadville, actually. You know, the home of the unsinkable Molly Brown and Baby Doe Tabor. And the truth is, ma'am, all modesty aside, I really do know my stuff."

"A mining engineer?" She seemed to be mulling over something.

"Sure am. I went to the Colorado School of Mines. You know, in Golden. And I'm working at a mine not far from here."

"A gold mine?"

He laughed. "All the mines in Cripple Creek are gold mines."

"Well, excuse me. I'm from New Jersey, and we don't mine gold there," she said saucily.

"What a cryin' shame," he said drolly, keeping his face straight.

Her lips curved into a smile—sweet, pink lips that he already liked to watch—and she gave a pretty little laugh. Good, she had a sense of humor.

"Well, Mr. Hollinger..."

Ty pushed his cap back on his head with a finger and stopped her right there. "Now, look, you can't go on callin' me Mr. Hollinger. My name is Ty. Short for Tyson."

"You certainly do talk a lot," she said, "Ty."

"I have a lot to say."

"About the Nola Jane?"

He looked at her for a second. Was she serious? "Forget about the Nola Jane. It's just a black hole in the ground that'll suck you dry. Even if you knew mining, which you don't."

"Why are you trying so hard to convince me of that?"

"Yeah, Ty," piped up old Joseph Stedman, the county clerk, from the other side of the counter. "You got dibs on luck around here?"

Ty settled his hat on his head and whistled with exasperation. "Now you keep out of this, Joe. You know better than most what gold fever'll do to a man."

"Or woman," shot back Joe. "This girl, here, she's Nola Jane Randall's great-granddaughter, and her ma, Lily Walton, it says here—" he tapped a finger on the page of his ledger book "—has clear title to the Nola Jane mine."

"Nola Jane Randall," repeated Ty. "Say, ma'am, that's mighty impressive. Now I see what's got you by the pants."

Abby seemed to think that was funny, too, but then that serious look came back into her eyes. "So you really think it's a waste of time?"

"Sure is." She seemed crestfallen and for a minute Ty was tempted to tell her the Nola Jane still had a hundred years' worth of gold in her—which she probably had, if you could afford to get it out—just to see her face light up with that dimpled smile again. "Say, ma'am—Abby, if you don't mind me callin' you that—why don't you come have a bite of lunch with me? I'd sure like to hear about your great-grandma. She's quite a name around here."

"Lunch?"

Those big, golden eyes fastened on Ty and he felt a hot weakness in his belly. "Well, maybe it's a *little* early..."

"Lunch. I'd like that," she said, and he breathed an internal sigh of relief.

"Aw, yer safe with Ty," Joe commented, "an' they got chili fer the special at Gracy's."

"Thanks, old-timer," said Ty dryly.

It was pleasant, walking along the wavy sidewalk with Abby. Abby from New Jersey. What a curious place to be from. A person was from Denver or Cheyenne or Butte or, just possibly, Salt Lake City, but not New Jersey. His mind couldn't even conjure up a picture of the place. "You live in one of those high rises?" he asked.

"No, I live in a house, an ordinary sort of house in an ordinary sort of neighborhood. In Newark."

"You work?"

"Do I ever. Two jobs. I have two children. Twins, actually. Boys."

Children. His heart sank. She was married. Drat the luck! Then the words just popped out, all by themselves, and he could have bitten his tongue, but it was too late. "Are you married, Abby McAlister?"

She stopped short in front of Assay Office Antiques and looked up at him. "No," she said quickly, "I'm divorced, recently divorced."

A grin glued itself onto his face. "Say, that's great. Me, too, only I've been divorced for a couple of years now."

"Great? I'm not so sure..."

"Well, I meant it was great you're not married, I mean, you know..."

But she didn't reply to his garbled statement. Then they were at Gracy's, where he held the door open for her very carefully, the way a gentleman did for a lady.

Now, why exactly had he felt so darned protective the minute he'd heard Abby asking Joe about gold mining? Good question, Ty thought. He was doing it simply and purely out of the goodness of his heart. He had a big heart and wasn't ashamed to admit it, a big heart and loads of sympathy for everyone and everything, from a wounded bird to a jilted woman. Never mind that his helping hand got slapped aside painfully from time to time; he never gave up on people. He'd think the best of all the souls he met until they proved otherwise. And it didn't hurt if they were pretty as a picture like Abby. Even if she *was* from New Jersey.

She started to take off her parka and appeared a bit surprised when he helped her. Didn't eastern men know how to treat women? They ordered chili, and he convinced her to have a beer "because the chili was a little bit spicy."

"Are you planning on moving out here, you and your boys?" Ty finally asked.

"Oh, no, I'm just looking around. I got curious. Well, I found a diary, Nola Jane's diary, and it made me want to see Cripple Creek. I couldn't move. I have two jobs and the boys are in school, first grade, and, well, I was raised there. All my friends . . ."

He knew she was too good to be true. He supposed it wouldn't hurt—one lunch—then goodbye, pretty baby. After all, what would a divorced woman with two little boys do in Cripple Creek? "So you came out to look at the mine."

"Do you know where it is?" She leaned forward on the table and her breasts pushed against her sweater. He switched his eyes abruptly to her face.

"Sure. It's a couple of miles southeast. Not far. But there isn't much to see."

"What would it take to start a mine up?"

"Equipment—maybe thirty, forty thousand dollars' worth. A crew. Then you have to ship the ore to a refiner. The closest is in El Paso, Texas. The cost of mining and shipping and extracting eats up your profit."

"But gold's going up. It's going to hit five hundred dollars an ounce soon."

"Maybe."

"It is. The dollar's weak and inflation is increasing. So people hoard gold and the price rises."

"You studied this?"

"I'm a bookkeeper, and I try to follow the stock market. But, really, anybody can figure it out."

"Listen, Abby, there've been boom and bust periods with gold for years now but no one's opening gold mines, or hadn't you noticed?"

"What about your boss? I thought you worked in a mine," she said stubbornly.

"That's different. It's a big operation with lots of capital. And even so, my boss is worried about throwing good money after bad. He may decide to close up after a while if he doesn't hit a good vein."

"Not if gold keeps going up."

He cocked his head and regarded her with amusement. "You sure you're plannin' on goin' back to Newark?"

She flushed then, her cheeks turning as pink as wild roses. "Of course I am," she said.

The chili was tasty and just as spicy as Ty liked it. Abby seemed a bit taken aback by it, though, and he asked Thelma for a glass of ice water for her.

"Wow," she said after a time.

"Good, isn't it?"

He asked her about her job, just to get away from the subject of gold mining. It seemed she worked awfully hard, and her no-account ex-husband didn't even send her any money. He wondered if she had a boyfriend, and then decided she couldn't have or she wouldn't be out here all by herself. Or would she?

"Where would you buy mine equipment?" she asked out of the blue.

"Mine equipment? Well, there's a place in Denver.... Now what on earth do you want to know for?"

"Just curious. And how would a person know what to buy?"

"Any miner could make a list in five minutes. Say, Abby..."

"I see." She thought for a minute.

"You aren't really considerin' mining, are you?" he finally asked.

She leaned forward, her eyes sparkling with excitement. "Wouldn't it be something?"

"It'd be damn hard work. And heartbreak."

"Why are you so discouraging?"

"Look, Abby, I know mining. It's all I do know. And I'm good at my job. I've blasted and surveyed. I've loaded ore, I've frozen in those damn holes, and roasted in others. I tell you, it's not for a nice lady like you."

"I can work hard," she said firmly.

"Can you stand to lose everything, to see your life's work go down a black hole?"

That stopped her. A line appeared between her eyebrows. Good. She had the sense to worry about that. Ty sipped his beer and then leaned back in his chair, stretching his long legs out under the table and hooking his thumbs in his pockets. "So," he said more gently, "tell me about your kids."

She eyed him quizzically. "Do you really want to hear about my kids?"

"Sure. I love kids."

"You don't have any of your own?" she asked carefully.

"No."

"Well, you might change your mind about loving kids if you knew mine."

"Doubt it."

Abby eyed Ty uncertainly, as if not sure how to deal with him, but she did start telling him about her boys.

At least she was off the subject of gold for the moment.

"My kids are twins, identical twins. They're almost seven. Boy, I can hardly believe that. I love them but they have a way.... Well, I guess it's worse with two; they egg each other on. Sean is a little quieter, but not much, and Benny is the manipulator. People have a terrible time telling them apart, but I never dress them alike. I read in an article that it's hard for twins to find their own identities, so they should always be treated like individuals."

"Can you tell them apart?" Ty asked, curious.

"Of course. They're two different boys. Well—" she gave him a little smile "—sometimes they switch clothes and fool me for a minute or two."

"They must be a handful."

She nodded her head. "They are. Sometimes..."

"It must be real hard working two jobs and tryin' to raise those kids," he said sympathetically.

She shrugged, obviously not wanting to complain. He liked that in Abby. She seemed to meet life squarely and obviously didn't try to dodge responsibility. And there was no complaining about it. Heck, he'd sure like to make it easier for a girl like that, but what could he do? She was going back to New Jersey, probably any day now. Damnation. It'd been a long spell since he'd liked a woman as much as he liked Abby McAlister, and she was leaving. Sometimes Ty wondered at himself: he sure could pick 'em. He sat, watching her talk, watching her lips move and her big eyes fix on him, watching her hand brush back a tendril of dark, glossy, curly hair. He almost regretted that he'd ever laid eyes on her.

"You must be bored to death, listening to me blab," Abby was saying.

"Not a bit. Your accent is a little funny, though," he said, grinning.

"*My* accent." She grinned back at him. "Now you tell me something. Where's Leadville? And where's Golden? And what exactly does a mining engineer do?"

"Where's Leadville? Heck, I thought everybody... It's in the mountains west of here. It was a real famous silver mining boomtown, one of the first. You heard of Molly Brown? There was a movie...."

"I guess so. I must have seen it. Didn't Debbie Reynolds star in it?"

"That's the one."

"Do you have any brothers or sisters?"

"Sure do. Three sisters, all older than me. They say they spoiled me rotten, but I never saw it that way. I just figured they gave me a lot of security."

Abby smiled at that. "Gosh, I always wanted to be a part of a big family. I'm an only child."

"Well, it's got its ups and downs. But I guess I like knowing they're all there when I want to call home."

"Why'd you come here?" she asked.

"The mines around Leadville closed up. Same old story."

"And Golden?"

"That's a town outside of Denver where I went to school. Here." He rolled his empty beer bottle over for her to see, and then tapped the picture on the label. "That's Golden, in those flat-topped foothills. Home of Coors beer."

She was leaning her chin on one hand, fiddling with her beer glass with the other. She had pretty hands and wrists. He wanted to take one in his grasp and feel the bones under the soft skin.

"I always wanted to be in mining, I knew that. My dad's a miner. Well, he was. Lately he's been unemployed a lot. Seems like my folks always struggled to make ends meet. We were poor, but then everybody in Leadville was, so it didn't matter. We were happy, anyway, and things seemed to turn out all right.

"Heck, I've worked all over. Idaho, Montana, Arizona. As long as I move around I can work. Maybe that was one reason Sheila left me."

Abby looked down. Had he embarrassed her? "Hey, there's no hard feelings between Sheila and me. Well, not too many, anyhow," he hastened to explain. "That's all past now."

"She left you," Abby said.

He shrugged.

"I'm sorry."

"I'm not, not anymore."

"So, what does a mining engineer do?" she asked then, back on track, as hard to turn as a runaway locomotive.

He swallowed the last of his beer. "Lots of things. I do surveys underground, I see to the shoring, check the geology of the mine, the kind of rock, that is, supervise drilling, whatever's needed."

"So you know about gold veins and where to look and that sort of thing?"

"As well as anybody, I reckon. Course, it's always chancy. There're never sure things in mining." He narrowed his eyes and asked, "Didn't you say you were goin' back home soon?"

"Oh, I am. I'm just curious, though."

A small silence fell between them. Ty had a feeling she was going to start in on the Nola Jane again. He leaned forward and rested his forearms on the table.

"Look, Abby," he said, "I know all about gold fever. Hey, it's been behind historical movements, made men go to California, into these mountains, all the way to Australia. I know what you're feelin'. But believe me, there's no way anyone's going to get rich quick mining gold—not you, not me, not anybody."

"My great-grandmother did."

He shook his head. "That was different. Times were different. Miners only made three dollars a day and there was a refining mill right here in Cripple Creek. And three railroads."

She sat back in her chair, and he could see her withdrawing from him. He hated to hurt her, to dash all her hopes but, dang it all, a person had to face reality.

"Well," she said then, "I guess I better get going. Thanks an awful lot for lunch."

Hell, he couldn't let her go off like that, all depressed and disappointed.

"Want to take a ride up to the mine?" he offered. "See the old gal in person? She's pretty run-down, but maybe you ought to take a look yourself."

"Could I?" Her eyes brightened and that dimple came back to the corner of her mouth. "Do you mind?"

"Heck, no. I'll drive you on up there. Like I said, it isn't far."

The wind was raw outside and a few snowflakes blew down Bennett Avenue, chasing the dust devils. "Wouldn't believe it was May, would you?" Ty asked, leading the way to his vehicle.

Abby ducked her head into her parka. "I can't believe it. Back home it's summer."

"That's what two miles high does for a place. Tomorrow it might be summer here, too." He stopped by an old Jeep. "There's no top on this thing. You goin' to be warm enough?"

"Oh, sure. Don't worry." She was clearly so excited the cold wasn't going to bother her at all. It only made her cheeks and the tip of her nose red.

"Now, wait a minute." Ty rummaged around behind him and came up with an old orange parka. "This is from hunting camp. I knew I had it in here somewhere. Put it on over yours."

"What about you?"

"I'm fine. Why, I've driven through blizzards in this old thing and been warm as toast."

"Do all Westerners say outrageous things like that?" Abby asked teasingly.

"Heck, no, only the ones who want to impress pretty gals from New Jersey. Now hop in, Abby." He held her hand while she climbed into the rusty old Jeep.

Lord, it felt good to be this close to a female. It had been...my God, two years since his divorce, since Sheila had cut out on him with that tinhorn salesman from Wyoming. Two years of casual dates and women who meant little to him, who hadn't touched him where it counted. He'd almost stopped looking.

Ty knew he was holding her hand for too long. She looked at him out of her big golden eyes, a little surprised, a little uncomfortable, and he let go.

It was a three-mile ride up to the Nola Jane mine, south along Highway 67, then east onto a rough dirt road to the foot of Gold Hill. He pointed out the narrow-gauge railroad tracks that paralleled the road for part of the way, and the old abandoned mines, whose names had once been world famous: the Mary McKinney, the Chicken Hawk, the El Paso, the Gold Dollar, the Joe Dandy.

"This is a very interesting area. It didn't look like gold country to the cattle ranchers who settled here. There weren't the usual outcrops, no evidence of quartz or formation of iron pyrites like there usually are in gold country, so nobody bothered prospecting. It was only crazy old Bob Womack who had faith all those years."

"Bob Womack. My mother mentioned him," said Abby, bouncing around like a ball as Ty steered the Jeep over some ruts.

"Well, he was right. The bowl that Cripple Creek sits in was once a volcano. When it blew its top off, the gold got compressed through fissures. Course, Womack didn't know about volcanoes and such. He just had faith. Did you see his old cabin back near the railroad station? It's still there."

"No, but I will."

"It's in what's called Poverty Gulch. Ironic, isn't it? And, sure enough, old Bob died broke. Sold the Gold King mine for peanuts. But he was happy. Drunk and happy. Or so they say."

"Do you know how Cripple Creek got its name?" asked Abby.

"Well, there're a few stories. There's one I'm partial to, though. The Welty family were ranchers here, long before the gold discovery. One day, as they were building their log cabin by the side of the creek, a log rolled on one brother. Then Levi Welty discharged his rifle by accident and hit his own hand. Then a pet calf jumped the stream and broke his leg. So they called it Cripple Creek."

"You sure do know a lot about this area," Abby said, holding on to the seat as they bounced over a rock.

"I'm interested. I could tell you about Leadville, too, or Aspen or Idaho Springs." He glanced at her and noticed how red her nose was. Reaching behind him, he pulled out a wool cap, beat it against his knee to dust it off and then offered it to her. "Here, put this on. It's cold."

She took it gratefully and pulled it on. He liked the way her curls stuck out around the bottom. No self-consciousness in Abby. He sure liked that in a woman.

The Jeep bounded over a branch in the road. Abby put her hand out for support and inadvertently clutched his knee.

"Sorry," she said quickly.

He finally pulled up at a small clearing. Some bushes grew against a green hillside, and a rusty bucket lay on the ground, along with a few splintered boards and some broken glass. Abby climbed down and looked around, obviously bewildered.

"This is it?" she asked in a forlorn voice.

"Yup. The Nola Jane. No neon signs, are there?"

"Where is it?" Abby was biting her lower lip, her dark brows drawn together in a frown. Maybe he shouldn't have brought her up here—there was nothing more depressing than these old abandoned mines. They tugged sadly at a man's heartstrings, brought to mind images of bygone days when men trudged in and out of the black holes, glad to be working, because the earth provided a good healthy living, then, and there was always the hope of striking it rich.

Ty studied Abby carefully for a long moment and suddenly he wanted to reach out, pull her to him and hold her. He wanted to tell her that he understood her sad, lost feelings.

"I don't see a mine," she was saying, turning around in place, craning her white neck. He supposed that since he'd brought her to this place he'd better satisfy her curiosity. "Over there." He pointed to a thicket of serviceberry bushes. "Wait a sec, I've got a lantern." He dug into the back of the Jeep again. "I knew it was here somewhere."

He led the way to the hillside, pushed aside branches and stamped on them to create an opening. "Now, the Nola Jane is what we call a slope mine. That means she opens into the mountainside at an angle. Most of the mines around here go straight down into rock. It's a lot cheaper to mine a slope mine; not so much blasting to do."

They approached a collapsed wooden framework. A few cross ties were scattered on the ground. "Careful," he said, taking her elbow, and then muttered, "hope I recharged this thing," as he turned the lantern on near the mine opening. It worked. Its surprisingly bright beam shone into the darkness.

"Is it safe?" Abby asked at his shoulder, peering at the cold, unwelcoming black hole in the rocky hillside.

"Well, I wouldn't go very far inside. But this whole valley is solid volcanic rock so the mines don't cave in, like you hear of in coal mines and such. We're lucky here, hardly need any shoring. No, what you have to worry about in these mines is dead air, carbon dioxide. Pockets of it form when the barometer drops. The low pressure sucks the oxygen out of the air and you can suffocate. But not so near the entrance, of course."

He stepped inside and held his hand out to her. She took it without hesitating and he loved the feel of her soft skin. Her hand was mighty cold, though.

was chill and damp in the mine. Ty expected it but he wondered what Abby thought. There were a few 'isted iron car tracks scattered on the wet floor. The ceiling dripped and crystals hung, reflecting various colors in the light from his lamp.

"It's wet," she said wonderingly.

"Sure is. Those crystals up there are copper sulfite. They're formed from the water dripping."

The shaft opened up before them, straight and dark, pregnant with echoes, dripping patiently, still, after a century. He felt Abby's arm against him and realized that she was shivering. But then she straightened and seemed to shake off the moment's weakness.

"This was Nola Jane's mine," he heard her whisper into the void. "She was here."

"Well, I don't reckon she drilled or blasted," Ty said, "but she must've come into the mine sometimes, I guess."

"Did it look the same then?"

"Probably not. First of all, the shoring was new, and there were tracks and ore cars and men pulling the cars. There were ventilation pipes to get air to deeper parts of the mine, and fans and things."

"So where's the gold?" she asked steadily, her eyes big with questions in the lamplight.

Ty laughed. "It's all around us in the rock, locked in the ore. You don't often find free gold—oh, a few sparkles sometimes—but mostly it just looks like rock. It has to be refined. Costs about four hundred dollars an ounce to get gold out and there's maybe five ounces of gold per ton. So you see..."

"But if you hit a vein, I mean, that's where the gold is really concentrated, isn't it?"

"Some veins are better than others," he cautioned.

They walked on, the carbide light bouncing off the rough, oily-looking sides of the shaft. Above his head, Ty could see the darker thread of rock that this drift followed—the gold vein. He was going to point it out to her, but then he hesitated. Why should he show it to her and get her hopes up when he knew the impossibility of her reopening the Nola Jane? He hated to quench her enthusiasm and he sure would like it if she had a reason to stay around Cripple Creek but, in all conscience, he couldn't lead her on. It was best she never saw it; it was best her gold fever got cured.

Reaching behind him, Ty took her hand to help her over a pile of rubble. Her cool, silken flesh beneath his work-roughened hand felt awfully good; he imagined if he rubbed her fingers for a minute they'd feel as warm as kitten fur in the summer sun. And he wondered what her lips would feel like beneath his. Would they be as soft and pliant as he imagined? Or her neck? She had a delicate, feminine neck, slim, with soft, velvety skin.

And here they were, thought Ty, miles from anywhere, in the bowels of a mountain. Alone. He'd never been in a mine with a woman, he realized. What would she do if he kissed her?

Geez, man, get a grip. What was he doing thinking those things about a lady he'd just met?

"Is that gold?" she was asking, pointing to some glittering flakes on the wall.

Ty snapped back to attention. "That? Heck no, that's fool's gold. Iron pyrite. It's just shiny rock. But it's fooled a lot of people."

"Oh." She sounded disappointed.

"Seen enough?" he asked.

"How could I get some samples to be assayed?" she asked him.

"You'd just chip some pieces off... Wait a minute, you aren't really planning on doing that, are you?"

"It's the only way to find out how much gold there is in the ore, isn't it? To find out if it's worthwhile reopening the mine?"

"Well, yes," Ty replied reluctantly, "but I told you, there's no profit in it, Abby."

"You said it costs four hundred dollars an ounce to get the gold out. If gold's selling for five hundred or if it goes even higher, that's at least twenty percent profit. Pretty good according to modern business practices."

Boy, was she stubborn! "Abby, it just isn't that easy, believe me."

"Why not?" She stood in the cone of light, her hands on her hips. There were droplets of water in her dark curls and he was sure she was shivering.

"Because... well, just because it never works out in practice the way it does on paper. The price of gold could drop, for instance, but it still costs you the same to extract it."

"I want the ore assayed," she repeated with infuriating resolution. "What do I do? Just tell me and I'll come back myself and do it."

"Darn it, Abby, I couldn't let you do that," Ty said.

"Why not?"

He kicked the toe of his boot into the wet ground. "You are truly bein' unreasonable, you know that?"

"Why?" The question echoed off the damp walls of the mine and hung in the cold air.

Ty gave up. "Okay, okay. But it'll cost you. I warn you, assaying is expensive. And whatever you find won't make a lick of difference."

"Just tell me what to do," she began.

"Aw, heck, all you need is a pick. I've got one in the Jeep." Why was he doing this? He didn't have to. Was he nuts or something?

She followed him outside and waited while he searched through the paraphernalia in his Jeep. He located a small pick and a broken-sided cardboard carton in which to put the pieces of ore. "I guess this'll do," he grumbled half to himself. "This is crazy, plumb crazy."

Abby put a hand on his arm. "I appreciate this very much, Ty. You're an awfully nice man to do this for me."

He looked down at her for a long moment, wanting to say something, but he wasn't sure what. She looked so serious, so dead set on her plan, so damned innocent and pretty, that all he could do was swallow and clear his throat and turn back toward the mine.

He chipped off a few hunks of rock from various places in the shaft. He even took a piece from the roof, where the vein ran, just to be fair. It didn't matter anyway, he told himself. A lady from New Jersey wasn't going to be opening any gold mines, now, was she?

"Okay, we're set. We'll drop this off at the assay office. That suit you?"

She carried the pick for him as they left the mine. "Yes, thank you." She stopped and turned, the glare of the lamp shining in her eyes. "I mean, really, you didn't have to help me like this."

"Sure I did," he answered gruffly.

The drive back to town was just as cold and bumpy as the drive up had been. But it was a lot quieter. Abby kept looking at the box piled with pale striated gray rocks that sat between her feet. Ty kept his eyes on the rough road, but he was terribly aware of Abby next to him, bundled in his orange hunting parka and wool hat. A snow flurry whipped flakes around the windshield and Ty settled his cap on his head more firmly and squinted. "You know," he finally said, "whatever your assay report says, it won't really mean anything."

"Why are you trying so hard to discourage me?" she asked.

"'Cause I like you, Abby McAlister."

She was looking down at her hands. Ty put the brakes on abruptly and turned, sliding his arm along the back of her seat. The tendrils of her hair tickled his forearm. "I don't want you to waste yourself on a wild-goose chase," he said softly.

She looked up and their eyes locked. Yes, she felt it, too—that current between them, that warm, shivery feeling that meant something could happen, something wonderful. He stared into those golden eyes a long time before steering his Jeep back down the dirt road toward Cripple Creek.

They dropped the box of ore samples off at the assay office. Bob Holloway, the assayer, gave Ty a hard, searching look, but Ty only shrugged. The lumps of rock were tagged and put away.

"Preliminary results'll be in tomorrow, ma'am," Holloway said. It was a good thing Abby didn't catch the wink Bob gave Ty over her shoulder.

He pulled up in front of the Imperial Hotel, yanking on the emergency brake so the Jeep wouldn't roll down the steep hill.

"Thank you," Abby said quietly, not meeting Ty's gaze.

He hesitated a second, and then blurted out, "Can I buy you dinner?"

She studied him for a minute. "Ty... I, ah... don't think it's a good idea."

"Why not?" He drew his brows together in puzzlement.

"You see—" she fumbled for a good excuse "—I only got divorced recently and I'm...well, never mind. I just don't think it's a good idea. But thanks a lot, I mean it. Thank you for everything today." She turned away and started getting out of the Jeep.

"Wait a minute," he said. "Will I see you again?"

She handed him his parka and hat. She looked tired all of a sudden. The wind blew a lock of dark hair across one eye and she reached up to push it back. "Sure," she said, "it's a small town." Then she turned and walked up the steps to the hotel, and left Ty sitting there in his Jeep, as cold and empty as the abandoned Nola Jane mine.

CHAPTER FOUR

THE DESK CLERK stopped Abby as she walked into the lobby. "You're Mrs. McAlister, aren't you? I've got a message for you."

Now how...? wondered Abby. No one knew she was here, unless it was the kids or her parents. Had something happened to one of them? Apprehension squeezed her heart as she took the note.

It was, however, from a Mr. Kevin Wayne, of Wayne Consolidated Mining, leaving a number and asking Abby to give him a call at her convenience. She'd heard his name already from Karen Lockley; Wayne was the Canadian mine owner. But how on earth did he know she was there—or where she was staying?

Abby fumbled through her change purse and dropped the coins into the pay phone. A man answered, "Wayne Consolidated, Kevin Wayne here." He had a well-modulated voice with a slight accent—Canadian.

"This is Abby McAlister, Mr. Wayne. You left a message for me at my hotel?"

"Yes, indeed, Mrs. McAlister. I thought you might be interested in talking a little mining, eh?"

"Me?"

"Why, yes. You do own the Nola Jane?"

Doesn't news travel fast, thought Abby. "Actually," she replied, "it's in my mother's name."

"I see. And have you made any decisions about the mine?"

"Decisions?"

"Have you considered selling it?"

"Well, I really haven't had a chance to think about it."

"Then let me give you something to think about, Mrs. McAlister. I'll write you a check for twenty thousand dollars if you'll sell her to me."

"Twenty thousand dollars?"

He laughed lightly at her reaction. "That's correct. You see, the mine I'm working now isn't far from the Nola Jane. Should I need to tunnel through...Anyway, I won't trouble you with details. Let's just say I'd like to protect my investment if it works out that way. I'm simply trying to cover any eventualities that might arise in the future."

"I see," said Abby pensively. In fact, she didn't see at all, but she intended to find out just why Mr. Kevin Wayne would be offering her a considerable sum of money for a so-called worthless hole in the ground. Something was not ringing true. Still, there was no point in putting the man off entirely—twenty thousand dollars was more money than she would see in her bank account in a lifetime.

"I'll tell you what," said Abby. "Give me a little time to think about it, Mr. Wayne."

"Well, of course. Take all the time you need. And I look forward to doing business with you, Mrs. McAlister."

"By the way," asked Abby then, "how did you know about me? I mean, my being here?"

"Cripple Creek, in case you haven't noticed, is a very small town. Well, do keep in touch, and enjoy your stay."

"I will, and thank you, Mr. Wayne." She hung up and stood there a long time, thinking, wondering just what was really behind his offer. Of course, there was the possibility that his motive was straightforward and up front, that he might have to tunnel into her mine at some future date and he was merely covering all bases. At any rate, she decided, in the morning, first thing, she was going to check on her samples, just in case. One never knew. Maybe Nola Jane had left a fortune locked in that black, dripping mine.

Abby had decided to dine at the hotel, but then suddenly, as she stood in front of the mirror and combed her hair, she changed her mind. She'd skip dinner; she didn't need the calories anyway, for Pete's sake. Then, too, for all she knew, Ty might be having dinner downstairs tonight. It would be awkward.

It was peculiar, but she didn't want to run into him. In fact, she realized, she'd wanted to get away from him by the end of the afternoon. The excuse she'd given when she'd turned down the dinner invitation had been pretty lame. So why *had* she said no?

Over and over in her mind Abby toyed with the nagging question. She came up with dozens of reasons she would have loved to have had another meeting with the handsome, friendly Westerner, whose deep, lazy drawl fell sweetly on her ear. In fact, there wasn't a single negative thing she could come up with except, perhaps, the fact that he'd tried awfully hard to dissuade her from opening the mine. Too hard? Or had he merely been protective—a nice guy trying to tell a lady the facts of life?

Abby sat on the edge of her bed and kicked off her shoes, staring unfocused at the patterned carpet. Ty Hollinger. What a man—a real man, and yet sweet and gentle, with a very masculine manner that was both confident and caring. She recalled him as plain as day then, his long, lean, muscled body, the blond curling hairs on his strong forearms, the sinewy neck and that boyish haircut—a chestnut color streaked in places by the powerful Western sun. Oh, and his eyes . . .

She lay back on the quilt, shut her eyes and sighed. Those eyes of his—those brown sparkling beautiful eyes with the long dark eyelashes fringing them. If she tried hard enough, she could almost see each spiky lash. He had great skin, smooth, the color of honey, almost without a wrinkle, save for humor lines at the corners of his eyes and deep hollows on either side of his mouth when he smiled. And, she recalled, he had beautiful ears, nicely shaped, close to his head, with small lobes, just enough for a person to nibble on.

So why hadn't she wanted to see him again? Lord, he'd sent her ego sky-high, done wonders for her failing self-image. He'd made her feel special and warm and liked. So what the devil had gotten into her?

A little voice, as if from an elf who sat on her shoulder, whispered in her ear, "Cold feet, you nerd, you got cold feet. Chicken."

"Baloney," said Abby out loud, but she fell horribly short of convincing herself.

When shadows were creeping out from the corners of the room, she shook off the thoughts of Ty Hollinger, grabbed her bath towel and diary and headed down the hall to the public bathroom. A good long soaking was what she needed. All this business about Ty and the twenty-thousand-dollar offer for the mine had her wound up as tight as a spring. She couldn't pull off one of her therapeutic screams in the hotel, but she *could* indulge herself in a nice relaxing bath.

Abby filled the big old enamel tub and stepped into the steamy water gingerly, letting out an ouch and an ah as she settled into the water. She supposed, what with four baths on the third floor, and it being off-season—the hotel seemed practically empty—that she could bathe as long as she pleased without someone pounding on the door.

Drying her hands, she picked up the diary carefully, rested her head against the back of the tub, and began rereading a section dated March 12, 1894, that had stuck in her mind, especially after her talk with Kevin Wayne.

It's been weeks since I've had a chance to write, Dear Diary.

My thoughts have been scattered and I have not known what to say. You see, I have become a widow. My husband, to my eternal shame and horror, became involved in an argument at the Nugget Saloon. It is being whispered around town that Mike Mann fought with a gambling man over a disreputable woman. Be that as it may, my husband was shot and killed and buried on the hill. I feel the loss, yet, strangely, I feel a sense of relief, although I shall never admit that to anyone.

I should have listened to my parents. Our marriage was a failure. The whole town knows of those women who brought paternity suits against Mike. And he had to pay them off, huge sums that we could ill afford. I was so humiliated, a new bride with stars in my eyes. I don't know how I ever lived through it.

Well, I have learned and I have endured and now I can put it all behind me. I suppose I could call it a stroke of luck, although Mike, for all his big spending ways, left me utterly penniless. Nevertheless, I am no worse off than when I married him.

I detest black. It is my worst color, but Mama says I must wear it regardless. Drat Mike Mann! And drat his clever way with women!

I have moved back into the house on upper Myers Avenue with Mama and Papa. Every day I help Papa at the store, but I think overly much about my namesake, the Nola Jane mine. It is really the only thing of substance Mike left me. I also realize now how little time my husband spent mining, and I wonder if the Nola Jane has real value after all. Probably I am getting gold fever. How terrible.

The other day, after church, George Rausch approached me and offered me a thousand dollars for my mine. I promptly turned him down, rather curtly, and there was much snickering in the crowd as our neighbors climbed into their carriages. Mama says I am daft and must sell the worthless mine, but Papa stands up for me. Maybe he has gold fever, too. If I get another offer, I will pay closer attention, but I have never liked Mr. Rausch, having found him unscrupulous, and therefore I shall never sell to him under any conditions.

Abby drew more hot water from the old brass tap and

lazed back again, turning another yellowed page and reading on.

June 18, 1894. Dear Diary, I have done it again. Today at the store I spoke to Mr. Laraby, who owns the Bennett Avenue Bank. I asked him about money to purchase new equipment for the mine and he asked me if I was unbalanced, thinking about mining. *A woman*, he exclaimed, sneering at me. The man is pompous and vicious and should I strike it rich, he'll not see a penny deposited in his stuffy mausoleum.

It is all over town now. Nola Jane Mann is trying to reopen Mike's mine. Everyone is laughing and last night Mama cried and said her friends will not talk to her on the streets. Papa is even starting to question my sanity. What shall I do? I cannot sit in this gold-crazed town and wear my black and wither away. What should I do?

Her poor great-grandmother! Why, it was hard enough being a career woman in this modern day and age, but inconceivable for Nola Jane. The ridicule the woman must have faced! And yet, she still had the pluck to forge on with her plans.

Abby drained the tub and put her cardigan over her nightgown, but her thoughts were lingering in her great-grandmother's day. She kept picturing Mike Mann in that saloon, wearing his gold brocade vest and black broadcloth coat, drunk as a skunk. And who had the other woman been, the one Mike had gotten into the argument over? An image of a blond woman in a red flouncy dress with a red feather stuck in her pompadour kept coming to mind. And then poor Nola Jane, standing on that cold hillside in March, burying her husband, hiding her shame from the world. Kind of the way Abby had felt when Steve had walked out on her and the kids: mortified, scared, alone and penniless, left with a nebulous future. Boy, Nola Jane had had guts to face all that and then somehow come out of it a very wealthy woman.

Another parallel struck Abby: the offer made to Nola Jane for her mine. Abby had just had an offer—a big one, at that—and still was undecided. What was she going to do?

Take it a step at a time. In the morning she'd find out if the ore was worth anything and then any decisions she might have to make would be a whole lot easier. She had to keep in mind, too, Ty's warnings. He knew his stuff, or seemed to, anyhow. And what was she doing thinking about gold and mining?

This is only a vacation, Abigail McAlister. Get your head out of the clouds.

Early the next morning Abby telephoned Mrs. Howell and the twins. It seemed that both boys had missed their mother the past day and Benny had had a terrible nightmare. But Abby talked to them at length and assured herself that they were doing fine.

"We're going to get a pizza tonight," said Sean expectantly.

"That sounds yummy," Abby said. "And just think, in a few days, Mommy will be home and we'll do something special together."

"What?" asked Benny.

"Well... We'll plan it when I get back, okay?"

"Bring me a present!" piped up Sean, and Abby promised them both something straight from Cripple Creek.

She ate a quick breakfast at the hotel, pleased with her willpower of the previous night, double pleased that the waistband on her slacks was a little less snug that morning. When she left the dining room, she peered into the bar, where they served coffee in the morning, but it was empty. She shrugged, shouldered her purse, and headed out to the street.

It occurred to Abby to drive her rental heap the four blocks to the assay office, but she decided against it. First, she needed the exercise, and second, it was a lovely morning to walk, sunny and clear, not a cloud on the mountainous horizon.

It really was a charming town, decided Abby as she marched, huffing and puffing, up bumpy Bennett Avenue. Especially when the sun was out and warm on her shoulders. All the little shops appeared neat and tidy, their storefronts painted colorfully or the brick veneer recently cleaned. These people cared about their town. There was the lady's boutique and the Mother Lode Saloon, the knit shop and the grocery—Nola Jane's papa's grocery? Of course, on the hillside there were a few sad old shacks that could have used a good painting but, still, they fit in somehow alongside the proud, quaint Victorians. It was hard for Abby to envision Cripple Creek as it had been in Nola Jane's day—a bustling city of over fifty thousand inhabitants. There had been hundreds and hundreds of buildings then, and all that remained of most of them now was a stone chimney or one crumbling brick wall or an occasional hole in the ground. Cripple Creek was littered with reminders of the good days gone by.

Two blocks ahead of Abby was the train depot. The little engine was sitting at the station puffing billows of black smoke into the clean air. The boys would adore a ride on that train, she knew. And they'd love the Western flavor of the town, and the burros that supposedly roamed the streets at will. The twins sure would like it here....

She walked along Bennett Avenue, drinking in the sights, looking into the distance toward the Collegiate Peaks, almost purple in the morning light. This sure would be a terrific place to raise two boys....

"Good morning," said the assayer when Abby pushed open the door and the bell dinged above her head. "You're up bright and early, Mrs. McAlister."

"To tell you the truth," said Abby, catching her breath, "I couldn't wait another minute to see your report."

"Well, now," he replied, "a report takes several days, but my preliminary tests show a real top-grade ore here."

"Really!" exclaimed Abby, her heart surging with adrenaline.

"Really." He laughed. "What did you expect?"

"I don't, ah, know. I thought you might tell me it was plain old rock or something."

"There's plenty of plain old rock, as you put it, in the samples, but plenty of gold, too."

"Gold," breathed Abby. "Oh, my goodness!"

"The Nola Jane always did have a good vein in her," he was saying, but Abby was barely listening. *Gold,* her brain kept repeating, *gold, gold, gold!*

Then suddenly her eyes widened and she asked, "Vein? What vein?"

"The vein running through your mine, of course. Didn't you see it?"

"Well...I...ah, I guess I did but, um..." That good-looking Ty Hollinger with his soft, deep voice, his "ma'ams" and his heavy-duty sex appeal must have known the vein was there! He *had* to have known! He had just conveniently forgotten to point it out. Oh, and to think she'd melted every time he opened his mouth!

"Something wrong, ma'am?" asked the man.

"I, ah, no. Everything's fine. In fact, everything's great."

"Careful. Before you know it, you'll have the fever."

"I think I already do," responded Abby brightly, her head swimming. Then she asked, "Do all mines here have veins?"

"Most of the good mines do. Although there're a few that were played out years and years ago."

"But the Nola Jane isn't one?"

"No, ma'am. The story around these parts is that your great-grandmother only took what she needed and left the rest to her female descendants. I guess the story must be true, huh?"

Abby left the office bubbling with excitement, whistling as she almost sprinted back down Bennett Avenue toward her hotel. *Gold, gold, gold!* Dear God, if there was a way of getting it out of the mine and processed she'd be a rich woman!

Suddenly she stopped short, her joy replaced by a flash of anger. Ty Hollinger. That... On the other hand, maybe she was so angry she was missing something, blocking, as they said in group therapy. Maybe there was a very logical explanation for why Ty had failed to point out the vein of gold running through her mine. Maybe—*now let's give him the benefit of the doubt here*—he assumed she knew about the vein, that he was so used to seeing them that he simply never thought to indicate it to her. *I mean, what right do I have to judge him so quickly?*

Her thoughts spun around again. *Gold!* She felt suddenly hot all over, flushed with fever and excitement. A thousand questions flew through her head, but Abby was unable to grasp or hold on to any. Later, when she'd calmed down, then she'd think about all the wonderful possibilities.

She found herself in Karen Lockley's used-clothing shop. She was bursting to tell someone her good news, and besides, she planned on going up to the house and looking around some more, so she'd best tell Karen, her neighbor, not to be alarmed.

"Well, congratulations," said Karen. "You must feel like a very rich lady."

"I do," said Abby with a huge smile, "but I guess, like a lot of other mine owners, just knowing there's gold there doesn't get it onto the market."

"They say it's expensive to mine it, all right," put in Karen.

"And the price could drop, too."

"It could."

"Still..." mused Abby.

"Still..." agreed Karen.

"Still, I'm going to look over the house again. Try to estimate what it would take to fix it up."

Karen laughed then. "Face it, neighbor Abby, you've been bitten by the gold bug."

"That's silly."

"Is it?"

"Well, anyway, I just don't want you or your daughter to be alarmed if I'm rattling around up at the house."

"We won't be."

"Well, see you later."

"I imagine I'll be seeing a lot of you, Abigail McAlister." Karen winked knowledgeably.

Abby climbed in the Ford and started it up; the old steam engine down the way had nothing on black smoke when it came to this piece of junk. Nevertheless, after several false starts, the motor finally sprang to life and she chugged up Myers Avenue toward her home—no, thought Abby, her *house*. Home was in Newark, New Jersey, with Sean and Benny and trusty Mrs. Howell. It was flagging cars on the highway and rubbing scratchy eyes while poring over ledger books at the Holiday Inn. It was worrying about the utility bills and the dentist and the seedy teenagers riding the school bus with the kids. It was fumes from cars and bouncing checks and roof repairs on the house. And it was needing a new dryer and wanting that dress in the store window at the mall but knowing she couldn't afford it. It was Saturday calls to her folks in Florida and dreaming of a way out.

She sat for a long time in the car and stared at the little purple and red house longingly. What ifs tormented her mind and she tried very hard to think of reality and forget about gold. She tried hard, all right, but everywhere Abby looked, everything she saw had this funny, unexpected hue to it: everything was just a little bit shiny and golden.

CHAPTER FIVE

TEN IN THE MORNING, Ty thought, and he was already feeling as if he could hoof it on down to the Mother Lode Saloon and drain a mug or two of beer. By eleven, he'd be stark raving mad if he didn't find some way of relieving this tension, but hellfire and damnation, drinking wasn't going to cure him!

It was Abby, no denying it, who was driving him crazy. He couldn't get her out of his head; he was elated and miserable at the same time, hot and cold, impatient and unable to concentrate. He saw her face on the ceiling, heard her voice in his head.

Why had she turned down his dinner invitation last night?

He rolled over in his creaking old brass bed and flung an arm over his eyes. Why? She'd liked him—at least he'd thought she did. But then maybe she didn't like him at all: maybe she was just being polite or something.

"Hell's bells," he swore, forcing his naked body out of bed and stomping into the cold bathroom.

"You're an honest-looking guy," he told the mirror as he rubbed at the stubble on his chin. "Heck, you're not so bad lookin', either. So what'd you do to turn her off?"

Ty showered and shaved and tried to comb his hair down flat, but it persisted in sticking up at the crown.

That was absolutely the last time he was going to get the four-ninety-five haircut. He padded downstairs to the kitchen and scrambled three eggs, made toast and sat at the table, but sure as the sun had risen, his appetite wasn't there. Frustrated, he pushed himself away from the table, grating the chair on the linoleum floor, jumped up and angrily scraped the whole mess into the cat's bowl. Gertrude, his huge orange cat, looked up at him through marmalade-colored eyes, said, "Meow," and sashayed out of the kitchen.

"Ungrateful woman," he called after her. Then he stood in the middle of the floor, hands on hips, and thought: what now? He had the whole day off because he had to work that coming weekend, when some equipment was due to arrive from Denver. So how was he going to kill the time?

He could go fishing. Or he could do that spring tune-up on his Jeep. Or he could rake the lawn in front of his rented Victorian house. Or he could drive on down the hill to the hotel and ask Abby McAlister who she thought she was, driving him crazy like this.

He opted for the last choice. After grabbing his jean jacket and trusty old Broncos cap, Ty climbed into his Jeep and ground his way down Bennett Avenue before he could talk himself out of it. But at the hotel, he was told she'd gone for the morning; the clerk, a trainee, had seen her driving away in an old clunker, a black Ford, the girl thought.

"Well, where'd she go?" demanded Ty.

"How would I know? Geez," said the girl, shaking her head, "I'm not into mind reading, mister."

Ty drove up and down the dusty roads searching for her car. Then he drove south out of town toward the Nola Jane mine, but there weren't too many decent roads around Cripple Creek and she couldn't have been dumb enough to drive up a rough dirt road just to sightsee. Or could she have? Was Abby stuck somewhere, in trouble? Oh, no....

His search proved futile. Disappointed, he drove back to his place. If he'd taken Myers Avenue, which ran parallel to Bennett, he'd have driven straight past her car and her house. As it was, Ty jumped out of his Jeep, anxious and frustrated, and never saw the Ford parked two short blocks away.

Ty's rented house dated back to the 1890s. It was a two-story Victorian with dormer windows, a widow's walk off the master bedroom upstairs, a wrought-iron fence and tiny green yard, lilac bush and all. To save a month's rent he'd painted the place, lavender with yellow and mauve trim. It was tidy and charming, and on this particular morning, he hated it. He hated his cat, the serviceable furniture, the gingerbread around the porch, the hardwood floor that he paced, his boot heels clicking restlessly. He hated everything.

"I should have told her about the vein," he grumbled to Gertrude, who yawned. "I should have moved heaven and hell to convince her to reopen that damn mine!" Gertrude stretched, scratched at the upholstery on the couch, circled and settled lazily back down. "Sure! I should have been a jerk and told her anything she wanted to hear, but no-o-o! Not good ol' Ty Hollinger, nice guy!"

The clock dinged one o'clock. He felt like throwing an ashtray through the thing. How was he going to stand life in Cripple Creek without Abby? She'd gone, left for Denver and New Jersey, and she wasn't coming back, either. And all because he'd been honest.

He strode to the kitchen window, held the lacy curtain aside and gazed out. For the first time in years he'd met someone special, and now he'd blown it. And he couldn't even say *why* she was special, just that she was. Abby was neither fantastically beautiful nor incredibly sexy. And her figure, although round in all the right places, wasn't the best he'd ever seen. Her face was real pretty and certainly youthful, but she'd hardly stop traffic. Yet there was something delicate and graceful to her; it was in the way her hand brushed her dark hair aside, in the manner that she walked and spoke. And, Lordy, how his heart had pitter-pattered when she'd laughed self-consciously. And she did have the most beautiful eyes, unforgettable eyes—that golden color that glowed just before dusk after an evening rain.

How long Ty stood there staring directly through the Ford was anyone's guess. He was gazing, unfocused, into the middle distance, when suddenly the undefined chassis of an old black Ford Galaxy became sharp and clear.

"Well, I'll be," he breathed, "her car! That's gotta be Abby's car!"

It wasn't thirty seconds before Ty was standing at the door of her house, panting, the fever in his head making him dizzy. He was raising his hand to knock when...what? What was that terrible, wrenching scream?

"My God!" Ty whispered, alarmed. "Abby!" He never thought. Just put his shoulder to the old splintered wood and gave it a bone-cracking shove. Another one. Abby was in there, in danger, maybe hurt!

The frail wood gave way around the rusted hinges and the door crashed in. And so did Ty, awkwardly, half falling over the mess he'd made, a hand on his shoulder as he yelled out, "Abby! Where are you?"

From where Ty stood looking frantically around the living room, he could see no one. Then she rounded the corner from the kitchen, her cheeks flaming scarlet, her eyes as big as saucers. "What the . . . ? Ty?"

"Abby."

"You . . . you broke my door in!" She didn't look as if she were injured. But then . . . she didn't appear angry, either. Of course, she *did* look sort of embarrassed.

"Are you all right?" he asked, catching his breath. "I mean, I heard this awful scream . . ."

"Oh, my," she said quietly, her gaze dropping from his face to the rubble on the floor. "Oh, gosh."

"But what happened?"

"I, ah, er, screamed, Ty."

"I know that."

"It's a way of . . . of releasing tension. We do it in my group therapy sessions."

It would be a warm day in winter before he understood *that* one. So he made her explain.

"A bunch of us women, and a few men, too, get together and talk out our problems. Sometimes we scream. It's simple."

"Screamin' is not talkin', Abby."

"Look," she said, staring down at her shoes, "I feel silly enough as it is. Can we just drop the whole thing?"

"Okay. I don't get this screaming business, though," he said finally.

Ty stuck his hands in his jeans pockets and rocked back on his boot heels. He was feeling mighty embarrassed himself, if truth be told. And, wow, was his shoulder smarting! His bemused look went from Abby to the broken door and back. He shrugged, then winced at the pain in his shoulder. "Ah, I," he began, "well, guess I better mosey on down to my place and get my tools." *And wipe this sheepish look off my face,* he thought.

If Ty was clumsy breaking in doors, and tongue-tied around pretty women, he knew he could make it all up with his hands. When he returned, he began by setting up a couple of makeshift sawhorses on her front lawn, rolling up his shirt sleeves, and building her a new front door out of the old one and a few boards he found lying behind her outhouse. A fast trip to the hardware store and *voilà*, there he had it, a usable, secure door that would last a lifetime.

"I don't believe it," said Abby, coming from the kitchen, where she'd been scraping dirt off the shelves.

"Ah, it's nothing," replied Ty, grinning. "Anything else? How 'bout my cleaning up the potbelly over there and fixing where the pipe goes into the roof? It looks pretty leaky."

"Well, sure. I mean, this is awfully kind of you, Ty."

"No problem. Just remember to get the stovepipe cleaned out before you use it too much. The darn things can be fire hazards."

"Oh, I will. And thanks."

He fixed the roof with tar paper and flashing, sealed it and did his best to clean out the stove, readjusting the joints in the pipe and making sure they wouldn't leak smoke. Abby came in and out of the living room, moving things around, sweeping, getting dirty and dusty. He offered her the clean red and white kerchief he always carried in his back pocket—a rag was about the handiest thing a man possessed—and she tied it around her head like a sweatband so that her dark hair curled up around the edges.

He was filthy by four o'clock, but then so was Abby. They decided to do a few more odd jobs, and then call it a day. "I hate to ask," said Abby, wiping her hands on the front of her already grimy turtleneck sweater, "but I just can't get the kitchen sink to drain. The water isn't turned on, but I got a bucketful from the pump out back and it sure would be easier to wash things if I could use the sink."

"No problem." Now, plumbing came as easily to Ty as breathing. He got his big wrench out of his tool kit and headed happily for the sink. The problem, he could see immediately, stemmed from the gooseneck underneath. Probably the water trap was plugged up and didn't even require replacing, just a little cleaning and some putty. He stretched out on his back and eased himself under the counter, his long legs sticking out on the cracked linoleum floor.

"Gosh, that looks uncomfortable," said Abby, leaning over to watch.

Ty took his eyes off the pipes for a moment and got a quick look up her turtleneck. He switched his glance back to the sticky joint instantly and swallowed hard. "It's a simple job, really," he sputtered. *Don't stand there like that!* he wanted to yell, his poor brain churning with uncivilized thoughts. No wonder cavemen had dragged their women off by the hair...

"Where did you learn all this stuff?" she was asking, still bent over.

"I, ah, from my dad, I guess." He twisted the fixture hard with the wrench. *Don't you have something else to do, Abby?*

"Your dad?"

"Yeah, like I said, we were a big, poor mining family in Leadville. We had a great old house, though, and on weekends we all pitched in and fixed it up until it was darn near a showplace."

"Sounds like fun."

"It was. Thing is, Dad and I were the only two men around, so this sort of work fell to us."

"And your sisters and mom painted and varnished..."

"And gardened and refinished. You know."

"You went to... where did you say? What school?"

"Colorado School of Mines. If you're into that sort of thing," he bragged shamelessly, "it's the Harvard of mining. A tough school. Very few applicants get accepted."

"That's great. For you, I mean."

"Yep. Like I said, though, mining and engineering just kinda came natural to me."

"Bookkeeping is my thing."

"I'm not so good at that. Guess I'm lazy. I never even balance my checkbook."

"I could do it for you. If I stayed around, that is."

He wanted to ask her just what she was planning to do. She was fixing up her house, but was it to live in or to rent out? But he didn't ask; he was afraid, maybe, to hear the wrong answer.

"So you've lived all over Colorado and where did you say? Montana?"

"Yes and no. More like Arizona and Utah. But I like Cripple Creek a whole lot, and I'm hopin' there'll be years of work for me here. It's my kind of town."

"You're not footloose, then?"

"You mean like a rolling stone that gathers no moss? No, not me. I'm a settling-in type. I only moved around a lot in the past out of necessity. I went where the work was." Ty twisted down hard with the wrench, forcing groaning sounds from his throat, straining his forearms. "Lordy, but this is stuck tighter than a wolf in a den!"

"I take it, then," said Abby, bending over a tad more, "that you think there will be more and more work in Cripple Creek. More mines reopening."

"This blasted nut won't move!" He put all the pressure he could on the pipe. Suddenly it gave way, a hundred years' worth of sludge in the gooseneck pouring into his eyes. His head jerked up and away automatically, his temple slamming into the pipe. "Son of a gun!" he hollered. "Ouch!"

"Oh, Ty...Oh, darn! This is all my fault." Her hands, soft and gentle, were on his forearms and she was pulling him out from under the sink and then helping him up. "Oh, look at you! You're covered with that stuff! And your poor forehead. Oh, Ty, I'm afraid it's bleeding a little. Oh, no." She pulled a kitchen chair over and carefully pressed him down onto it. Then she was taking the kerchief off her head and rinsing it out in the pail of well water and saying, "This is so unsanitary... We'll have to fix you up right."

"It's fine. I'm okay," he mumbled, but subsided as she put the cool cloth to his temple and dabbed tenderly at the gash. Then she was rinsing out the rag again and wiping the mucky sludge from his eyes and off his nose and cheek. She was standing so close to him that her breast was brushing his bruised shoulder and sending shock waves straight down to his...

"Abby," he said, choking, "that's okay. I'm perfectly fine. Honest." In a minute he'd be putting his hat in his lap to hide himself, for goodness sake! "Abby, don't..." Holy cow! "Abby, gosh, stop this!"

"What's wrong? Am I hurting you?"

"Yes! No! Really, I'm fine." He squirmed in his seat.

"Well, there's a big knot coming up on your forehead and I think I should get some ice." She brushed his shoulder again, and sweat popped from every pore in his body.

"My gosh, you're hot," she said matter-of-factly, and Ty thought if he didn't pull her into his arms in a minute and kiss those pink lips, he was going to go as nuts as a caged timber wolf.

"No. Now, listen. Let me up here and I'll finish with the sink. Come on, Abby, I'm perfectly fine."

Ty fixed two of the front windows while Abby drove into town and got some bread and lunch meat and a six-pack of Coors. Then, when her Rent-A-Wreck stalled a block from the house, Sir Galahad was under the hood tinkering and within minutes the Ford purred like Gertrude beneath his touch.

Abby was under the hood, too, exclaiming over Ty's clever use of his hands. "Boy," she said wonderingly, "Steve, my ex, was the biggest klutz in the world when it came to cars and stuff like plumbing. Dad, too. It sure is nice to have a handy fellow around."

Ty's head swelled so big it was a wonder he didn't get it caught under the hood.

He built a fire for her in the potbelly—a couple fires wouldn't hurt until the chimney sweep came—loaned her his broom, propped up the broken leg of the old couch with a cinder block and found her an Indian blanket for upholstery. The place was taking shape, but it was still not quite livable, and when she announced,

"I'm going to stay here tonight," he wasn't at all sure she should.

"That's not a very good idea," said Ty, standing in her living room with his hands on his hips.

"Why not?"

"Because there's no lock on the door and, well, the bed is pretty old back in that room and I don't know about these windows..."

"I'll be fine. I checked out of the hotel this morning and got some bedding from Karen's shop."

"And there's no electricity, either."

"I'll get some candles."

"What about having to use the outhouse?"

Abby cocked her head to one side. "I could shower at your house. I mean, if you don't mind."

He answered her so quickly he stuttered.

TY HAD NEVER REALLY LISTENED to running water before—at least not like this. He heard every drop hit the enamel; he heard the splashes on the shower curtain; he wondered, tormented, whether the droplets were coming from the shower head or off her breasts, or maybe her cute round bottom. His brain worked feverishly while he sat, seemingly relaxed, in the easy chair with his beer, stroking Gertrude's back, wishing it were Abby's.

Then, while she used his hair blower to dry her hair and sat on the edge of his bed—his *bed* for God's sake—Ty climbed in to take his turn in the shower. Difference was, he used cold water first, and then turned it to hot.

He was sure, he was so sure he was going to pull her into his arms the minute he walked out of the bathroom that his newly washed skin was already covered in a fine sheen of perspiration. He combed his hair and shaved—for the second time that day—and he put on some after-shave lotion. He whistled, rubbing circles on the steamy mirror as he grinned like the Cheshire cat.

Frowning momentarily, he shook his damp head. Sure, he was going to pull her into his arms. Course he was.

With only his underwear and a clean pair of jeans on—no shirt, he wasn't going to need it—Ty strode out of the bathroom, his still damp feet making prints on the hardwood floor. "Abby?" Where was she?

"Downstairs," she called back. Damn.

Reluctantly he put on a clean shirt and walked down the stairs. "Abby?"

"In the kitchen, Ty. I was just putting away your beer and the lunch meat. I hope you don't mind?"

"Sure, that's fine." He padded into the kitchen. God, she was a sight for sore eyes! She was bent over his refrigerator, tidying, her rear end presenting quite a pleasant picture, her newly washed hair all damp and shiny, curling up slightly around her ears. "Abby," he said, the lump in his throat making him sound hoarse, "Abby..."

She turned around. "Yes?"

"Abby...I..."

"Yes, Ty?"

"I...ah...well."

"It is getting late, isn't it? And you must be beat. I suppose I better get on home. Do you have a candle or two I could borrow? I'll replace them tomorrow."

"Ah, sure. But it's not that late."

Abby smiled charmingly. "You are such a gentleman, Ty Hollinger."

A gentleman, he thought. Boy, did she have *that* wrong. If Abby could read minds . . . "Why don't you just stay here?" he asked suddenly. "I mean . . . in the guest room. It's warm and comfortable . . ."

"I'll be fine down the street, Ty. Really I will."

"Are you sure? I mean, are you absolutely positive?"

"You are so sweet. Of course I'm sure. Honest."

"Can I at least walk you home?"

He did get a blush out of her, anyway. "If you want to," she said softly.

The two blocks passed too quickly. And then they were at her door and Abby lit a candle and stood on the threshold, her hand on the newly sanded wood, smiling, the light flickering in those beautiful golden eyes. "Thanks for everything, Ty. I really mean that."

"It was nothing." He'd almost ground his toe into the dirt and said shucks.

"Well . . . good night."

"You sure you'll be okay?" he asked persistently.

"I'll be fine."

"Well, bye, then."

"Good night, Ty," she whispered as she closed the door.

HE TOLD HIS BOSS a ridiculous lie on the phone the following morning—something about having to work at home on the survey sketches for that new tunnel—but it worked. And besides, Ty knew he'd get all his work done that weekend and wouldn't put in for overtime or anything, so there was no loss on either side. He hung up and smiled to himself, then pulled back the kitchen curtain and checked on Abby's car. It was still there, all right.

He found her mixing paint in the kitchen. "Good morning," he said cheerfully as he poked his head through the back door. "Need some help? I've got the day off, it seems."

"You do? Oh, great," she replied, "I could use some help."

"Then I'm your slave for the day, ma'am."

They painted the kitchen lavender and white—Ty had lots of lavender left over from his house. And Abby scrubbed and bleached the old cracked linoleum floor and splurged on curtains from the hardware store. "You know," she admitted as she reached and stretched to hang the lacy material, "I'm as careful as they come with money. I've had to be. But every once in a while I just spend on something. Like these curtains. I had to have them no matter what." His eyes followed the contours of her sweater as she reached up, fussing with the rod.

"You fixin' to stay?" he finally ventured to ask.

"Oh, I don't know. Probably not. You know I live in New Jersey."

"This is a weird vacation, then, isn't it?" He wondered if his terrible disappointment showed.

"Not really," she said, the fabric pulling tighter across her breasts. "I like to work like this. It's relaxing."

Ty climbed up on a chair next to her and held one end of the curtain rod. "So you really are going home?"

"I have the house there, Ty, and the kids."

"I know."

"Besides, you said yourself that reopening the mine was a long shot."

"I never said that. What I said," he corrected, "was that I didn't think you could make money at it. Anyone can reopen a mine around here. It takes money, though, and a lot of hard work . . ."

"Let's not get into it, okay?" Abby said. "I keep changing my mind enough as it is."

"All right," he replied as they slipped the curtain onto the rod, "but just remember, as much as I'd like to see you stay here—" he held her gaze for a moment "—I'd move heaven and earth to keep you from reopening that blasted mine of yours."

"Let's drop it, okay?" She let go of her end of the curtain, laughed suddenly, and everything went back to normal between them. Sort of.

The back steps leading into the kitchen were falling down. Ty worked on them until they were as sturdy as a rock. He then fixed the swinging gate between the wagon wheels and propped up one corner of the sagging front porch with cinder blocks. He bought two new panes of glass downtown while Abby picked up a pizza and they drove back up the hill in his Jeep, laughing and bouncing around like two newlyweds returning to their dream home. Trouble was, Ty knew, they were far from married. Heck, he still hadn't even kissed the lady!

There was a sadness in Ty that afternoon as they sat on her couch and ate the gooey pieces of pizza. He was growing miserably fond of Abigail McAlister, even though all along he'd known she was going to leave soon, most likely forever. Oh, at first it had been easy to woo the woman from Newark. It had been fun and romantic and a pleasant way to pass a few quiet days in Cripple Creek. Then it had turned from fun into something else. Well, what now? he asked himself. He sure did want to pull her into his arms and nibble that tomato sauce off the corner of her mouth, but was that the wise thing to do? Wouldn't he just be pursuing a hopeless cause? Damn.

"Is something wrong, Ty?"

"Not at all," he answered brightly, too brightly.

They put a second coat of paint on the kitchen shelves and Ty fiddled around the outside of the outhouse, securing the half-attached door. Then they cleared the yard of the major debris and made a trip to the dump above town, unloading the old boards and rubble they'd piled up in the back of the Jeep. The sun was slipping behind the mountain by then and Abby was talking about the twins and how much they'd love Cripple Creek and how she should have taken a ride on the narrow-gauge train.

"I just wish I had a better feel for it," she said pensively as Ty pulled out his parka from between the seats and helped her into it. God, just touching her like that . . .

"A feel for what, Abby?"

"For Cripple Creek. For the mine." She averted her gaze.

"You aren't still thinking . . ."

"This is not a safe subject," she began.

"I agree." His hands lingered on her shoulders too long. "I think, Mrs. McAlister," he said softly, "you should forget about gold."

"And sell out to that man?"

"What man?"

"You know, I told you, to Kevin Wayne . . ."

"What?"

"He made me an offer."

"He did?"

"But I was sure I told you, Ty. He offered me twenty thousand for the Nola Jane."

"Twenty thousand! And you turned him down!" His fingers automatically gripped Abby's shoulders too tightly.

"I wasn't sure. I'm still not. And you're hurting me."

He released her instantly but without apology. "Take the money. Look, I knew this guy once. He put every cent he had into his mine. Lost everything. He's never gotten over it. Please, Abby, take the money."

"I can't make that decision yet."

"Abby, take it."

She began to climb into the Jeep. "I think we'd better go now. It's getting cold out."

For too long Ty stood there studying her, wondering, positive she'd lost her mind. Sure, he thought, his anger growing, he could try to persuade Abby to stay, he could have her all to himself then. But what about when she went broke, when her spirit was destroyed and she had nothing left? It could happen. How many times had he seen it? In fact, it most likely would happen that way. Blast it, he couldn't let her do it!

He climbed into the driver's side in one fluid, angry movement. "Take the damn money," he said under his breath, grinding the transmission into first. The tension between them was palpable, and by the time they pulled up in front of Abby's house neither was speaking. Abby stepped down and looked at him questioningly, but he didn't relent. Her shoulders drooped and then she began walking toward her door. Ty merely sat there, gripping the steering wheel with white knuckles, his brain churning with frustration. Why did women have to be so all-fired stubborn!

Suddenly he hopped out of the Jeep. "Abby!" he called after her.

She kept on walking.

"Abby! Stop right there! We have to resolve this."

Finally she paused and turned. "We can talk in the morning," she said quietly.

"We can talk right now."

"Not when I need to scream, we can't." She went inside and closed the door.

Something in Ty seemed to let go. His body was no longer under his control. It was as if he stood aside and watched himself take long strides, covering the distance between them. Then he was inside her house and she was turning and without thinking, he grabbed her shoulders and pulled her around to face him. Her eyes, wide and startled, were fixed on him and he started to say something, but gave up.

There was nothing else to do: Ty's head dipped and he covered her mouth with his, pulling her up against his chest and crushing her to him. For an instant Abby tried to pull away but then suddenly, as suddenly as his own emotions had altered, her arms were going around his neck and her lips yielded and neither could breathe. It was as if stars were exploding overhead and showering them with burning cinders all over their flesh. Hungrily, Ty searched her mouth with his and held her to him with reckless need.

In the end, she stirred in his arms and pulled away. "I..." she began, her chest rising and falling unevenly, "I think that was a terrible mistake."

Ty tried to catch his breath. "I don't," he said simply. Then, before she could utter another word, he did an about-face, marched out of her door, purposely leaving it open behind him, and sauntered down the walk toward his Jeep. He didn't even bother to glance back when he heard the sound of her door slamming.

CHAPTER SIX

A LONG-DISTANCE RIG crawled by Abby, raising dust, and the trucker leaned out his window and whistled admiringly. Abby didn't even notice him. She held up her sign, subliminally aware of the long line of traffic, but focusing her mind on debating the agonizing question.

Should she stay in Newark where she was safe, where there was the boys' school, where she had jobs, friends, her self-help group? Or should she sell her house, pack up and move to Cripple Creek? Every time she thought of relocating, her heart gave a terrible leap of fear and anticipation. She lay in bed each night going over the pros and cons of a move. Once she'd even taken a blank piece of paper, made two columns and listed all the reasons for going and all the reasons for staying.

Both columns ended up being nearly equal in length, and Abby knew the decision boiled down to one thing: what did she want to do?

Her radio buzzed. "Stop your line," came the tiny voice at the other end, "convoy's ready here."

After obeying orders, her mind reverted instantly to her problem. Cripple Creek. Friendly Karen, incredible scenery, pure air, the ramshackle purple and red house. That nice solid school building, practically close enough to the house to hear the kids playing outside at recess.

There was, of course, the gold in the Nola Jane mine. The *vein* of gold. How could she keep flagging cars and adding up ledger columns for the rest of her life, knowing every waking minute and even in her dreams that the gold sat there awaiting her?

And there was something else in Cripple Creek, too. Or, rather, someone. Ty Hollinger. She turned the sign from stop to slow and blushed all the way down to her work boots. Ty. How could she forget the way he'd pulled her into his arms and kissed her? The tall handsome Westerner with those beautiful sable eyes and those darkly fringed lashes—he'd kissed her! Oh, sure, she'd been mad as a hornet at him, but still . . .

Then she thought: she was thirty-one, for Lord's sake, and she certainly was too mature to allow romance to get in the way of sound business sense. She tried desperately to leave him out of her calculations but, darn it all, he just wouldn't remove himself.

Decisions. The big drawback was, as always, money. She'd have to sell her house, the only thing of value she owned. She might lose every penny of it—her grubstake—and then where would she be? Fright clutched her stomach. She'd be alone and broke and far away from anyone or anything she knew. Did she have the courage?

To stay—she almost groaned aloud—meant the same unrelenting routine, the worry, the grind of work and no time and no hope. But she could manage, she knew that.

On May twenty-fifth, she went to a realty office recommended by Denny, the night auditor, and listed her house for ninety-two thousand five hundred dollars.

"That's a bit low, Mrs. McAlister," said Sandy, the realtor she spoke to.

"If I sell it, I want it to go fast," said Abby.

"*If* you sell it? Mrs. McAlister, you need to be sure if you list your home with us."

Abby drew in her breath, feeling anxiety gripping her heart again. "I'm sure," she said. But she wasn't.

On the phone, her mother listened patiently to Abby's anguished arguments on both sides of the question. She sighed, and then said, "Honey, you have to do, first of all, what's right for the boys. They're your responsibility."

"I know. And moving could be the best thing I'll ever do for them. Mom, how do I know?"

"You don't. Oh, Abby, I wish I were there with you."

"Nola Jane went to Cripple Creek. It worked out for her."

"Her parents were with her, she was young, honey, and didn't have any children."

"I know," said Abby, suddenly discouraged.

"But you say it's a nice place. Oh, dear, it's so far away..." Her mother sighed again.

"Look, Mom, do one thing for me. In case I decide to move. Could you get some papers drawn up selling the mine and the house to me for a dollar? I'll pay whatever it costs you to get it done. And I'll take care of the taxes from now on. I need to own the property if I'm going to mine it."

"Are you sure you'd have to sell your house in Newark?" Lily asked.

"I'd need the money to buy equipment and pay a crew. No one's going to give me a loan, you know. I've figured and figured and it's the only way, Mom."

"But what if you lose it?"

"If I lose it, well, I'll start over. I can always sell the mine to this Kevin Wayne I told you about. I could open a bookkeeping service in Cripple Creek. Start out small. I'm not afraid of hard work."

"Oh, honey..."

"The house would be mine. No mortgage. I don't need much. I could manage."

"Abby, you sound like you've already decided what you're going to do."

"No, I haven't, Mom, really."

Her group therapy sessions were becoming less comforting. She wanted so badly to tell Joann and the others of her dilemma, but after the last reaction to her talk of gold mining, she was afraid to. The group was supportive, but only within certain boundaries, it seemed. This was one choice she'd have to make all on her own.

Mrs. Howell gave Abby a message one afternoon when she got home from work. It was from the real estate lady: she was to call her right away. Abby was hot and tired and caked with dust. She flopped down on a kitchen chair and rubbed at the line her hard hat had made on her forehead.

"Mommy, I'm hungry!" yelled Ben.

"Can you come to the school play next week, Mommy?" asked Sean. "I'm a bumblebee."

"I'm a flower!" put in Ben.

"What night is it?" Abby asked.

"Thursday night, Mommy, and we have to bring cookies, for after."

"Oh, gosh, I'm sorry, boys. I work on Thursday night."

Their faces fell.

"Mrs. Howell will take you," Abby said cheerfully.

"Aw, they think she's our grandma." Sean's mouth was sulky. He grabbed an apple and pulled on Benny's arm. "Come on, let's go play."

Damn, she thought. Double damn. She was angry at herself, at Mrs. Howell, at Steve, at the school. Why couldn't they have their darn play on another night?

She got up and opened a can of diet pop, washed her hands and splashed her face with cold water. Mrs. Howell's neat handwriting on the pad of paper by the telephone jogged Abby into action.

She dialed the number and asked for her agent, Sandy.

"Good news, Mrs. McAlister. I showed your house and the gentleman's come in with an offer. Ninety-one five. Of course, you can make a counteroffer. I did tell him it was a very good price..."

"It's a deal," said Abby firmly.

"Well, I'm sure we can get another five hundred..."

"Sell it, Sandy," replied Abby. "Like I said, I'm in a hurry. I'm moving to Colorado."

It took two weeks to take care of all the details, to pack and throw out, to quit her jobs—both of them—to say goodbye, close bank accounts and pay bills. She arranged for Sandy to have power of attorney at the closing of her house and to rush her check to her in Cripple Creek, care of general delivery. Sandy looked at her as if she were crazy. *"Cripple Creek?"* And she even found time to bake cookies and attend the end-of-the-year school play, featuring Mrs. Bluestein's first grade.

Very early one June morning, Abby tied down the last rope on the U-Haul trailer, locked her front door and left the key in the mailbox, took a deep breath and got into the green Dodge station wagon.

Mrs. Howell was there to say goodbye, tears in her eyes. "You'll send me postcards, won't you?"

"I promise. Thank you for everything."

"Bye-bye, kids," said Mrs. Howell, wiping her glasses. "You be good boys for your mother."

"Bye, Mrs. Howell," chorused the twins, solemn-faced, still half asleep, each clutching his favorite toy. Sean had a figure of Rambo and Benny had an army truck.

Abby swallowed, near tears herself. She was leaving, she was risking everything, for once taking her life into her own hands and not waiting passively for something to happen. But, oh, it was scary and lonely out there on the brink! She put a bright smile on her face, started the car and said decisively, "This is it, kids. And we're not looking back."

"Mommy! Sean took my truck!" wailed Ben.

"I told him he could have my Rambo!"

But Abby didn't hear them; she steered the car away from the curb, felt the U-Haul trailer jerk after her and turned toward the New Jersey turnpike and points west.

THE BOYS RAN like wild little animals upon being let out of the car after four solid days on the road. They loved the house, they loved the dirt road and the hillside, they'd already examined every square inch of the property and climbed on every purple and red wagon wheel.

It was late in the afternoon and Abby was only going to get a few essential boxes out of the trailer. She'd make up her bed, open the suitcase they'd been living out of for four days. All their clothes were dirty. There must be a laundromat in town. Of course, there was that ancient wringer washing machine in the shed out back. She recalled, vaguely, her grandmother using one. She wondered if it worked.

There were so many things to do. She needed groceries and didn't have the energy to go buy them. Besides, that would mean sitting in the car again. Tomorrow she'd see about getting the electricity and water turned on and call the telephone company. Then there was the mine. Just how did a person go about opening a mine? What on earth would she do first?

A dusty car drove into the driveway next door and Karen Lockley got out. She yelled something and waved and came hurrying right over to Abby. "You came back! Abigail McAlister, you really did it!" she said, hugging Abby and laughing. "Boy, am I impressed!"

"Oh, Karen, it's good to see somebody I know. I'm really wiped out. That was a very long drive."

"Better than a covered wagon, though," replied Karen. "Now, where are those two boys of yours?"

"Probably in the outhouse."

"Say, they can use my bathroom if they want."

Abby laughed. "They love the outhouse. They wouldn't use a real bathroom if you paid them."

"Abby, are you really here for good?" asked Karen.

"Yes, I'm here for good. I sold my house, I sold everything I couldn't carry and here I am."

"If you need anything, I mean anything, you let me know. That includes advice, a shoulder to cry on, the bathroom, whatever. You have a bed to sleep on and all?"

"Yes, don't worry, I'm all set."

"Now if the fellow down at the electric company drags his feet getting you hooked up you tell him I told him to get a move on, you hear?"

"Oh, Karen, thanks, I really appreciate everything."

"I've got to get back to the store now. Janet's watching it—she gave me fifteen minutes." Karen rolled her eyes. "She's got a date. You know."

"See you later."

It had definitely improved Abby's spirits to see Karen. She had one friend, at least, someone she could talk to if she got lonely. She supposed she wouldn't have a whole lot of time to sit around feeling lonely, though.

Karen backed out of her driveway just as Sean and Benny ran out of the outhouse. She stopped her car and leaned her head out of the window. "Hi, boys! I'm your Aunt Karen!" Then she waved and grinned and drove away.

"Who was that, Mommy?" The boys looked puzzled.

"That was your Aunt Karen. Well, not really your aunt. She lives next door and she's going to be a good friend of ours."

"Is she a cowgirl?" asked Benny. To him, everyone in the West was a sheriff or a cowboy—or cowgirl.

"No, she has a store in town, a secondhand store."

Abby went back to unpacking. She pulled out sheets and pillows and blankets and carried them into her bedroom. Then, as long as it was handy, a box of kitchen utensils. And, of course, a carton of dishes in case she had the energy to buy some groceries and fix dinner.

Thank heavens it was cool up here in Cripple Creek, but even so, Abby was soon sweating and pushing her hair off her damp forehead. Then she just had to lug out her favorite old rocker. It would make her new house look like home. And the small Oriental rug—that would look so nice in front of the potbellied stove, especially when she refinished the old floor.

"Mommy, when are we going to eat?" Sean asked. "Where's my *Star Wars* book?"

"Did you find Tigger yet?" pressed Ben. Tigger was his favorite stuffed tiger.

"Tomorrow, kids, okay? We'll unpack the rest tomorrow."

"Can we eat now?"

Abby sighed but then brightened. "Hey, I bet there are some potato chips left in the car."

But they were soggy because Sean had spilled his pop on the bag. "Okay, soon, boys. Hold on. Let me get a few things put away before it gets dark. Remember, we have no lights except some candles."

The chair was heavy and unwieldy but Abby got it through the door finally. The rug was easier. She just dragged it in and unrolled it as far as the old couch, which she didn't have the energy to move.

She put the toothbrushes in the bathroom, a glass, towels. She tried not to look at the gaping hole covered by a piece of plywood where, someday, a new toilet would go to replace the missing one. Ty had said he could put one in for her... She shook herself angrily. She couldn't depend on Ty, even if he was still around.

Water was a problem. There was the pump in the backyard, and the bucket.

She might have to ask Karen if they could use her shower, just until she got the water turned on.

She walked outside and stood on the doorstep looking at her yard, at the purple and red wagon wheels, at the squat, dark spruce trees along the side of the low house, the aspen trees by the back door, the grass that was much too long already and the shed that leaned crazily against some bushes bordering on Karen's yard.

It was hers, all hers. She owned it, lock, stock and barrel.

The town lay below her, dozing in the late afternoon sun; she hadn't realized that her house sat on such a steep hill above town. An occasional trail of dust marked a car's route along one of the dirt roads. Abby laughed to herself at the thought: she lived on a dirt road! Only Bennett Avenue and a couple of the side streets were paved.

Nola Jane must have stood here like this. The house had been her parents' and then, when they had died, hers. But she couldn't have lived in it for long before she struck it rich and moved to Colorado Springs. How different Cripple Creek must have looked to her! The whole valley had been filled with buildings, the town's avenues lined solid with banks, hotels, department stores. There were schools and churches, elegant homes, a stock exchange, five newspapers and streetcars. Eighteen passenger trains arrived every day. According to Nola Jane, it was the most exciting place in the world.

It was so different now. The strange thing was, the gold was still here, but nobody wanted to risk mining it. There must, there *must* be a way, Abby thought fiercely. There had to be.

A trail of dust was approaching her, a vehicle climbing the hill up Myers Avenue. She started out to the curb, to get another box from the trailer. The distinctive churning of a Jeep engine came to her, a familiar churning. She knew that Jeep! She stopped short halfway down the walk and felt her heart bound in her chest.

"Mommy! Mommy! Benny fell off the fence," screamed Sean, running up to her, panting.

The Jeep stopped in front of her house, the dust blew away and there he was. He sprang lithely out of the rusty vehicle, looking adorable, shining his endearing smile on her. His sleeves were rolled up and his worn jeans fit his hips perfectly and his stride was unencumbered and sure... just as she'd remembered. No, better.

"Abby," he began, stopping before her, his dark eyes devouring her. Then again he said, "Abby."

"Hello, Ty," she said, feeling a little shy and pleased and excited. Automatically her hand rose to push back her tangled hair.

"Mommy! Benny fell. I think he's dead!"

She didn't hear him, but Ty did. His eyes switched away from hers reluctantly. "You say your brother's dead? Think we should go see?" he said to Sean.

The boy shut up instantly, tilted his head back and studied Ty. "Are you a cowboy?"

"Nope, I'm a miner," said Ty, taking Sean's hand. "Now where's this dead feller?"

"A miner," said Sean, considering, then disappointed. "Oh."

Ben wasn't dead; he'd only scratched his neck tumbling off a wagon wheel. "It's okay," he said bravely. "I'm not a crybaby."

"Let's see about that scratch. You don't want to get gangrene. Then we'd have to cut your head off. Say, which one of you is which?"

"I'm Sean."

"I'm Ben."

"You are not," admonished Abby. "Ty, I'm sorry, they do this sometimes. *He's* Sean and *he's* Ben."

Ty looked from one to the other. "You'll have to wear name tags, for a time, anyhow."

"Who're you?" asked Sean.

"I'm, well, Uncle Ty."

"Boy, Mommy, how come we have all these uncles and aunts and stuff we didn't know about?"

"This is Ty Hollinger, and he's a friend. He helped fix our house up."

"They're both the spittin' image of you, Abby." Ty shook his head admiringly and stared after the boys as they scampered off. "Cute as buttons, but I'll be danged if I can tell them apart." Then he took her hand in his and grinned down at her. "So...you came back."

"Yes." She liked the feel of his hand—warm and strong and reassuring.

"For good, Abby? Or is this another vacation?"

"For good, Ty," she said resolutely. "I sold the house. I'll never go back."

"You did it," he said wonderingly. "Well, I sure am glad."

Abby looked down. "I thought, well, I wondered if you'd still be here."

"Course I'd still be here! Would I leave knowin' you were coming back?"

"*I* didn't know I was coming back."

"But I did, Abby McAlister."

He carried some boxes in for her, saying, "You look tired. This is hard work."

All Abby had to do was say, "here" or "there", and the boxes were set down seemingly without any effort on Ty's part. He was lean, his stomach absolutely concave, but the muscles in his forearms stood out when he lifted something heavy. His hair looked almost blond in the late sun and she hadn't remembered that his eyebrows were so thick or that his neck was so strong. But those eyes, deliciously brown, warm and soft and humor-filled—oh, yes, she remembered those eyes.

Before long he'd brought in boxes of clothes, the boys' bunk beds, all of Abby's pots and pans, her brass floor lamp and the kitchen chairs.

Then he dragged the old wringer washing machine out of the shed in back, rigged up an extension cord to Karen's house, filled it with buckets of water and tried it out. Nothing happened.

"Now just hold on here a blamed minute," he mumbled to himself, returned to his Jeep and came back with something. He lay on the ground under the machine, fiddled, banged and yanked at things, then got up and turned it on again. It worked.

"I can actually wash our clothes!" Abby cried. "You're magic!"

"Oh, it wasn't anything, just a little belt in the motor. People just don't understand these things," Ty said, slapping the noisy, chugging machine.

"That's enough," she said, "please. You make me feel guilty. I can't even feed you. There's not a bite of food in the house."

"I'll take you out."

"Ty, I don't even have the energy to change my clothes."

"I'll go buy some groceries."

"I'll do it tomorrow, really."

"You have to eat. And the kids..."

She sighed. "I'll think of something."

The boys came in, complaining about being hungry again.

"See?" Ty said. Then he kneeled down and asked, very solemnly, "Ever seen a burro, guys?"

"No," replied Sean, "but Mom promised we could."

"Where are they?" asked Ben, wide-eyed.

"Well, now, I just happen to know where they are today. I might take you to see them."

"Please!"

"Ty, you don't have to do this," Abby said.

He ignored her and talked to the boys, mischievous and grinning. "Shh! It's a secret. We can't tell anyone else where they are." He put his finger to his lips and winked at Abby. "And there's a new baby burro with the herd."

"Can we go? Come on, let's go!"

And before Abby knew what had happened, Ty squeezed her hand, assured her he'd be back with some food and was gone with the boys, his Jeep kicking up a cloud of dust.

Abby sank down on the top step in front of the door, leaned her face on her fists and watched the dust sift slowly back down onto Myers Avenue. She wasn't sure whether to laugh in relief or cry from exhaustion. Ty certainly had taken over. Oh, she didn't mind at all; in fact, it was delightful to have someone she trusted. Funny how Ty was always there when she needed him. He'd been at the courthouse, he'd taken her to the mine, he'd fixed up her house. And now he'd taken the boys off her hands, given her a breathing spell, some time alone, perhaps the most valuable thing he could provide just then. She'd have to thank him somehow, show him how very much she appreciated his thoughtfulness. She'd have him over for dinner when she got the house fixed up.

Slowly Abby pushed herself up, went inside and began putting away pots and dishes. The kitchen was shaping up. She hung some clothes in the bedroom closet, which had no doors, and put away towels and sheets. There were no dressers and she hadn't been able to bring her old ones along, but she thought maybe Karen could help her find a couple. Maybe she even had some in her shop right now.

She kept glancing out the window. How long was Ty going to entertain Sean and Benny? They got a bit wearing after awhile, especially to someone not used to kids. Why was Ty doing this? Did he really like kids so much? Maybe he was trying to get on her good side, pretending to like kids. No, not Ty, she decided, he didn't pretend.

When Karen got home from the shop Abby ran over with shampoo and a towel and asked if she could take a shower. Ridiculous, all this running around to other people's houses to shower. She'd get her water turned on tomorrow, no matter what!

When she got out of the bathroom, Karen asked her, "Hey, was that Ty Hollinger I saw with your boys downtown?"

"Yes. Were they behaving?"

"If you call talking a mile a minute with ice cream smeared from head to toe behaving. I didn't know you knew Ty."

"Oh, well, I just met him when I was here before. He was awfully nice to me."

"Hm," remarked Karen, head to one side as she studied Abby, "nice, huh? Ty Hollinger. Hmm."

"Come on, he's just being polite."

"Oh, sure. Listen, Abby, he's one great looking guy. Of course, I don't know him real well but, you know, it's a small town. I sure don't recall hearing of Ty dating anyone around here."

"I'm not dating him. I'm not the least bit interested in men. I have a mine to open."

"Oh, sure."

"Thanks for the shower, Karen."

"Any time."

As Abby crossed to her own yard she wondered if her explanation to Karen had been really truthful. She wasn't interested in men, that was a fact. But could she truthfully say she wasn't interested in Ty? There was no sense lying to herself. She *was* interested in him, she liked him. And here she was, showering, washing her hair, rummaging through the suitcase for perfume and hand cream and mascara, for Pete's sake! And clean jeans and her pink plaid shirt that flattered her coloring. And looking out the window every five minutes, looking for Sean and Benny? Or Ty?

When she was all dressed and feeling a hundred percent better, they still weren't back. My goodness, where were they? It was almost seven. Desultorily, Abby got a couple of small end tables out of the trailer before locking it up for the night. And then she wondered: did she really need to lock anything up around here?

One table she put by the old sagging bed in her bedroom, the other by the couch. She stood back and viewed the effect. Not bad. Sort of funky cute, a little bit like a room she'd once shared in college.

She wandered outside. The boys must be exhausted by now, getting crabby and stubborn, fighting. If they were too awful, he'd be disgusted, dump them on her and leave.

Or... would he wait until the twins were asleep and then try to kiss her again? And would she let him?

Abby stood there, watching the shadows lengthen in her unkempt yard, watching the sun send long fingers of light over the top of the hills to glow on her barn-red house. Had Nola Jane once stood there in front of her parents' house, waiting for Mike Mann to come calling on her? Had the dust motes hung dancing in the sunbeams the way they did now?

Ty arrived then, the old Jeep grinding its way up the hill from town. The boys jumped out and ran to Abby, their cheeks red with glee, and chocolate ice cream dried in patches on their faces, on their shirts, even on their shoes.

"Mommy! There's turquoise in the streets after it rains! Uncle Ty said so!"

"Oh," said Abby, giving Ty a sidelong glance. "Turquoise?"

"Sure is," he was quick to reply. "Honest. All these hills around here are loaded with it. When it rains real hard, the turquoise rises up and floats in the puddles. Honest."

Benny tugged on her shirt. "We saw the baby burro. Uncle Ty said we can feed it carrots!"

"We saw this neat train and the engineer blew the whistle!"

They were dancing with excitement, trying to talk at the same time.

"Uncle Ty says we can go fishing with him!"

Abby met Ty's amused gaze over their heads. "Did they drive you crazy?"

"Heck, no. I just kept feedin' them."

"Thanks an awful lot."

"I brought you dinner, and me, too." He held up a box. "Fried chicken. And a six-pack of cherry Coke. What do you think?"

"It sounds wonderful. Ty, you're so good to do this."

"Hey, don't Westerners have a reputation to uphold? We're known as neighborly folk."

"Mommy, I gotta go to the bathroom again," said Ben.

"Me, too."

"Go on. Then you guys are going to brush your teeth with a bucket of well water and get your pajamas on," said Abby.

"Oh, Mom! It's early!"

"Uncle Ty said he'd tell us a story."

"I'm not tired."

"Boys," said Ty sternly, "get ready for bed or I'll never let either of you steer my Jeep again."

"You didn't!" gasped Abby.

"You weren't supposed to tell," said Sean.

"Oops." Ty made a face. "Sorry."

"Ty," said Abby, "that's dangerous."

"Not really," he whispered. "I had my knee against the wheel all the time. My dad used to do that."

"Oh."

Ty finally got them into their sleeping bags. It was starting to get dark so he lit a candle. The boys loved it. "We're like Daniel Boone," Sean said drowsily, staring at the flame.

Abby knelt on the floor, blew the candle out and kissed each child's cheek. "Good night, kids. Sleep tight. This is your first night in your new home, you know."

"Night, Mommy."

Then there was only the two of them, alone, in the darkening living room. Abby felt nervous and a little dazed by everything that was happening, by the wrenching changes in her life, by the future. By Ty Hollinger's presence.

"So," he said softly, "ready to eat?"

"By candlelight, no less." Abby tried to be lighthearted but her voice sounded shaky to her own ears.

Ty lit a couple of candles and put them on the rickety old kitchen table. "I bet you're starved."

Suddenly Abby realized that her stomach was absolutely empty and about to growl. "I am," she said in surprise.

They ate chicken with their fingers, although there was silverware somewhere in one of the boxes, Abby knew, and drank the sweet Coke out of the cans. The room grew darker until there was only a wavering circle of light around the table.

"This place is comin' along fine," Ty commented, glancing around.

"It needs a lot of work. But when there's water and electricity it'll be wonderful."

Ty looked at his drumstick thoughtfully. "You goin' to get a job?" he asked carefully.

"I'll be working, don't worry," Abby replied, sidestepping the question.

"You sold your house in Newark, you say?"

She nodded.

"You plannin' on starting a business here?"

"You could say so."

"Damn it, Abby, you know what I'm fishin' for! Are you opening that derelict old mine?"

"Yes."

Ty hit his forehead with his palm. "Didn't you listen to me a bit?"

"Yes. But I studied the facts and decided to go ahead." Her heart hammered painfully. She didn't want to start another argument, but he had to accept her judgment.

Ty looked at her for a long time, as if assessing her willpower. Then he gave a short laugh and shook his head. "You take the cake, woman. I don't know whether you're smarter than the devil or plumb crazy."

"You're not mad?"

"No. Everyone to his or her own poison, I say. It'd be like tellin' someone hell-bent on gettin' married not to go through with it."

Abby smiled at him over the box of chicken bones. "Gee, I'm glad. Now we don't have to fight over it anymore."

"I never wanted to fight with you, Abby," Ty said gently, and she knew her cheeks were turning pink with pleasure and nerves and anticipation.

Ty built a fire in the potbellied stove. "Now, you get that stovepipe cleaned out, you hear?"

"It sure gets cold here, doesn't it?" Abby remarked.

"It's the altitude. You need a jacket every night, all summer long."

"It's so different..." Abby began.

Ty turned the flue down and went to sit on the couch, settling his lean frame back against the rug-covered couch and patting the cushion next to him.

Abby's feet felt like lead and her stomach was jumping. She was hot and cold all over, on fire with expectation but paradoxically deathly afraid. She sank down into the cushion and it sagged beneath her. Her fingers clutched the can of Coke as if it were a life preserver.

"Aw, Abby, I know this is a big move for you," said Ty. "I'd like to help, to make it easier for you."

"You already have," she whispered, searching his face. "I don't know what I'd have done..."

"You'd have done fine." Ty pried her fingers off the Coke and held her hand. "You're some woman, Abby."

Abby's skin glowed with the warmth of his touch. Candlelight flickered on his face, shadowing its contours—his deep-set eyes, his wide mouth with its full lower lip, his long neck with its Adam's apple.

"I think we're both having the same thoughts," said Ty in a whisper so deep and caring that Abby's heart clutched with fright and desire. Hadn't it been obvious since his Jeep drove up that they both longed to embrace, that their first meeting the month before had not been a whim but something deliciously, incredibly right?

The fire crackled as he leaned toward her and brushed her lips tantalizingly, so lightly that Abby thought she was dreaming. Then he pulled her closer, so that her chest was pressed against his and their lips touched.

"You are so pretty and so soft," Ty whispered against her mouth. "And I've been waiting weeks to do this."

His breath was sweet and his skin so smooth, his hands strong and knowing. He ran his tongue along the curve of her lips and darts of white-hot pleasure shot through Abby; a shower of sparks drifted onto her skin, raising delectable goose bumps, and she felt herself going under, drowning. Abrupt fear flickered in her brain.

Ty pulled back. "You're afraid," he said with infinite understanding.

She nodded, her eyes wide, her body quivering with powerful, contradictory urges.

"I'll wait then," he said simply, touching her cheek with his fingers until her eyes closed in relief and regret.

She stayed there on the sagging couch, hugging her arms around herself, while Ty got up and went toward the door.

"Thank you," she finally whispered, not looking at him, ashamed, thrilled, sad, relieved.

"Night, Abby," Ty said and she barely heard the quiet snick of the front door as it closed behind him.

CHAPTER SEVEN

MAYFLOWER VAN LINE has nothing on me, reflected Abby as she breathed hard, dragging the heavy wing-back chair across the yard. She should have asked Ty to help yesterday but he'd already done so much. How did a body collect so much stuff, anyway?

"Excuse me, ma'am, but could I help you there?"

Abby gasped and dropped the chair. When she looked up there was a man standing in front of her, a big man—six foot three if he was an inch. She could tell right away he was someone official by his Western-style trooper's shirt. Did he think she was trespassing?

"Rob Loring," he was saying, tipping his wide-brimmed Stetson hat to her. "I'm the sheriff of Teller County and I was just passing by. It looks to me like you could use some help."

"Abby McAlister," she replied, putting her hand out to him, relieved that he didn't seem to be interested in arresting her. "And I sure could use some help with this chair, if you don't mind."

Now there was a good-looking man. A big man. Not only was he tall but he was large-boned, as well, and there was not a pinch of extra flesh on him, either. He had short graying blond hair, a long handsome face, green eyes and weathered skin. Sheriff Rob Loring must have been in his mid to late forties, Abby guessed, as she stood watching him pick up her chair as if it were a toothpick and carry it easily into the living room.

"Over here okay?" he asked.

"Perfect. And this is awfully kind of you," said Abby gratefully. "I mean, in Newark, all the police do is give out tickets."

"I'm sure they do more than that," he replied with a smile as big as the Colorado sky.

"Bang! Bang!" came a little voice from the kitchen—Sean's. He was holding out a finger, pointing it at the sheriff.

"Bang, bang, yourself, young man," said the sheriff gravely.

Abby frowned at her boy. "That is not polite, Sean. Guns are no joking matter."

"I was only pretending, Mommy."

"Quite all right, ma'am," said Rob. "Just as long as his finger isn't loaded."

"Around here," said Abby, "you never know. I've got two boys, actually—twins. It can be murder when they're running wild."

"I heard about the boys," Rob said. "Miz Lockley, Karen, told me. To be honest—" he looked down at his size-thirteen boots "—Karen asked me to check in on you."

"That was very thoughtful of her. In fact," said Abby, "everyone in Cripple Creek is just wonderful. I'm not used to people going so far out of their way to be helpful."

"We do try, ma'am. Folks in Teller County here pride themselves on being neighborly." He looked around the cluttered living room. "Is there anything else I can help you with?"

"No. Really. Carrying that chair was more than enough. And thanks."

He tipped his hat once more. "My pleasure. And I want to officially welcome you to the town. We sure can use enterprising young people in these parts. Especially," he said, "Nola Jane's great-granddaughter. I wish you well."

"Thank you," replied Abby, flattered.

"I better be getting off to work then. That is, if you won't be needing any help."

"I'm fine, really."

"Be seeing you soon, Miz McAlister."

"Abby."

"Be seeing you, Abby." He ducked through the door and drove off, leaving a cloud of dust behind the official Teller County Blazer.

"Wasn't he nice?" said Abby to Sean, who was pushing a truck between her feet.

"Yeah. Did you see his gun, Mommy?"

"I did." Abby had never liked the things but didn't want to make a big deal over it to the boys. "And will you please stop tripping me with that dump truck?"

"Yes, Mommy." But he gave her foot just one last little nudge anyway.

"I need a sitter," said Abby as she heard something in the boys' bedroom crash, followed by Benny's instantaneous scream.

There was lunch to get for the boys, the U-Haul to return to the gas station, the rest of the utilities to be hooked up, a dozen errands to run. And Abby wanted to get up to the mine, as well, and give it another look, by herself this time.

"Come on, you two," Abby called to the twins, who were tearing apart their toy chest, "we have things to do. Let's go. Front and center, troops."

She dropped off the U-Haul trailer, charging it on her Visa—why pay now?—then ran to the grocery store and the hardware store for light bulbs and a new hammer. She'd have sworn she packed one but couldn't seem to locate it. Then it was off to leave a deposit at the electric company. The local company headquarters turned out to be in the assay office. "Hardly need a branch office for this one-horse town," said Bob Holloway. After a quick stop at the post office, she decided that if she was going to trudge around the mine, she'd need some decent boots or something waterproof. *Guess they're going to have to be used, though.*

The boys had a grand old time in Karen's shop, ripping through the used toys, exclaiming and fighting over a secondhand bicycle. "They're always like this," explained Abby to Karen. "Indians."

"They're cute at that age, though," commented Karen. "Wait till they hit the teenage years."

"So I've heard."

"If it isn't a beer it's worse—drugs. You know."

"Drugs? Here?"

"We're not immune, you know, just because we're at ten thousand feet."

"Ugh!"

"You're telling me. Here," said Karen, "try on these boots. They were Janet's and she hates them, says they're uncool. I don't think she ever put them on her feet."

"Boys will wear anything. At Sean and Ben's age, anyway."

"Not girls. Say, those fit pretty well, don't they? Boy, they sure wouldn't fit Janet anymore."

"They fit great! Oh, perfect. I'm going to try to get the car up that road to the mine and tromp around a bit."

"You really going to reopen her?"

"I certainly hope so. I've got to look into so many things, though, and I haven't the slightest idea where to start."

"There're plenty of men around here—out of work ones—who know mining. Maybe you could hire someone."

"I could, I guess. Oh, and by the way, speaking of men, thanks for sending over Rob Loring."

"Was he able to help?"

"You bet. And—" Abby paused, smiling "—he sort of blushed when he told me you were the one who sent him by."

"He would. He's pretty shy, really. A big teddy bear."

"He's very nice looking, too."

"Are you fishing, Abby?" asked Karen, laughing, brushing back her long curtain of brown hair.

"Yes."

"Okay, I confess. I've been seeing Rob for a year now."

"Serious stuff?"

"I hope so!"

"Mommy! Benny bit me!"

Karen settled the dispute between the squabbling boys and then turned to Abby. "You know my daughter baby-sits."

"She's how old, Karen?"

"Fifteen. Going on thirty, I might add. She's very mature, and she can be very responsible, Abby. I wouldn't recommend her if I thought otherwise."

"I'm sure you wouldn't."

"Plus she's got all this free time on her hands now with school out for the summer, and there's this boy from Victor...You know."

"You don't approve of him."

"I don't approve of all the time they spend together. He drinks and drives, too. And every time I try to talk to Janet about it, she gives me a bunch of you-know-what. I'll tell you, Abby, there's a lot to be said for having a man around. Janet respects Rob, but me? No way. She's so rude to me it's embarrassing. And now she's getting rebellious, what with this kid, Hank, hanging around all the time."

"And if Janet was busy..."

"If my daughter was busy, maybe she'd have less time to talk back to me."

"It would be great having a baby-sitter who lived right next door," reflected Abby.

"Shall I call her?" Karen asked expectantly, her hand poised over the telephone.

"Sure, why not? And see if she could cope with the boys for a couple of hours this afternoon, would you? I still want to go up to the mine and I'm afraid I might get stuck or something and have to walk out."

THE BOYS TOOK TO JANET amazingly well. Abby had been afraid that they were so used to Mrs. Howell that there would be a problem—a new home, a new sitter. It did take time to adjust.

"I'll teach them to play Monopoly," suggested Janet, who was the spitting image of her mother, a few pounds lighter, a few years younger but just as tall and buxom and strongly built. "And then maybe, if it's okay with you, Mrs. McAlister, we could walk into town and get an ice cream," she said.

This was the rebellious, rude teenager?

"I wanna ride on the train!" piped up Sean.

"Me, too!" yelled Ben.

Janet looked to Abby for help. "I suppose they can. I'll give you some money."

"Oh, no money. I know the engineer and he'll let us on for free," said Janet. "Only tourists have to pay."

While Janet took the twins next door to fetch the Monopoly game, Abby changed into jeans and her new used boots and a jacket, since the sun was darting in and out of billowy white clouds and the temperature—in June—was still hovering just below seventy degrees. Gee, she thought, in Newark it would be ninety-five in the shade! Had it really only been a few weeks ago that she'd been flagging cars on those hot, steamy highways?

Driving down Bennett Avenue, Abby thought about Ty. Where was he? At work, probably. She wondered if the mine he was employed in was near the Nola Jane and if, while she was so busy getting settled in, she'd see much of him. It would have been a whole lot simpler, too, if Ty were driving her up to her mine in his Jeep. She'd certainly feel more secure. As it was, she wondered if her station wagon was going to make it at all.

In a lot of ways, decided Abby, it was awfully nice to have a man around. Of course she'd had Steve around for eight years and their relationship had not always been so nice. There'd been arguments over just about everything—especially in the end. And Steve had generally had his head in the clouds, always scheming, always looking for the easy way out. But Ty, on the other hand, was not a schemer. His feet seemed to be planted firmly on the ground. Oh, he wasn't rich or ambitious or anything, but he seemed content and well-adjusted. Happy.

Ty. He sure was good-looking. There wasn't a thing about him she'd change. Even that haircut, which made his hair stick up around the crown and over his temples, was adorable—boyishly charming. And those eyes. Abby's heart pounded a little too heavily just envisioning them, fixed on her, thoughtful, lovely and dark and warm.

Suddenly she caught herself. *You're going off half-cocked, McAlister.* Good looks and a winning personality did not a relationship make. There was still far too much risk in intimacy, and she'd better keep that knowledge in the forefront of her musings.

As Abby turned onto the dirt road that led to the Nola Jane mine, she felt a twinge of excitement stir in her stomach. What would it look like to her now that she was a resident of Cripple Creek and the owner of the mine? Would she back down and be afraid to take that leap? There were always her bookkeeping skills, after all, and surely she could make ends meet if she budgeted sensibly. Money, Abby knew only too well, was right at the top of her necessity list.

The car rocked and rattled along the road, protesting, but doing amazingly well. There was this spot, though, remembered Abby, where the route was narrow and steep and very rocky. The spot where she'd grabbed Ty's knee for support. He had awfully nice knees... She saw the steep section ahead, gunned the engine a little, and up went the station wagon. Abby only banged her head on the roof of the car once.

"Phew!" she breathed at the top, where the road leveled off. "That was hairy." She knew for a certainty, that she'd have to trade her car in on some sort of four-wheel-drive vehicle if she did indeed reopen the Nola Jane. Maybe Ty could help her...

Ty! Was he all she was going to think about?

There it was. The clearing, the piles of orange mine dump rubble, the brush half blocking the entrance to the mine—greener now in June, and a whole lot thicker. She'd have to clear the road first thing, bring up a shovel and a big pair of hedge clippers. Maybe Ty had some clippers she could borrow.

When Abby stepped out of the car she did so almost reverently, as if the earth she stood on was hallowed ground. In a way it was, to her; it was Nola Jane Randall's legacy. And how apt it was that there had always been a daughter to bequeath the mine to. Until Abby.

She walked through the undergrowth that had sprung up, closing the way, since she and Ty had forged their path many weeks before. There was the gaping aperture into the side of the mountain, black and cold looking, forbidding yet paradoxically welcoming to her. A chill seized Abby as she stood staring at the hole in the hillside, thinking about Nola Jane, who had once, so very long ago, stood on that same ground, her heart pounding in anticipation, alone in her quest, so very alone. The enormity of her great-grandmother's undertaking struck Abby like a blow. And here she was, in this modern age that allowed a woman to go just as far as she pleased in a career, worried about her own future. The thought made Abby feel about the size of an ant.

You've got to do it, you've got to reopen the mine, her brain commanded. And she would do it, by golly, she would!

But where to start?

There was equipment to be bought and men to be hired and licenses and insurance to take out, dozens of other things, no doubt. So much to be done.

Abby switched on the flashlight she'd brought along and entered the mine. Ty had said it was relatively safe inside—relatively. Still, Abby moved down the tunnel cautiously, a little like a child groping in the dark. Her heartbeat quickened with each step and once she turned around to see the opening that was now merely a pinpoint of light. Boy, was it *dark*. What if her flashlight went out? She'd be lost in that cold, damp blackness, all alone... It had seemed safer with Ty. Her footsteps echoed, splashing a little; unseen water dripped on her. She stumbled over a twisted metal track. It smelled damp and musty in the mine.

She laughed out loud at herself but didn't like the ghostly sound. Then she tried to picture the mine as it had been, full of men with picks, burros hauling cars piled with gold-bearing ore along shiny new tracks. The mine whistle was blowing; outside the railroad rattled along on its local route, taking men to work. Wagons picked up ore and carried it to the refinery in town. Teamsters swore.

And the Nola Jane had just been one mine out of dozens, hundreds even.

The shaft curved ahead of Abby and forked. She remembered the way Ty had taken, to the right, and followed the path along the old rusted tracks. She began to talk to herself, realizing that she was more than a little fearful in this cold, damp place, alone, miles from the nearest human being, miles from help should she need it. Thank God Janet knew where she'd gone!

Abby whistled a tune for a time, listening to it echo off the silent rock, bouncing up one tunnel and down the next. "Eerie," she said.

Why had she come here?

She turned around at another fork and experienced a moment of utter panic—which way? Which way had she come? But then the terror subsided; she'd come from that tunnel, of course she had. "Don't be such a chicken," she said out loud, half laughing, holding her flashlight high.

What did Nola Jane want her to do? she wondered, stopping as if listening for some sort of advice from down the corridors of time. "Wow," she said, "you're really going crazy now, McAlister. Must be this dark hole in the mountain . . ."

"No it ain't."

If it was possible for someone to leap out of her skin, Abby did it. She darn near had a heart attack, as well. And she definitely screamed, and screamed again, dropping the flashlight so that its beam lay along the ground uselessly. She plastered herself against the dripping wall. Suddenly, irrevocably, she believed in ghosts.

"Didn't mean to scare ya, missy," came a disembodied voice from out of the deep, cool darkness. At first all Abby could see was a strong light beam swaying toward her and a shadowy silhouette of a man behind it. Then the light dipped, zigzagging across the earthen floor until it rose again to shine in her eyes, blinding her. The next thing she knew there was something being pressed into her nerveless hand—her flashlight—and she could finally see the features of a lean, bent old man with gray hair sticking wildly out from beneath a miner's hard hat.

Abby tried to speak, but nothing came past the lump in her throat.

"I ain't no ghost, if that's what yer thinkin'."

She swallowed convulsively. "Are . . . are you sure?"

"Positive. But folks round here'll tell ya I'm daft, they will."

"Daft?" Dear God! What was she doing here, in this cold damp place, talking to a wild-looking old man who'd told her people thought he was crazy? *Of course he's crazy!* And what in the name of God was he doing here anyway?

"I know what yer thinkin', missy, but yer wrong."

"You haven't the slightest idea what I'm thinking, mister." There, that was better, wasn't it? Under control, sort of.

"Gibbs is the name, John Gibbs."

"Would you mind telling me just what you're doing here?"

"Lookin' for Abigail McAlister. That's you, ain't it?"

He was scrutinizing her sharply and Abby's courage went flying like a bat down the dark tunnel. "I'm Abby," she managed to say. "So what? Why do you want me? And how did you get here?"

"Got here through a crosscut, if you really want to know. Thought I'd look the old gal over."

"This is private property, Mr. Gibbs."

"Now yer right on that score, missy. But I kind of thought you might be wantin' a bit of company. Maybe some free advice."

"Don't tell me," she replied. "You're a miner and you want to warn me not to reopen the Nola Jane. You're going to tell me I'll go broke and . . ."

"Now hold yer horses." He rubbed at the gray stubble on his chin. "I was going to tell you to do it. To get the Nola Jane up and runnin'. She's got the best damn vein in her I ever seen and you'd be a blamed fool—pardon my expression—if ya didn't start mining her."

Abby leaned against the wall, feeling a little easier. "I must say," she began, "that's a refreshing viewpoint."

"So what're you gonna do?"

"I'm not sure." *Who am I kidding?* she thought with a spurt of knowledge. "I'm going to reopen the Nola Jane, that's what I'm going to do." Holy Toledo, she'd finally made the decision.

"You said you came in here through a crosscut," she said, suddenly relieved. "Do you work somewhere nearby? I mean, did you see me come in and somehow follow me?"

"Nope to both questions. I haven't got a job right now and I didn't exactly follow you. I hang out in the mines."

"Hang out?"

"People say I live in them. Ya know, missy, all the mines connect underground."

"Well . . . do you live in the mines?"

"Maybe I do and maybe I don't."

He was strange, all right, decided Abby. Really weird. Maybe he was even truly crazy. On the other hand, he seemed harmless, and there was a sort of kind and knowing twinkle in those faded blue eyes.

"Are you living in the Nola Jane right now?" ventured Abby.

"Maybe." He motioned with his hand, as if to say, "Let's go this way." "Maybe I'm just watching over the old gal here and makin' sure nobody jumps yer claim."

"Who would jump my claim?"

"Follow me," he said, retreating down the long dark shaft. "If you want, that is."

Why, exactly, Abby followed him she never quite knew. It did occur to her that he could very easily get her lost and then leave her, and yet she believed him when he said he was watching over the Nola Jane; it was in those sparkling old eyes—honesty.

"So you work . . . worked," corrected Abby, "in the Cripple Creek area?"

"All my life."

"But there's no work now?"

"There's some."

"But you can't find a job?" She hoped she hadn't gone too far.

"Nope." There it was, that honesty in his voice again. "Like I said, folks round these parts'll tell ya I'm daft. But I ain't. I just like living my own way."

"You mean like living inside the mines?" Abby followed him dutifully down one winze and then into another. It all looked the same to her; they might have been going in circles.

"Some of the old mines," he said over his shoulder, "are real hotboxes. Warmer than houses. Never did like houses."

So he did actually live in these dark, dank holes. But then, to give the old man the benefit of the doubt, maybe he had a point, not that she'd ever live in a mine, but just because he did, it didn't mean Mr. John Gibbs was a certified nut.

As they trudged along, he pointed out features unique to a mine—many of the same things Ty had shown her. "And once you get the ore into the trucks," he was saying, "it really starts costin' you. Gotta ship the whole lot to El Paso, missy. And if it's a poor grade of ore, then there you are, broke as an old wagon."

"But you encouraged me to reopen," said Abby.

He stopped short and she darn near ran into him. Then, slowly, he tipped his head back, shining his light upwards, blinking his eyes when a drop of water fell into one from the rock ceiling. "There," he said simply.

"What?" asked Abby, puzzled. "I don't see anything."

"There." He waved his hand impatiently.

"You mean that stripe?"

"That vein, missy."

"That's the gold vein?"

"You bet yer pretty little head it is. As rich as any in these old Rocky Mountains."

Abby was speechless, speechless and mesmerized. About four feet above her head was a dark stripe of rock, no more than five inches wide, running in nearly a straight line the length of the shaft. That was gold? But it just looked dark, like any old granite or something. It wasn't anything special at all!

"Yes," Gibbs said. "It'll make you a rich woman, missy. Just gotta get it out of the rock and processed."

"Wow," she breathed, still staring up. "So that's the gold."

"Twenty, thirty thousand'll do it, too. Buy you yer equipment in Denver and hire you a crew for six, maybe seven weeks till the first check comes in from El Paso."

Finally Abby dragged her stare away from the vein. "Twenty *or* thirty thousand dollars? Which is it, Mr. Gibbs?" she asked. "I mean, I'm not made of money. My resources are very limited."

"It all depends on the equipment. If you buy right, then twenty thousand. If you buy like most folks would do, then thirty."

"You do talk in riddles, John Gibbs."

"All I'm saying is that you gotta know yer stuff when you're dealing with these city slickers. And you gotta be able to hold firm on yer offer. If you get turned down, then you go elsewhere."

"It all sounds pretty confusing. What do I need, a list of equipment?"

"A list of the *right* equipment, missy."

"And where would I get that?"

"From a mining engineer," he replied offhandedly.

"I see." Without a bridging thought she was thinking about Ty. He was a mining engineer, wasn't he? He could help her. On the other hand, Ty had led her directly beneath the gold vein and never once pointed it out. Why? she asked herself again. Was his silence really meant to protect her from her own folly, or was there something she was missing? But no, of course there wasn't—if ever she'd met an upright guy it was Ty Hollinger.

"What do ya think?" Gibbs was asking. "Is it worth opening the Nola Jane, giving the old gal another chance?"

"I think it is."

"So do I, missy. It's time folks round here realized the gold in these hills could bring new life to this has-been town. It can be done."

They made their way back through the maze of drifts and crosscuts and shafts toward daylight. When Abby saw the entrance to the mine ahead, she felt small-minded and foolish for her previous notions about John Gibbs getting her lost. He was a nice old man, and knowledgeable—a character, true enough, but Abby liked him just the same.

And then the summer sun was on her shoulders once more and she was momentarily blinded. It felt good. She turned to Gibbs. "Thanks for all your advice in there," said Abby. "And if you want, I mean, I hope this doesn't embarrass you, you can stay in the Nola Jane all you like."

"I just might do that." He seemed to be lingering, as if uncertain. He rubbed at his beard with an age-splotched hand.

"Is there anything I can do?" asked Abby carefully.

"You could," he said, staring over her shoulder, "let me help with the equipment list. I got a degree in engineering, you know."

"Oh," replied Abby, "I . . . ah . . . well, I know this engineer in town and I'm sure he'll be able to . . ."

"Hollinger?"

"How did you know . . . ?"

"He won't be havin' time fer that."

"I don't understand."

Gibbs cleared his throat. "You see, if I were to do your list, maybe even help you in Denver . . . I wouldn't ask for a thing, not until your first check from El Paso came. Then you could pay me whatever you pleased. I don't expect no handouts, missy, and I don't expect you'll believe I got all my marbles upstairs till we make some money."

"I don't know what to say."

"Say you'll give me a shot at it."

"But I told you, Mr. Hollinger . . ."

"And I told *you*, missy, that that fella he works for'll never let Hollinger get involved with the Nola Jane. No, sir. The man's jealous enough as it is."

"What are you talking about?" demanded Abby.

"That Mr. Wayne your boyfriend there works fer."

"Mr. Wayne?"

Abby barely remembered the drive back down the rough road and along the curving ribbon of highway into Cripple Creek. She never saw the June sun sparkling off the distant spires of the Collegiate Peaks, or the softness of the green rolling hills surrounding her new home. The things that had brought her to Cripple Creek—the lovely new sights and sounds and smells—were suddenly tarnished and ugly.

Ty, working for Kevin Wayne, the man who'd made her the offer on the mine, the man whom Gibbs said was jealous. Of course. Ty had known all along the value of the vein. That was why he'd conveniently neglected to show it to her. That was why, no doubt, he'd made it a point to meet her, get to know her, discourage her. His next move, she was suddenly certain, would be to persuade her to take Wayne's offer.

I wonder how much Wayne is paying him?

Brakes squealing, Abby pulled up in front of her house and rested her forehead on the steering wheel. She was peripherally conscious of the sounds of her boys' laughter, but only one thought beat at her brain: Ty Hollinger could have been forgiven for doing his job, and he certainly had been a great help to her, but why, why did he have to go and carry it a step further—why did he have to romance her, as well?

CHAPTER EIGHT

TY WAS ON HIS WAY out the door after a late lunch break when he heard footsteps running up the steps of his front porch.

Abby, he thought happily, and went to meet her.

Her hand was raised to knock when he got to the screen door, but she lowered it the minute she saw him and stood there. Something was wrong. Uh-oh. He registered her stance, which was stiff, and her face, which was white, and her hands, which were clenched into fists down by her sides.

"Hi," he said weakly, searching his mind. Was she mad that he'd walked out on her last night? Was she...?

"I've been to the mine," she said tightly. "I met John Gibbs there."

"Oh, sure, Gibbs. Crazy old codger."

"He's my new mine foreman," she announced coldly.

"Oh."

"He told me a few things."

This was not like the Abby he knew—the sweet, kind, lovable lady. This was a hard-eyed antagonist. "Why don't you come on in? No sense standin' there on the..."

"He told me, for instance, that the Nola Jane has a rich vein of gold in it..."

"Well, sure, but..."

"And he told me that you work for Kevin Wayne!" she finished.

"Oh." Ty opened the door for her and she stalked in, then whirled to face him. Even though he knew she was mad, he couldn't help admiring the way her hair bounced and the way she moved, so ladylike and graceful. But her words drew him back to reality.

"How dare you stand there and say oh like it wasn't important!"

"It isn't important, Abby. What's the difference who I work for? That's got nothing to do with us—or with your gold mine."

"Oh, no? Well, John Gibbs told me a few things that opened my eyes. Boy, am I dumb!" She paced back and forth across his floor angrily. "Wayne wants the Nola Jane so he sent you to . . . to seduce me!"

Automatically Ty opened his mouth; he was sure his jaw hit the hardwood floor. Seduce her? Wayne sending him to seduce her? He clamped his mouth shut and searched for something to say—anything. He felt as if there were dozens of bees buzzing in his head, and he couldn't think. "Abby . . ." He coughed into his hand and tried again. "Abby, I never . . ."

"You be quiet! You tried so hard to convince me not to open the mine, didn't you? Just so I'd sell to Wayne, isn't that right?"

"No, it isn't one bit right!" Ty was starting to get angry, too. How could she believe this stuff?

"Oh, of course you wouldn't admit it. No, not you! You're a real good liar, Ty. You lied to me. You even . . . you even deceived my kids!"

"Now, you just hold on one minute there. I never lied to you. You didn't ask me who I worked for. I would've told you. And, darn it, Abby—" his brows drew together into a dark bar over his eyes "—I never, I never deceived those boys!"

She stopped and folded her arms, facing him. "Ha!" she said, scoffing.

"And I didn't tell you about the vein because I didn't want you to start up that damn mine in the first place. That's true and you know it. I was only tryin' to save you a lot of grief."

"Ha!" Abby repeated, her eyes sparking golden fire.

Ty tried to put a hand on her arm but she pulled away. "Aw, come on, Abby. You don't really believe that bull about me tryin' to get you to sell your mine."

"Oh, no? You must have thought I was really stupid to fall for your line." She thrust her chin forward and Ty could see angry tears brimming in her eyes. "How much of a cut did he promise to give you?"

"A cut? What in tarnation are you gettin' at? What kind of man do you think I am?" Ty started pacing the floor himself. "Who in hell told you that?"

"Nobody. I figured it out myself," she said loftily.

"Well, you figured wrong."

"Ha!"

"Will you quit sayin' that?" Ty stopped in front of Abby. "Now, look, you're upset. Maybe I should've told you about the vein and Wayne and all that, but I just didn't want to complicate things. So, I made a mistake but, I swear to you, Abby, you ask anyone in this town, I am not a liar and I wouldn't do anything illegal or even unethical. I like you, too. I like you a lot and I'd never hurt you."

"Well—" Abby swallowed "—you hurt me a lot, buster. I feel dumb and used and deceived."

"Oh, damnation, what can I say? I'm sorry, forgive me..." Flowers, if only he had a bunch of flowers to offer her—or candy. Women liked chocolate, didn't they? It soothed their nerves. He looked down into those fury-filled eyes and took a stab. "Can I . . . can I buy you dinner tonight, Abby?"

"No! Oh, Ty, I can't forgive you. You took my golden dream, my whole future, and you made it ugly."

"No, Abby, believe me, I never did that." He couldn't reach her. She was too mad and upset. She'd calm down and see he'd just made an error in judgment.

An errant tear rolled down her cheek and Abby brushed it away impatiently. "Oh, why do all my men have to be cheats!" she cried.

"Now don't you go lumpin' me in with your Steve. I'm not like that. If you were my wife and those two kids were mine, I'd fight tooth and nail to keep you. I'd never run out on a woman."

"Easy to say!" Abby took a deep breath; Ty could see her trying to compose herself. "I'm going now. I don't think you better take the boys fishing. Thank you for everything you did for us, but I really think I can manage now."

"Wait, Abby." Ty looked at his watch. "I've just got to get back to work now, but let's talk about this later, okay?"

She looked at him sadly and shook her head, her lower lip trembling a little. "No, I don't want to talk. You go on back to Kevin Wayne. And, Ty, you tell him I will never sell the Nola Jane, to him or anyone else. You tell him that for me, will you?"

"Abby . . ."

But she left him standing there and ran down the porch steps, leaving the screen door banging after her.

Ty took off his Broncos baseball cap and threw it on the floor. "Damn!" he said. Then he spun around, as if looking for a way out of the mess he was in, kicked the cap and said again, explosively, "Damn!"

Wrenching the Jeep around the curves, Ty drove out to the Golden Slipper, Wayne's mine, too fast, cursing himself all the way. *Look at it from her point of view,* he told himself. It looked bad. It looked as if he'd deliberately set out to convince her to sell her mine. *Oh, boy,* he thought, *you did it this time! You really fixed yourself good this time, Tyson.*

She was hurt; she was outraged. He could have kicked himself in the backside all the way to El Paso County. That crazy John Gibbs, filling her mind with idealistic nonsense. *Open the mine.* Oh, sure! She'd go broke, she'd be banging her head against a stone wall. Kevin Wayne was barely making his payroll, even with lots of capital behind him.

It was lucky that no one was in the trailer that served as an office for the Golden Slipper mine. Ty didn't want to talk to anyone. He finished up some work, checking surveys, figuring shoring loads in a new tunnel, ordering some supplies. He could have put on his hard hat with its carbide lamp and gone down into the Golden Slipper. Usually he liked to see the guys working on the face, to say a few words to them, maybe even get his hands dirty drilling some dynamite holes and setting off the charges. Yeah, sure, he liked the guys and they liked him, too—but not today.

The phone rang. Irritated, he answered it. It was Kevin Wayne calling from home. "Did you order that new jack-leg drill?" he asked. "I'm going to Denver on Friday and I could pick it up."

"I'll call them in Denver and tell them, Mr. Wayne."

"Thanks, Ty."

Ty hung up. Was it true that Kevin Wayne wanted the Nola Jane that much? he asked himself. Now, Mr. Wayne was a hardheaded businessman, sent down here by his father's company to turn a profit. But would Wayne try to cheat a woman out of a mine? He'd offered Abby twenty thousand dollars, a good price, about as much as you'd have to put in the mine to reopen it. So she'd be taking no risk at all, and she'd be twenty thousand dollars richer. Nothing to sneeze at.

And another thing occurred to Ty. Just how rich was the vein in the Nola Jane? Grudgingly, he admitted to himself that he was curious. And that nut, John Gibbs, well, the man knew mining, all right, but he was completely eccentric. For Lord's sakes, people said he lived in the mine shafts. And the old man had been known to claim that he knew every crosscut and every winze between Victor and Cripple Creek, six miles apart, and that he could walk underground from one town to the other. Crazy!

Or was he?

Ty drove straight from work to the Mother Lode Saloon. He needed a beer or two and the low-key company the bar offered—no searching questions, no deep conversations, just plain, unassuming fellowship. The Mother Lode, like all Western-style saloons, was long and narrow and dim, with a polished wooden bar along the right-hand side that had a mirror behind it. A few tables filled the back of the room and a squat old jukebox constantly played country and western music or oldies but goodies from the fifties.

When Ty walked in, the Platters were crooning "The Great Pretender" and he felt the words pierce his gut like a knife. That's what Abby thought of him: the great pretender.

The assayer, Bob Holloway, sat nursing a beer and Barb, the bartender, was drying glasses behind the bar.

"Howdy, Ty." She nodded. "The usual?" Barb was tall, thin as a whip and sharp as a tack, besides being a darned good bartender and a tough lady for a Saturday-night drunk to deal with.

He nodded, grasped the cold glass and took a swig.

"Bad day?" asked Bob Holloway.

"I've had better," said Ty glumly.

"That new gal, Miz McAlister, came by today and got her electricity turned on. She's hell-bent on openin' that old mine, ain't she?" said Bob casually.

Ty took a long draught, his Adam's apple working, and then set his glass down. Boy, he couldn't get away from it, could he? "I guess that's her business, Bob."

"Pretty gal."

"Yeah."

Bob turned on his bar stool to face Ty. "You know, that ore of hers I assayed was pretty goldarn good. Better than the Golden Slipper's ore. It might assay out at seven, eight ounces per ton. You know, Ty, gold's been climbin' like crazy lately. It's over five hundred an ounce now." He shook his head wonderingly. "Maybe a soul could make a buck."

"And maybe not," growled Ty.

"Where's that lady from?" asked Barb, coming over to lean an elbow on the bar in front of Ty, unabashedly listening in.

"Newark," he muttered, "New Jersey."

"Cute kids she's got. Saw 'em with you yesterday," said Barb. "Think she's gonna stay here?"

Ty shrugged and finished his beer. Automatically Barb refilled it, talking all the time. "My brother-in-law—say, you know him, don't you, Ty? Big Fella, Tap Crenshaw?—he's a good miner. If Miz McAlister's lookin' for men, you just put Tap's name in with her. He hasn't worked in six months and my sister's ready to cry."

Ty wanted to laugh. As if Abby would pay any attention to him! "Now listen up," he said. "Abby McAlister is doing her own thing. I want to go on record as having tried to talk her out of it. It's crazy."

Old Joe Stedman, the county clerk, doddered in and hitched his skinny behind up on a bar stool. "Howdy, Ty," he said. "Hear Miz McAlister's got old Gibbs as her mine foreman." Joe cackled, drank half a glass of the beer Barb slipped in front of him, and then wiped the foam off his lips with the back of a hand and cackled again.

Ty put his head in his hands, wanting to groan. This town was too damn small.

The jukebox was blaring "Elvira" by the Oakridge Boys. Usually Ty loved the music, the comfortable old smells of cigarette smoke and stale beer and the gossipy patrons in the bar, but tonight he felt as if they were all pinning him to a wall, pulling off his wings, his legs, and ripping out his heart. They didn't know about the fight he'd had with Abby that afternoon, so he really couldn't blame them. But how much more of this torture could he take?

And yet, if he went home, he'd knock around his house, lonely and hurting and knowing Abby was two short blocks away. Warm, soft Abby, with those sweet, curving pink lips and smooth white skin and lovely golden eyes.

Sheriff Rob Loring came into the bar just as the jukebox changed songs again. This time it was "Smoke Gets in Your Eyes." Wonderful old song. The words were true, so true. He'd never really listened before. Oh, boy, did Ty ever have smoke in his eyes!

Loring nodded. "Nice gal, that Abby McAlister," he began. "Just met her this morning, Ty. Hope she gets the Nola Jane going again."

Ty stifled a groan this time. Magically, there was a fresh beer in front of him and he drank it down like a college kid in a chugging contest.

A couple of the boys from the Golden Slipper wandered in. "Missed you today, Ty," Billy White said.

"I was busy."

"Come on down tomorrow for sure," suggested Hank Donovan. "We hit this here new vein. Looks real promisin'."

"Sure will," said Ty, a belch rumbling up inside him.

Billy was looking down into his beer. "I hope this new vein pans out. If Wayne closed the mine—" he shook his head sadly "—I'd have to move again, and Dotty's just beginnin' to like this town."

"Say, did I hear about some rich lady from back East who's openin' the Nola Jane?" asked Hank.

"She isn't rich," mumbled Ty.

"So it's true? Well, I'll be," said Billy. "That's one gutsy lady."

Ty finally went home. Nobody in the Mother Lode was talking about anything but Abby McAlister and the Nola Jane mine. As he left the bar, the jukebox was reverberating with the rousing song, "Up in Cripple Creek," about a miner lonely for his lady and wanting to get off the mountain. He drove home, meandering a little on the dirt roads, with the song's chorus echoing

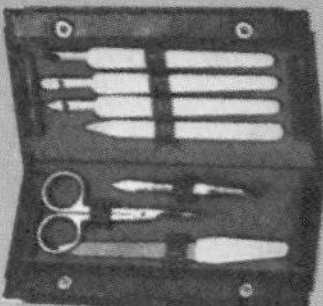

in his ears, feeling maudlin, buzzy in his head and sorry for himself.

HE STRODE AROUND HIS HOUSE, kicking at things and then threw himself on his bed without even taking his boots off. Gertrude finally settled down on his stomach and slept peacefully. But not Ty. Abby was just down the street, so close. Probably asleep now, lying there with her pretty eyes closed and her pretty lips open a little as her breath went in and out, in and out.

He fell asleep just like that and dreamed confusing dreams about Abby and the Nola Jane. At three in the morning he woke up with a start, feeling as dry as Death Valley, drank two glasses of water, pulled his boots off and fell asleep again.

At nine, as he drove up to the Golden Slipper, he felt sick and shaky, cranky, tired and miserable. What had happened to his normal good nature? He could usually disregard the small annoyances of life. Well, he supposed, this was not a small annoyance. Heck, no. It loomed larger and larger over him, like a thunderhead full of cold rain. He couldn't imagine not seeing Abby again, he couldn't imagine not speaking to her, not touching her. He wanted her worse and worse every moment—or was it only because he couldn't have her?

Kevin Wayne was about fifty-five, Ty guessed, a tall man with graying hair, a receding hairline, a neat gray beard and large, nicely modeled features. He was from Vancouver and thus, to Ty, hardly distinguishable from any Westerner in the United States, although he said "out" and "about" in a funny way and had an odd habit of ending some sentences with "eh?" He expected his employees to work hard, but he was fair to them, if very exacting.

"Morning, Ty," he said, looking up from some papers he was studying.

Ty said good morning as he reached for the coffeepot on the electric ring.

"We've got ourselves a good possibility in the south crosscut," Wayne said.

"So I heard." Ty held the coffee cup in one hand and massaged his temples with the other.

"Oh?"

"At the Mother Lode last night."

"I see." A hint of a smile touched Wayne's lips. "How about taking a look, eh? I want the boys to blast out that shaft as fast as possible."

"Sure."

"Think the old jack-leg drill will hold up till Friday?"

"Should."

"Good, good."

Ty put on his hard hat, with its bright carbide light, which had been recharging all night, and walked out to the ore skip, the small, cramped metal cage that transported men down into the mine and brought them up. He waved to the man in the hoist house, rang the bell, the standard signal to send the skip up, got into it and rang the operator again to send him down. He switched on his light and watched the dripping walls slide by inches in front of his face, feeling the dank, icy blackness enfold him. But it was a neutral darkness to Ty, and held no terrors; he knew every inch of the Golden Slipper as well as a man knows the neighborhood he lives in. The descent was more than a thousand feet, and Ty's ears popped twice as the skip moved quickly and steadily down the narrow shaft. Finally the cage lurched, slowed, then came to an abrupt halt on the floor of the shaft, deep within the bowels of the earth. He walked along the familiar, unlit routes that turned and twisted and dripped endlessly, his light bouncing off the rough, dark granite walls and the water that slid down them. After a ten-minute walk, he heard the muffled stutter of a jack-leg drill up ahead and the whine of the ventilation fans.

Unerringly, he made his way to the south shaft, where the new vein had been found.

The boys heard him coming and yelled up the drift to him. "Fire in the hole!" Then they scrambled toward him, their lights puncturing sharp holes in the blackness. The four miners joined Ty, ringing for the skip to take them up above the station where the dynamite was set to go off in a few minutes, when its sixteen-inch primer had burned down. It was the age-old routine of mining, basically unchanged for the past hundred years.

The blast reverberated in the passageways, a trapped explosion that buffeted the men's ears; if they'd been closer, the concussion would have broken their eardrums.

The men would clear the ore rubble from the shaft, send it to the surface, then begin again drilling holes in the new face, jamming the dynamite in the holes, creating a five-hole burn or a seven-hole burn, lighting the primers and then getting out of the way. Over and over, endlessly. It was hard and dangerous work, but it created a closeness among the men that was rare, except perhaps among mountain climbers or test pilots or men at war.

Twenty minutes later, Ty shone his light on the newly exposed rock face. There was a dark purplish line there. The vein looked good. He chipped off a few pieces to check later, took his pad out of his pocket and made some notes, and then checked the underground survey lines with his Brunton compass so they could be mapped on the master chart.

"Looks good, doesn't it?" pressed Billy, his face dark with dirt, his eyes shining white.

"Yeah." Ty nodded. "But you know it could peter out in another foot."

"Not this one. I sort of got a feelin'," said another one of the men.

Miners always had feelings; it was a superstitious profession. Some men wouldn't come to work without wearing their lucky socks or carrying their lucky lunch boxes.

"Mr. Wayne wants you to push this one," Ty said. "I'll check the shoring loads and have some lumber ready for you in the morning. Might even send in another crew."

"Wayne thinks it's a good vein," said Hank. "He knows his stuff, Ty."

"Yeah, sure. I hope so." Usually Ty was much more enthusiastic. Sometimes he'd take over the jack leg from one of the boys or light fuses. Today he just didn't care; he went through the motions—listened to Billy swear at the old jack leg and Harve tell a dirty joke—before he made his way back to the skip. Automatically he rang the bell—three rings to call the skip down—and rode up to the surface of the earth.

"Looks rich, eh?" Kevin Wayne remarked.

"Could be."

"This is the one, I know it. Hey, if we hit pay dirt, I'll give every man who works for me a bonus." Wayne was grinning, showing more emotion than Ty had ever seen in him before.

Ty spent the afternoon cross-checking the survey lines and plotting them on the master chart. He looked at the lines he'd drawn, the numbers he'd marked down, drew his eyebrows together in a frown, and then rechecked his figures. Yes, they were correct.

"Mr. Wayne," he said over his shoulder, "could you come over here a minute? I want to show you something."

Kevin Wayne leaned over Ty as Ty pointed to his figures. "Now, see that, Mr. Wayne? The new vein goes straight toward the northern boundary of the Nola Jane. It might even be the Nola Jane's vein if it doesn't veer off."

"Not likely. You know that, Ty."

"Maybe not, but if the boys keep blasting out that crosscut they'll reach the boundaries of the Nola Jane in a month at the outside."

"So?"

"Well..." Ty hesitated. "Then we'll have to stop blasting. And if Abby McAlister really does open that mine, she could hold us liable for violating the apex law."

"Not very likely," said Wayne. "Nobody upholds that old law anymore." The apex law stated that a mine owner could follow a vein that apexed on his property if it was a continuous, unbroken vein. Therefore, if Wayne's men were indeed following the nether end of the Nola Jane's vein, they'd be, technically, breaking the law.

"It could hang you up for a while though," said Ty.

"Oh, come on, Ty. That girl's never going to get the Nola Jane open, and even if she does, she'll go broke so fast she'll have to sell out. In a month, Ty, that twenty thousand I offered her'll look better than an offer of marriage."

There was an assured, sneering kind of sound to Wayne's voice that Ty didn't like. Wayne was right, of course; in a month Abby would be so glad to sell out and salvage a little something from the fiasco that Wayne's offer would look great. But supposing, having the advantage, Wayne lowered his offer? He could do it and Abby would have no recourse. And he might do it; Kevin Wayne was no slouch when it came to grabbing bargains.

Poor Abby. Why didn't she listen to him? Lordy, he'd tried, but she was so stubborn. But then, would he like a wishy-washy girl who swayed with every spring breeze?

Ty drove home that afternoon in a troubled state. He missed Abby and he was really uncomfortable with Wayne's plans. He was still tired, his stomach growled with emptiness and his eyes burned. He couldn't face the Mother Lode again, nor could he face his own empty house. If only he could stop at Abby's, if only they were still friends.

He passed the red and purple house on his route. Well, he didn't have to pass it, but it was only one block out of the way. Her dusty station wagon was parked in front, so he knew she was home. He craved a sight of her. Should he stop, knock on her door—the door he'd fixed—and apologize? He cringed at the thought. He didn't have the nerve. *Coward,* he thought. *Sniveling, yellow-bellied coward.* And what could he say, after all? He'd said it already, over and over.

Misery stuck in his gullet like a knife. He felt like a lost, lonely adolescent and the sensation wouldn't go away.

"Oh, ain't love grand?" he said to himself bitterly as his Jeep toiled up the hill toward his very empty house.

CHAPTER NINE

ABBY STOOD ALONGSIDE HER BED and pulled on her blue jeans. Then she looked down at herself. *Well, what do you know*. . . The old things with their patched seat and half-worn-out knees were loose! *I'll be darned.* She smiled. It was the first time Abby had really smiled in the past three weeks, long summer weeks since she'd argued with Ty, weeks in which she'd worked herself to a frazzle trying to outfit the Nola Jane.

Of course, her weight loss was due to mental as well as physical work. She'd had no idea how complicated it was to open a mine. Just learning all the terms had been like taking a history final. There were things like sprags, the scaffolding the men stood on to work, and bulkheads, the supporting logs that were spaced every thirty or forty feet. And air compressors to run the drill. There were ventilation pipes, air lines and ore cars that ran on the tracks and jack legs—drills, to Abby. And fans to push air into the deep reaches of the mine, and something called a stoper, for "runnin' raises", according to John Gibbs. That meant driving a hole upward, he translated for her.

Thank God she'd had John Gibbs to help her. The dear, sweet old soul. He was crazy as a loon in dozens of ways, but a knowledgeable engineer. They'd even driven to Denver together and bought the equipment, and she'd spent nineteen thousand five hundred dollars. Not twenty, and certainly not thirty.

"Mommy, Benny wants junk cereal!"

"And you don't, Sean?" called Abby, smiling to herself.

Her days had taken on a sameness. She got up early, got dressed and fed the boys. By then Janet would be there. Then it was off to the mine. Part of Abby's nineteen thousand had gone to buy a used but sturdy pickup truck, for which she'd traded the station wagon in Denver. The deal had cost her an extra sixteen hundred. Not bad, considering how desperately she needed the truck. It was almost eight by the time she got to the mine, and Gibbs was always waiting for her. They'd walk the shafts and stopes, move equipment around together—backbreaking labor for an old man and a woman. But they'd accomplished a lot. They'd put in new track where needed, set up the generator and strung electric lines. They'd placed the carts, ordered a portable toilet and laid the new ventilation pipes all by themselves. They'd obtained the workman's compensation insurance—although Abby still had no crew—and she'd gotten in all her account numbers from the state and federal government to set up her payroll. The papers her mother had drawn up to transfer the title of the Nola Jane and the house to Abby had finally come through. And so she was ready—nearly ready.

Three weeks, she thought while she scrambled eggs for the twins, three weeks, and she'd only seen Ty from a distance, and then only by pure accident.

He'd looked miserable, hadn't he?

"Mommy, Janet says we can keep Barney if we feed him. Can we feed him?"

"Please, Mommy, oh, please!"

"That blasted burro," grumbled Abby. "Eat your eggs, Sean."

"Mommy, what about Barney?"

"I'll see. I'll think about it."

"You always say that," pouted Ben.

Abby frowned as she scrubbed the egg pan. The acquisition of the burro was Janet's fault. The girl had helped the boys catch the fuzzy little thing on one of their hikes. They'd brought it home and fed it. Kellogg's Corn Flakes, no less. And now the burro wouldn't leave. The boys had named him Barney and they adored him. The animal had already eaten the single lilac bush in the yard and pushed down the outhouse, to the boys' lamentation. There was no loss there, though, because Abby had her toilet installed. Abby had come home once, exhausted, only to find the back screen door shredded and the beast in the boys' bedroom. Janet had apologized as if there had been no stopping the twins. And Karen, when Abby had told her, had smothered a laugh. Very funny.

No wonder I'm tired all the time.

But it all would have been okay if there wasn't this rift between her and Ty. That whole day, while Abby worked alongside John Gibbs, she couldn't get Ty out of her mind. She lifted rocks and cleared the entrance to one of the shafts and replaced a section of rail, but the harder the physical labor was, the more Abby thought about Ty.

"You sure are preoccupied today, missy," said Gibbs, as he wiped sweat from his forehead with an old bandanna.

"Am I?"

"You worried about opening?"

"Not really. I'm mentally ready, anyway. The worst I can do is lose my life's savings." She smiled grimly.

"It's only money, missy. Money'll git ya in more trouble than ya can dream. I had me plenty once. Yes, I did. And I got me a woman and a house and an automobile. And I got me headaches the likes of which you'll never know."

"What did you do?" panted Abby as she helped lift a rail.

"I got rid of them! I gave the lady my bank book and said, *Adios*, so long. Be seein' ya, gal."

"And you moved into the mines then?" *Ugh.* "God, that track is heavy."

"Didn't move up into the mountains just yet. Nope. That was back in the forties. Didn't move up to these hills till the late sixties, when all them hippies took over."

"There were hippies in Cripple Creek?"

"Missy, there were hippies crawlin' out of every corner of the country. Course, you were just a baby then."

"I was a teenager then. Well, almost."

"Maybe you was one of them." He grumbled something, then disappeared down the shaft to find his shovel, or so he said.

Abby took a long swallow of water from her steel thermos and sat down on the side of a cart, wiping sweat from her neck with her shirttail. She'd have to get a bunch of bandannas if she were going to work this hard every day. And to think, she'd been shivering the first time she'd come up to the mine. That first time, with Ty.

Why had he done it to her, romanced her and helped her and been about the best friend a girl could have, when all along he'd been working for Wayne? He could have told her who his boss was. If he had told her, they could have worked things out.

Maybe it's all a huge misunderstanding.

But it couldn't be. The facts were too plain.

Nevertheless, Abby missed him dreadfully. And not just physically, either. She liked Ty. She liked the way his mind worked, logically and easily. She appreciated his simple view of life, his wholesomeness. She adored his soft, deep voice and the way he looked her in the eyes and called her ma'am. He moved so beautifully, too, in long, relaxed strides that were confident and easygoing. There was no rushing Ty Hollinger or, for that matter, changing his opinions. He was just plain stubborn. Why couldn't he understand her need to take this one big risk? Couldn't he see that it was her way out, perhaps her salvation? Would Ty have been happier if she'd stayed safe and sound and flat-out broke in New Jersey?

He sure had looked awfully miserable when she saw him down the street the other day. As miserable as she was?

"Just gonna sit there all day?" asked Gibbs, as he emerged from the deep shadows. "Do I gotta do everything round here?"

Abby had a rough time falling asleep that night; she was consumed with doubt and worry and her thoughts always circled back to money. Why did money have to be so all powerful that the thought of her bills could cause her to break out in a cold, clammy sweat? Her mother wasn't that way, nor was her father. Maybe Steve had done it to her, although, to be fair, she'd fretted about the bank balance long before her husband had up and gone his merry way.

Abby rolled onto her stomach and fluffed up her pillow. She desperately needed new windows for the house; a real heating system would be nice, and she could sure use a clothes dryer, too, although the dry mountain air could always suffice until winter.... Money. If she had enough . . . but how much was enough?

Her mother had said just the other day on the phone, "You've got enough, Abby, when you don't have to clip coupons anymore."

Heck, Abby would always clip coupons. If she were a millionaire, for Pete's sake, she'd clip a coupon to save ten cents.

But Ty Hollinger wouldn't bother. A man like that didn't really care if he had change rolling around in his pocket or a wad of hundred-dollar bills. And yet he was content. He'd told her his whole, big poor family had always been happy. How did a person get that happiness?

If Abby could have screamed without waking the kids—not to mention Karen next door—she would have. Instead, she rolled over, snapped on the light and took the diary from the top drawer of her nightstand. Maybe she could read herself to sleep.

She flipped carefully through the brittle, yellowed pages until she found where she'd left off weeks before. Nola Jane had been ready to begin mining. In fact, her great-grandmother had a crew hired, as well, but when Abby had last been reading, Nola's crew had walked out on her—something about a threat from George Rausch, the owner of the Compromise mine.

Ah, thought Abby, here was the place.

I cannot sleep tonight. I have a crew again, true enough, but I can barely stand to mull over the mortification I have suffered in rehiring men. For two days I tossed and turned in my sleep, debating the question: should I traipse around the streets to find my new crew, or should I confront these cowardly men who were bullied by Rausch and walked out on me yesterday? I certainly knew where they all spent their free time: the Crystal Palace Saloon. The decision I came to was agonizing. I decided to confront them all at once and see who was man enough to take an offer of a job from a woman who would pay top wages. Perhaps some of my old crew would come back to work. I dressed sedately, as Mike Mann has only been dead and buried four months. I would have preferred to appear more colorful, but I'm afraid I looked grim when I held my breath and walked through those swinging doors of the saloon.

The smoke was appalling, as was the odor of whiskey, and I felt my gorge rising. If Papa could have seen me... But never mind, he did not. However, every other man in Cripple Creek did. I vow not a breath was taken for a full minute when I made my timely entrance. The place was as packed as a den of wolves, and I thought my lungs would burst from fear and no small measure of stage fright. The humiliation did not come until later, however, when I was again able to think and realize just what it was that I had done.

There were women there, too, in the saloon. I had seen these sorts on the street before, but they had been clad in frocks, and not the scant satin gowns they wore in the saloon. My eyes must have fixed for too long on the ample bosom one in particular displayed because she, of all the crowd, was the first to move. She turned away. Was the woman embarrassed? I know little of these saloon ladies and cannot possibly guess.

I must have cleared my throat as if to make a speech when a dapper, slick sort stood from his chair and approached me. "My dear woman," he said smartly, "have you lost your way—or perhaps your husband?"

There was some laughter at this, but I soon took command. He had left me such a wonderful opening, I could not resist. In a clear, loud voice I said, "Sir, I know exactly where I am. Is this not the Crystal Palace Saloon? And as for my husband, you are quite correct, I have lost him. He's buried in the Mount Pisgah Cemetery."

That closed the man's mouth and he took his chair again. I launched directly into my prepared speech. I told the men that I was in need of workers for my mine and that I would meet the normal wage being currently paid by any mine in the town, three dollars per day. And then I mentioned Rausch's name. I told them in a straightforward manner how George Rausch had bullied my workers. I called him a coward who would resort to blackmail, and I said that if they would not stand up to him, then I would in their stead.

The place was so quiet by then I vow I could have heard a pin hit the floor. I thought I'd failed and only served to make my plight worse, when suddenly a voice came through the smoke. "I'll work for you, Mrs. Mann," I thought I heard him say, but I could almost not believe my ears. Then another voice joined his, and yet another.

I was speechless by that time. I believe I muttered, "Thank you," but I am not certain. I do recall straightening my back and walking toward the door, and I am positive that man who first challenged me held open the swinging doors for me.

I lie in my bed now and die of shame. Word spread around Cripple Creek like fire in a barn: Nola Jane Mann went to the saloon begging. Papa must have heard, because he's been quiet and Mama refuses to meet my glance. I do not think they'll speak of it, however.

At any rate, I have my crew. And I suppose, while I am digging in my mine, the rumors will fade away. I tell myself that I don't care what people think, but I wonder if I am not deceiving myself.

Abby was wide awake, reading and thinking, when suddenly there was a scraping sound at the window over her head. She froze. The sound came again, like a scratching on the screen, as if someone were trying to get in. Her heart pounded furiously as she reached over and snapped off the lamp.

Slowly, carefully, her breath coming in shallow pants, Abby eased herself out of bed. She had to look out that window but, oh, boy, she was scared. She closed her eyes momentarily as she heard yet another scratch. Then she opened them and peered out. Her hand flew to her breast then and she stifled a cry when she realized it was Barney, the blasted, stupid burro!

"I'm going to kill you," she muttered under her breath. "I'm going out there and strangle you with my bare hands!" She grabbed her robe and went out through the kitchen, wondering just who she could call to come and remove the beast: the dogcatcher? The sheriff? They'd laugh at her and she'd never be rid of the thing!

The burro emerged from the night shadows, trotted up to Abby, and let out a mournful bray. Canaries of the Rockies, thought Abby, that was the nickname the miners had given the burros a hundred years ago. Well, this one didn't sound like any canary—it sounded more like a rusty gate. "Shh!" she said to the animal. "I suppose you're hungry. You're always hungry." It nudged Abby with its bristly, wet nose. "Stop that." There was no choice, she knew, but to feed the thing. It would keep up the racket all night if she didn't. Angrily, Abby went back inside and reached for the cornflakes, muttering to herself that she was going to go broke feeding two growing boys and a burro. *I can't afford this.* She went outside, though, and fed him, receiving a wet lick on her bare toes for her efforts. "Don't try to make up to me. You can't live here. You're not a pet."

She became aware of the familiar grinding of an engine—Ty's Jeep. He was climbing Myers Avenue, coming directly toward her house. She could see his headlights and ducked into the shadows while her breath came quicker and quicker.

What if he stopped? What if he didn't stop? *Oh, Ty,* she thought, *I miss you so much.* Was he coming to see her? Was he?

The Jeep was at the corner. His lights were aimed directly at the front door, and he'd come to a complete stop, his engine idling, breaking the silence of night. It was after midnight. What was he doing there? Had he come from a bar or something? Was he drunk?

She heard him put the Jeep into gear, and he started around the corner. He was going to park, of course he was! He couldn't take this terrible separation any more than she could. And she'd forgive him, too. She'd tell him that she believed everything he'd said about his job, about his not trying to stop her from reopening the mine on his boss's account. Ty would never have done such a low thing. Not Ty. How could she have been so stupid?

Abby's heart was ready to burst in anticipation. She could almost feel Ty's arms encircling her, taste his mouth on hers. Her knees were so weak she thought she might crumple standing there in her shadows. Oh, Ty...

But he kept going. He kept going right past her house and on up the street!

No, she cried silently, *no!* But the truth was staring her in the face. He didn't care anymore, and he was done with her. After a long time Abby finally forced her feet to move. She felt horrible, weak and lost and so miserably alone. She made her way back into bed and felt the ache that had begun in her stomach swelling upward into her chest. Finally it moved up her throat and became a wrenching sob. It was all her doing. She'd lost her temper and jumped to conclusions and ruined it all.

Scratchy eyed, Abby drove to the mine the following morning. She felt tired and confused, unable to rid herself of thoughts about Ty, and unable to separate past from present after reading the diary last night. She was besieged with one problem after another, it seemed. When was her life going to take on some order?

John was waiting for Abby, as always, near the entrance to the Nola Jane. There was a down-around-the-mouth look to him this morning, though. What now, she wondered darkly.

"I took me a trip into town last night, missy, to the Mother Lode Saloon. I was thinkin' that now we're getting pretty close to opening and you'd be needin' to hire a crew. Fifteen men or so, at least," he said, shaking his head.

"So?" asked Abby.

"Well, it's like this. Folks around here are wishin' ya well and all that, but I'm afraid the men are being hesitant when it comes to takin' a chance workin' for you."

"You mean no one, out of all these unemployed miners, wants to go to work?"

He nodded. "Ya see, missy, they've been disappointed too many times in the past. Guess they're afraid."

"The cowards," said Abby.

"Well, maybe. But there's nothing worse than puttin' in a week's work and then finding out there's no money comin'."

"But I'd never do that!" Abby walked around in a circle, her head hanging down, kicking at stones with her boot. "What am I going to do, John? I have to have a crew..." It came to her suddenly and clearly. Nola Jane had done it, and Abby would, too! "I'm going to the Mother Lode tonight," she announced staunchly, "and I'll talk to the men there."

John grinned, pushing his hard hat back on his head. "Well, I'll be tied and hornswoggled, missy. You got the nerve to do that?"

"I guess I'll have to work it up somehow, won't I?" Abby shot back.

That whole afternoon and evening found Abby marching around and whistling a tune. She'd do it, all right, and she'd get her men. What, she wondered, would she have done if she hadn't had her great-grandmother's lead to follow?

She told Karen her plan after dinner. "What do you think? I mean, is it too pushy of me? Should I put an ad in the paper instead?"

"Hold on there, Abby," replied Karen. "I don't think it's the least bit out of place for you to go straight to their nest. It's better if you tell them face-to-face that your intentions are good. Still..." Karen shook her dark head. "It might be hard on you. Going into the bar and all."

"I'm sure it will be. But how else can I get their attention? Call a town meeting, for Pete's sake?"

Karen laughed. "The Mother Lode it is, then. But maybe I ought to go with you or something..." She snapped her fingers suddenly. "I've got it! Rob can escort you!"

"The sheriff? *Your* Rob?"

"Sure. Why not? If the sheriff is standing next to you, Abby, then the men will have to know you're on the up and up."

"Do you think he'll do it, though?"

"If *I* ask him to he will."

"You're a pal, Karen," said Abby, turning to go back to her own house. "And tell Janet nine o'clock will be fine, okay?"

"Sure. Oh, and Abby, by the way, that burro tore up part of my vegetable garden. What are you going to do with him?"

Abby groaned. "Do you think his mother will take him back?"

At nine sharp, Janet knocked on the front door. With her was Rob Loring, and Abby, having grown as nervous as a cat, admitted she was glad to see him. "Boy,

I can't tell you how much your going along means to me," she said. "This morning my idea sounded great to me, but tonight . . ."

"You'll do just fine, Abby," he said and gave her one of his big western smiles.

Abby, like her great-grandmother, had given a lot of thought to her dress. She didn't want to appear too casual even though the Mother Lode was a blue-jean joint. On the other hand, she didn't want to seem too citified and put them off. She wanted to appear respectable but seem like just plain folk. She chose a khaki shirtwaist dress that had big pockets and shoulder pads and a wide rope belt. It was the kind of safari dress that could be worn just about anywhere. To do it up further, Abby put on a gold chain necklace, small round gold earrings and a chain bracelet. White flats completed the outfit. She looked somewhat dressy but not overdone. She also looked ten pounds lighter than she had been, and the feeling gave her a measure of confidence.

"All ready?" asked Sheriff Rob.

"As ready as I'll ever be."

He was a considerate escort, holding open the door of the Blazer for her, making polite small talk as they headed down Myers and turned onto Bennett Avenue. Nevertheless Abby was keyed up, her pulse beating too rapidly, her blood pressure soaring, no doubt, as the blocks sped by.

It was a beautiful summer evening in Cripple Creek. The sun had set behind Mount Pisgah already, but it was still light out, a golden light shadowed by dusk moving in from the east. Abby loved the town at this time of evening. It seemed more defined, the lines of the old Western buildings sharper, the pastel colors of the

Victorians muted in the late light. Frequently, in the evening, storm clouds would cluster over the valley and there would be a downpour for fifteen minutes. Then it could clear miraculously. Afterward, everything smelled sweet and fresh to Abby, washed clean. But tonight there wasn't a cloud to be seen. Was that a good omen?

She glanced sidelong at Rob. It struck her that she wished it were Ty sitting next to her, steering the Blazer with his competent hands. Why had Ty deserted her? *No, no Abby,* she reminded herself, *you deserted him, you fool.*

Holy cow, the Mother Lode! Abby's heart skipped three beats, then pounded furiously in her breast. God, where was her spunk, her nerve?

"You look as pale as a ghost," said Rob as he stopped and parked. "Sure you want to go through with this?"

"I want to go home," confessed Abby, "but I won't. I'm going inside the Mother Lode."

"Good girl. It'll show these men you're not afraid to take the bull by the horns."

Abby was terrified of bulls. "I wish you'd put that differently," she said, and tried to give him a smile.

"Ready?" asked Rob, as his hand reached for the knob.

Abby swallowed hard. "Oh, God, I guess so. I just hope this works, Rob."

"It will." He squeezed her hand reassuringly and again Abby thought: why wasn't Ty the one to stand beside her?

Then they were inside. It was a long room with a bar running along the right side; a tall, thin woman was pouring a pitcher of beer behind the counter. There were tables near the back and wooden posts stood in a line up the center. A jukebox played somewhere—yes, in the back—and the words of an old song filled the smoky air. She was assailed by the odor of stale beer and cigarettes and wood as well, old wood.

Rob nudged her. "Coming?" he said into her ear.

"Sure," replied Abby shakily as she took several steps farther into the room. A few heads turned in her direction, and then a few more. She heard a whisper or two when the song stopped playing: "That's her, that's Miz McAlister," and her heart played havoc against her ribs. Thank heavens Rob was there; without him, Abby was positive, she would have turned and run.

A silence seemed to fall over the room, as if an invisible hand had been raised somewhere. And those who had not at first noticed Abby did then. All eyes riveted on her, again as if by order.

She swallowed and swallowed, her throat as dry as cotton, but there was no turning back now. If Nola Jane had done it, she could, too.

Rob took a step forward, his boot heels clicking, the old wooden floorboards protesting noisily. "You all know me," he began, "and some of you probably know Miz McAlister here. Well, she wants to say something and I'm asking you to listen and give the lady a chance."

No one moved. Not even a cough or a sneeze or the tap of a glass being set down broke the close silence. Holy cow, thought Abby, holy cow. *Here goes.*

"Good evening," she started in, her voice too small, too shaky. She cleared her throat. "Good evening," she said louder. "I'm Abby McAlister, but I guess most of you already know that. And I suppose you all know why I'm here tonight."

Ah, there! A head nodded!

"I need miners. I need to hire a crew for the Nola Jane. I thought of putting an ad in the paper, but I figured no one would reply. I'm told," she said, her tone growing clearer as she continued, "I'm told that you aren't sure if I can make my payrolls. Well, I'll be totally honest with you. I can pay you for at least two months. And after that I'm hoping we'll all be set. But if not, then at least you've gotten some work in. And I promise that no one will work an hour that he isn't paid for."

Suddenly, in the middle of Abby's speech, she heard a chair scraping against the wooden floor. Then a gruff voice responded: "We've all heard that before, lady. I say, once bitten, twice a fool."

"I told you," repeated Abby, "I can pay..."

"I dunno," the man interrupted. Then he turned his head and searched the back of the room for someone. "You know the lady. What do you think?"

He emerged from the smoke-filled shadows, tall, lithe and easy in his gait. He moved toward her a few feet and then stopped, his glass of beer in one hand, a shoulder coming to rest negligently against a wooden post. Abby felt her stomach drop to her feet like lead. Why did he have to be here?

"Well, Ty?" another man asked, his face turned expectantly to Abby's nemesis.

Ty was studiously silent for too long, his dark eyes going from Abby to Rob and back, giving nothing away, nothing whatsoever. It seemed to Abby as if all the air had suddenly been sucked out of the room; she felt weak and breathless.

"What do you think, Hollinger? Can the lady keep her promise?"

"I think," began Ty finally, his gaze locked with hers, "that the lady here means well, boys, but she doesn't know what she's up against. You all know only too well the risks of gold mining."

Damn him, she screamed silently. Damn the way he was standing there so casually, so self-assured and easygoing, as if he didn't have a care in the world! This was her whole life he was talking about, her whole future!

"Wait a minute," said Abby abruptly, getting their attention once more. "I said I can make my payrolls. I've offered you good, solid work. And Mr. Hollinger is wrong. I *do* know the risks. I'm willing to go broke, flat-out broke. All I want is to give you some jobs. It seems pretty simple to me."

"I dunno," came a voice.

"Isn't a month's pay better than nothing?" asked Abby fervently. "Aren't *I* the one taking all the risks here?"

Ty straightened and set his beer down on a table slowly. "Take your risk, Abby. But remember, these are lives you're toying with. These men have families. They've been disappointed too many times before."

Abby felt herself flush with anger. How dare he stand there so insufferably superior, insinuating that she was ignorant and careless with people's lives!

She glared at him hotly, wondering if he could feel the wrath emanating from her. The room grew silent; not a soul moved. Everyone in the bar felt the tension flowing between the two adversaries like a high-voltage current. Abby could almost hear the smoky air crackle with it as she stood motionless, refusing to drop her gaze, refusing to turn tail and run. And in the background, suddenly loud against the gravid silence of the room, the jukebox played "Stand By Me" in blithe irony.

At her side, Rob cleared his throat and moved restively, like a big bear. He probably wanted to leave, Abby thought, and she didn't blame him a bit.

But Abby wasn't ready to make her exit. Oh, no, not quite yet. She found her voice and it emerged surprisingly clear and strong. "I've given you all my word. This town can come alive again, men, but it's going to take courage from all of us. Courage and trust. On Monday at eight in the morning I'll be up at the Nola Jane. I'll see anyone who wants to work then. I'm hoping you'll all be there."

By then, her nerve had failed, and seemed to drain out of her body and puddle on the floor. She had to get out of there, instantly. Suddenly Abby turned and headed toward the door across the respectfully cleared room. She didn't wait for Rob and she never looked back, but she could feel that one set of dark eyes boring into her back like burning embers. She pushed open the door and cold air struck her hot cheeks. Mercifully, the night hid her face.

CHAPTER TEN

ABBY WAS UP at the Nola Jane earlier than usual Monday morning, but John Gibbs was already there, puttering around, checking the wet cell batteries on the headlamps, counting hard hats, fiddling with the trigger mechanisms on the jack-leg drills.

"Will anyone show up?" she asked Gibbs expectantly.

"Don't know. Maybe," was all she could get out of him.

Abby paced, returned to her truck to check that she'd remembered the W2 forms the men would have to fill out—if there were going to be any men—and then paced some more.

John was not talkative that morning. He left the drills and went to the portable toilet, pushing at it to see if it was stable, opening the door, closing the door. Abby was nervous enough, but his behavior made her even more on edge. Why didn't he sit down or talk to her or admit that he, too, was concerned?

It's like being all dressed up for a party and then being stood up, Abby reflected, walking around aimlessly, kicking at rocks.

At 7:49 there was a noise, a grinding, bumping noise down the dirt road, and shortly a battered pickup truck arrived, dragging a cloud of dust. Two men climbed out.

"This the Nola Jane?" one asked.

"Sure is," replied Gibbs. "Sign up with Miz McAlister there."

A motorcycle with a burly man riding it roared up. "This the Nola Jane? Barb told my wife you had jobs . . ."

An open Jeep pulled to a stop, disgorging five men. "I guess we got the right place," one said to the others.

Abby was grinning; she felt as if she'd never be able to wipe that big smile off her face as she handed out forms and pens. "Thanks for coming," she repeated over and over. "I really appreciate your going to work for me."

In all, sixteen men signed on with Abby that morning. They were an assorted lot, dressed in worn overalls or jeans or work pants, scuffed work boots, all carrying thermoses and lunch boxes. They had uniformly strong, work-worn hands and weathered faces. Some were uncertain about this job, Abby could tell, some were devil-may-care, some were serious and worried, but they were all ready to go to work.

John Gibbs gathered them together at the mine entrance and passed out hard hats and lamps. "You mighta heard I was a crazy old coot," he told them, "but I know mining and I know *this* mine. If you work hard and honest for Miz McAlister here, this mine'll pan out real good. Yer families will eat and yer kids'll have new shoes. But you gotta give it yer all. An honest day's work is all I'm askin' from you."

"That's fair, old-timer," one man said. Others nodded or shifted their feet or settled their hard hats on their heads more firmly.

"Okay. We start blasting the north crosscut. I know there's a vein there good as any in the valley. Come on, men."

As they disappeared into the mouth of the mine, Abby hugged herself, still grinning like an idiot. She twirled around and said out loud, "Thanks, Nola Jane, thanks, Great-grandma. It's going to work! It's going to work!"

By late afternoon, there were a few loads of ore already emerging from the mine entrance in cars. Abby helped unload them. She was dying to go into the mine and see what they actually did in there, but didn't have the nerve to ask. Maybe miners didn't like women in their lair, like sailors who believed women jinxed a ship. But later, when she knew the men better, she'd go in with them and watch everything.

She got home at five-thirty, totally drained.

"Hi, Mommy! Barney likes Milky Way bars," said Sean.

"Janet made me drink a glass of milk. Yuck," said Ben.

"Mr. Wayne called and left a message to call him back. It was very important, he said," Janet told her. "He left his home number in case you were late."

"Wonder what he wants."

Janet shrugged. "Well, I'm going to go on home now, Mrs. McAlister, okay?"

"Thanks, Janet. I hope the boys were good."

"We were real good, Mommy," Benny assured her, a cherubic expression on his smudged, dirty face.

After a long, hot bath, Abby fixed dinner, watching Sean and Ben through the window as they romped with Barney. The burro lived in the shed, kept the lawn cut, fertilized it, too, and begged at the door for cornflakes.

He sure was cute, Abby had to admit, with his tiny, dainty feet and big ears. He was a pain in the neck, true, but the boys adored him. What on earth would they do with him in the winter—move him into the kids' bedroom?

For early July—summer in most places—it was still cool in the evenings. Abby wondered if she'd ever grow used to the dry, crisp climate as she decided to build a fire in the potbellied stove, just for a short time, to take the edge off the chill. She was getting good at starting fires: first she crumpled newspaper and then added kindling and small pieces of wood. Soon it was crackling cheerfully and warming the house like magic.

It was getting dark and she was in the middle of reading *Where the Wild Things Are* to the boys when she remembered Janet's message to call Kevin Wayne. She finished reading, tucked the twins in and decided she'd better make the call.

"Mrs. McAlister, so glad you got back to me," said Wayne. "I guess you had a good first day at the Nola Jane, eh?"

She guessed everyone knew about it; Cripple Creek was certainly a small town. "It went very well, thank you."

There was a pause on the line and the sound of papers being rustled or something. What did he want? "Mrs. McAlister," he began, "I've taken the time today to go over some of my figures from my first month of operation last fall. I'm wondering if you are looking at the costs in a realistic manner."

"Mr. Wayne," said Abby, irritated, "I am a bookkeeper. I believe I know enough about ledgers and profit and loss sheets to know what I'm doing."

"Um," he said doubtfully. "In that case, then, all I can do is restate my offer. I suggest you take it seriously and consider selling now. If you wait, the mine will drain you dry."

"You sound very certain of that." There was something in his tone, some sharp edge to his words, that Abby decidedly did not like.

"There are no certainties in mining, Mrs. McAlister. I'll tell you what. Give it a week or two and then call me. I can wait but—" he hesitated "—not forever."

"Thank you, Mr. Wayne," replied Abby, "but you won't be hearing from me." She hung up.

The incident left Abby feeling shaky despite her confidence on the telephone. And for a moment, while she'd had him on the line, she'd been tempted to blurt out her anger over his using Ty to get close to her. Maybe she should have, if for no other reason than to let Kevin Wayne know that she was not some flaky female come to the West with a head full of impossible dreams. He'd tried one trick to tempt her to sell, and he might just try another.

Abby paced the living room, thinking, her hands on her hips. She could talk to John Gibbs, tell him what had been going on with Kevin Wayne, alert him—just in case. Sure, that's exactly what she'd do. John would know how to handle Mr. Wayne in the future. The notion made her feel very much better. She stopped her pacing, snapped off the lights and walked into her bedroom, glad that she'd stood up to that man and stood up, actually, quite well.

But by the time Abby had her nightgown on, her face washed and her teeth brushed, she was still too keyed up to sleep. And besides, there'd been precious little time to keep up with Nola Jane lately. Maybe tonight she'd read herself to sleep and find out just how her great-grandmother had dealt with all her money problems. She propped herself up in bed with the diary and started turning pages, searching for the place where she'd left off. The next entry was dated October 10, 1894.

Dear Diary,

There was nothing else to do, no one else I could turn to. George Rausch has too much influence in this town. And, in addition, the bankers, all being men, turn me down without even looking at my accounts. I am quite tired of being patronized. I have even tried banks in Colorado Springs but the dastardly Englishmen running that place are no better.

I've decided I have to keep the mine running. If I give up, then my marriage, Mike's death, none of it makes any sense. I despise a world in which things don't make sense. Surely God, in His wisdom, would want things to make sense!

So I did what I had to. It was a bitter night, blustery and snowing a little. The town, however, was as busy as ever. The saloons and gaming rooms were raucous, the streets full of traffic, the hotels lit up like the firmament. I lied to Mama and Papa about my destination, put on a hat with a veil, bundled up in my oldest black cloak and walked into town, straight down Myers Avenue. I looked neither right nor left, but went directly to the Bon Ton and knocked.

Now, I'd been told Big Lil—Lily Francis, that is—had a soft heart for women in trouble. She had more money than she needed and, I hoped, would lend me enough to keep the mine going until I made a profit, which I surely would within a few months. Unfortunately, Big Lil, whom I'd only seen from afar, is a sporting woman, a madam who runs a house of ill repute.

So, I knocked. The door opened. From the interior I could discern cigar smoke and the cloying scent of cheap perfume. There were many men. I shudder to recall the familiar faces there. I tried to stay in the shadows. "Please call Miss Francis for me," I begged the negress who attended me. Shortly a rough voice asked, "Who wants Miss Francis?" and I saw her up close for the first time.

Big Lil is a strong-faced female of about forty-five. She is broad and substantially built with a narrow waist and a very large—excuse me, Diary—bosom; hence her name, I conjecture. Her hair is hennaed bright red and she wore a forest green satin gown that I watched most carefully lest the seams burst when she breathed. But I faced her bravely.

We went to the office and I tactfully admired the decor of her house, which was, indeed, impressive. To make a long story short, I talked, she listened, and I left with a bank draft to cover my expenses. Lil now holds a promissory note for a forty-nine percent share of the Nola Jane mine, with a clause allowing me the option of buying her out anytime at fair market value.

We shook hands and she let me out the door. "This is my thanks to ol' Mike," Lil said as I left. "He was one damn good customer—excuse me again—and an even better poker player."

Abby had to smile. Nola Jane. She could see her in

the Bon Ton, forcing her whole existence to make sense. Nola Jane had a certain lovable arrogance, Abby decided. Never mind God or man. Nola's world would be bent to her will.

Abby got up, made her way into the living room and put another log on the fire. It was so cozy and comforting to listen to its sputtering. She climbed back into bed, pulled the blankets up and picked up the diary again.

I was just leaving the Bon Ton when the wind sent a fearful blast around the corner. My cloak tangled around my legs and I stumbled backward, only to be brought up short by a pair of strong hands. "The wind is uncommon fierce tonight, ma'am," the owner of the hands said. "May I escort you back inside?" It was only then that I realized he thought me one of Lil's girls. Imagine my mortification! "Excuse me, kind sir," I said, "but I was just passing on my way home. . . ."

He did not let me go, but laughed and gave me a squeeze. I drew myself up, pulled aside my veil and said firmly, "I am Nola Jane Mann, sir, and I wish to pass."

Well, he was apologetic and belatedly introduced himself as Mr. Randolph Hutton, new to Cripple Creek—George Rausch's mine foreman, as a matter of fact. "That bounder," was my remark and Randy wanted to know why, so I told him of my tribulations with Mr. Rausch.

"So, you're *that* Nola Jane," he remarked. Oh, what a handsome man Randy Hutton was that first dark, windy night! I can still remember how his hands felt when he helped me. Oh, I am wicked,

wicked! A widow and respectable, and still I noticed what a lovely square chin Randy had!

Randy Hutton! thought Abby. Great-grandpa Hutton! My goodness, she'd never put two and two together before. Of course, this was Abby's own great-grandfather. So that was how Nola Jane met him. What a riot! Bumping into her future husband in front of a brothel! Abby turned back to the diary, amused and curious.

Randy said he'd call on me and explain Mr. Rausch's wish to buy me out. Was that an excuse to see me again? I confess, I am not averse to the company of such a well-set-up, soft-spoken man. Would it shock the town if I had a caller so soon after Mike's death? I yearn for company, yet I have six months to go before the year of mourning is out. But, truly, I have turned this town's opinion against me already by running the mine, so what harm can another tidbit of gossip do me?

So, that was how it started, Abby thought, putting the diary aside and yawning. She could picture the scene in her mind so clearly. Sliding down in the bed, she felt her tired muscles aching pleasantly, heard the cheerful snap of the last log burning down in the stove and closed her eyes. Nola Jane Mann-Hutton. What a story. And what a funny coincidence that Randy had been George Rausch's foreman. Like Ty. But Randy wasn't deceitful; otherwise Nola wouldn't have ended up marrying him. Idly, Abby wondered how Randy and Nola Jane had settled the matter of his working for Rausch. She'd read some more tomorrow and find out.

Too bad there weren't any more Big Lils around to back the Nola Jane, Abby thought sleepily. No, Cripple Creek was poor now and she'd have to finance the mine herself.

She dozed off, still caught in the past. Big Lil, Nola Jane, the Bon Ton. Cigar smoke and heavy perfume and, perhaps, a tinkly piano in the background. Oh, yes, she could see it, smell it, feel the hot, pulsating atmosphere of the Bon Ton. She stood facing Big Lil, a buxom redhead who wore too much makeup. The green satin dress showed off Lil's gleaming white shoulders and the woman's perfume made Abby's head spin. Abby felt the stays of her corset digging into her ribs, felt the drag of her long cloak pull at her shoulders. An oil lamp flickered on Lil's desk and Abby was trying desperately to convince the woman of something, something vitally important. She felt so insignificant standing in front of the madam; her own dress was black as she was still in mourning, although she did have a cunning onyx brooch at her throat. She wished she still had the diamond Mike had given her, but she'd long since sold it to raise money for the mine.

The oil lamp flared up, Big Lil's powdered face came closer, the heavy perfume made Abby cough and the whorehouse faded around the edges, wavering like the bright blaze of the lamp, then going up in flames as she was choked by...

Smoke! Abby, jolted out of her dream, flew out of bed and dashed into the living room.

She gave a smothered shriek. The room was filled with strangling black smoke and there was a roaring conflagration in the stovepipe. Her mind began galloping in panic. Water? Was there a hose, a bucket? The boys! Oh, my God, the boys first! Her purse!

She ran into the back bedroom. *Don't scare them!* Forcing herself to speak calmly, knowing hysteria lurked just under the surface, Abby shook the boys. "Wake up, Sean. Ben, come on, you have to get up."

They slept like the dead. They wouldn't budge. She shook them harder. "Sweethearts, babies, come on now." Oh, Lord, she'd have to carry them! They were heavy but she'd have to! She gathered them in her arms, heart racing. Smoke was beginning to billow into the boys' bedroom.

"Mommy?" Ben asked sleepily.

"There's a little fire in the stove and we have to go outside, honey, okay?" She was half dragging, half carrying the two boys.

"Ouch," said Sean, wiggling, making Abby nearly drop him.

"Come on, just a little farther." She was in the kitchen and they were all coughing; her lungs ached from the awful black stuff. The back door was just ahead.

"Mommy!" cried Sean, in a panic now.

They burst outside into the cold, clear night air and Abby pulled them into the yard away from the house and collapsed on the ground, coughing and hacking, while the stovepipe spewed noxious smoke and terrifying red flames into the night sky.

A light went on in Karen's living room, and she came running out in her bathrobe. "What happened? I heard a noise. Smoke! Oh, my God!"

"Call the fire department!" gasped Abby.

Karen ran, a shadow in the night. Another light went on across the street and a man stuck his head out his door. "What's going on?" he yelled.

"My stovepipe. On fire," said Abby.

"Damn city slickers," he mumbled and then ducked inside.

In five minutes a siren commenced wailing up the hill, growing louder as it drew near. The fire truck raced up; the volunteers jumped off. A hose was unrolled and dragged across the grass. Horrible orange light flickered on the moving figures like strobe lights on an unearthly dance floor. Men yelled and cursed and shouted orders and pointed the hose at the house.

Abby was aware that she was clutching the boys, that Karen and Janet were at her side, that she was shivering with cold in her thin nightgown.

"Wait a minute!" called one of the firemen. "Hold yer horses!"

"It's gone," whispered Karen.

Abby looked. It was true. The flames were gone, the smoke only wispy now. The house was a squat black silent shadow again.

People stood in groups up and down the street, talking, pointing, buzzing with excitement. But the eerie blinking was gone now.

"What happened, Mommy?" asked Benny in a tiny, scared voice.

"Burned itself out," said the fire chief. The rest of the men relaxed. Nervous laughs were heard from the ones holding the hose. "Goldarn thing burned itself out."

"Creosote fire," muttered a neighbor.

"Stovepipe caught. Needed cleanin'," said another.

Abby sank down onto the ground again and covered her face with trembling hands. The stovepipe! Ty had warned her. She'd meant to call . . .

"Want us to check inside, just in case something caught?" the fire chief asked Abby.

She looked up. "Oh, please, yes. That would be awfully nice of you."

"Say, ain't you that there Eastern lady what's openin' the mine?" asked one of the firemen.

"Yes," Abby whispered.

He shook his head. "Well, guess that pipe's clean as a whistle now, ma'am."

"Abby!" A man's voice reached her ears, a harsh, anxious call.

She was so glad to see him she could have rushed into his arms. She wanted to be held and comforted. But they were enemies, weren't they?

And yet he stood there, barefooted, his face an open book of concern and worry. He reached out a hand, as if to pull her close, but then, slowly, as if rethinking the gesture, he withdrew it. She didn't know whether to be thrilled he was there or turn from him in anger. She felt shell-shocked, unable to think, unable to weigh the meaning of his presence. She only knew she was terribly happy to see him. Ty. He always turned up when she needed him.

"Thank God," he breathed. "You're all right."

"We're fine. Scared to death."

"Son of a gun, Abby," he gasped. "What in tarnation happened?"

She hung her head. "The stovepipe."

"I saw the flames. I ran when I saw it was your house. You sure you're okay?"

"Uncle Ty," said Sean. "Is everything burned up in our house?"

"I don't reckon so. It was just in the pipe, it looks like."

The firemen came out of the house, leaving the lights shining from every window. "Not too bad, considering," said one man. "It'll need some cleanin' up, I guess. You got anywhere you can stay tonight, ma'am?"

Abby's head whirled. "Stay?"

"My place," said Ty firmly.

"Oh, no, I couldn't," said Abby quickly.

"Gosh, you could stay at my place," Karen remarked. "The boys could sleep on the floor and maybe Janet could move in with me."

"I've got plenty of room." Ty stood stock-still, staring down at Abby, waiting.

"But Karen's right next door and . . ."

"Don't argue for once," he said in an uncharacteristically sharp manner. "You and the boys are staying at my house."

"Ty . . ."

"Poor kids," he said, ignoring her completely, kneeling down and putting his arm around each boy. "You must be freezin'. Let's go on down the street and get you tucked away."

"Couldn't we stay here?" she asked the fireman.

"Take a look," was all he'd say.

The house reeked of creosote; it reminded Abby of her flag-girl days, when a road had just been paved—but it was much worse. And everything was covered with a thin film of black greasy soot. "Oh, no," Abby said, a catch in her throat.

"We'll clean it up," Karen offered. "Janet and I will help."

"Lucky nothing burned," said Janet.

"Is my Rambo okay?" asked Ben.

"Yes, honey, but he may need a bath," said Abby. Oh, Lord, the work ahead of her! And her new curtains—she'd have to wash them. And everything smelled like smoke and oil!

She stood there, looking at the ruin of her new home and blinking back tears. A strong arm slipped hesitantly around her shoulders and Ty said into her ear, "It'll be fine. We'll leave the windows open so it can air out."

"Oh, my house," moaned Abby.

"Hey, it's not burned to the ground," he said softly.

She drew in a shuddering breath. He was right, of course. Things could have been much worse. She'd just have to clean it up.

"That's a girl," Ty said, squeezing her reassuringly. "Now, troops, let's retire to the bivouac area. March."

She gave up trying to protest and followed him. What a procession they made. Abby in bare feet and a nightgown, Ty, also barefoot, in jeans and nothing else, carrying a twin under each arm.

He pushed open his front door and stepped aside to let Abby in. The warm air felt wonderful; she hadn't realized how cold it was outside. Ty followed her in and snapped on a lamp, setting the boys down, turning to study her in the light. He shook his head somberly, and she felt herself flush with heat. The fire was her fault, his look told her. Now here she was, standing barefoot in the middle of his living room, half clad, like a beggar.

"Come on, boys," he said finally, breaking the awkward silence as he held her gaze a moment too long. "It's bedtime. Again."

He tucked them into the double bed in the guest room, turned off the light and came into the living room to face Abby, who was sitting on a chair, dazed and trembling.

"You okay?" he asked.

She took a deep breath. "I'm a wreck but I guess I'll live."

"Your face is all black."

She rubbed a finger on her cheek; it came away smudged. Strangely enough, she didn't even care.

Ty got a jacket and gently laid it over her shoulders. "You need a drink," he said, disappearing into the kitchen and reappearing with two glasses of something.

She took it and swallowed. It burned going down. "Ugh," she said.

"Pretty bad, isn't it?" agreed Ty. "I prefer beer, but this is medicinal."

He sat down across from her, his elbows resting on his splayed knees, and regarded her. "You never called the chimney sweep, did you?"

"No," she said dully.

"You gave me a fright."

It occurred to Abby that she should be more upset about being in Ty's house in the middle of the night with only her nightgown on. Somehow, she couldn't muster up the energy.

Ty cleared his throat. "Well, you can use the bedroom upstairs," he said, "and I'll sleep on the couch."

"Oh, no." Abby's head jerked up. "I can't take your bed. The couch is fine. I couldn't sleep a wink, anyway. I'm too worried." She gulped the last of her drink, breathed in and coughed.

Ty rose and stood in the middle of the room looking at her. He seemed very young and very sexy and very manly, his belt still undone, his bare chest smooth and gleaming, with just a small patch of fine, fair hair on it.

Abby felt like shrinking into herself suddenly. What on earth was she doing here, alone with Ty? "Oh," she said, "I'll never sleep tonight. Why don't you go on upstairs and get some rest? All I need is a blanket. I'll be fine." She was going on ridiculously, she knew, trying to outtalk an uncomfortable situation. It didn't work.

Ty never stopped studying her. Finally he said, "I couldn't sleep, either, because..." Eventually he looked away. "Damn it, Abby, because you're in my house, so darn close and all I'd think about..."

"I'm going home," Abby stated abruptly, standing and heading toward the door. "Thank you very much..." She stopped short, confused. "The boys..."

"Oh, tarnation. You'd all choke in that hellhole. I apologize, I'll never mention it again."

"It's too late."

"Too late for what?"

She tensed, knowing he was coming closer, he was going to touch her. *Don't touch me, Ty. A woman can only stand so much!* "I can't stand this," she whispered, trapped. He was at her shoulder; he was turning her to face him. "Don't," she begged.

"Why not? What I feel for you, Abby, is so much.... When I thought you might have been hurt tonight, I felt, well, I never felt anything like that."

His jacket had slipped off her bare shoulders but his big hands held her arms and she wasn't cold. No, she burned, her skin was incandescent, her blood pounded and leapt through her veins. She was terrified, elated, desperate for it to be over, frightened that it might start. "No," she said.

But she didn't mean it and Ty knew that. He drew her close and bent his head, brushing her lips. "I waited," he said, "and I'm not a real patient man." And then his mouth was on hers, forcing her head back. She clutched at him, feeling cool, smooth skin under her hands, and returned his kiss with every ounce of passion she had.

Panic flared in her. No, she couldn't. She was melting, giving in. In a minute she'd let him do anything and she couldn't. The boys were there and it was all wrong. Ty was her enemy. Wayne had convinced him to seduce her....

She broke free and pushed him away; her skin felt bruised all over and she was bitter cold and shivering. "No," she gasped. "That's enough."

Ty regarded her sadly. "You're afraid. What is it, Abby? You're still mad at me, aren't you?"

She wrung her hands. "Yes. I don't trust you."

"What do I have to do," asked Ty angrily, "to prove I'm on your side?"

"I don't know. I don't know." She turned away. "I wish I knew."

"Well, one of these days I'll figure it out and then you won't have any more excuses. I'm going upstairs now. Good night." But he stopped. "I'll feel like a cad all night for makin' you sleep down here, but right now I'm mighty aggravated with you, Abby McAlister, and, damn it all, you don't deserve my bed!"

Abby curled up on the couch, quivering and confused and miserable. A big orange cat joined her after a time, purring much too loudly. Absentmindedly she stroked the cat, her heart jumping every time she heard a noise from upstairs, as she imagined Ty turning over restlessly, imagined his lean white body under the sheets. She couldn't get the picture of him out of her mind; he'd been so totally unselfconscious, even with his bare chest and the top button of his jeans undone.

She kept seeing, in her mind's eye, the flat paleness of his stomach and the patch of fair hair that disappeared down into his pants.

What was he thinking now? Could she dare believe those things he'd said—about caring for her? She lay there, paralyzed but sleepless, on the lumpy couch, unable to bear the thought of his naked body, just a few yards away, forbidden to her.

CHAPTER ELEVEN

"SITTIN' IN YER OFFICE AGAIN, I see," said John Gibbs as he passed by Abby's truck one morning in late July. "Won't be gettin' any work done with your nose buried in them papers of yers."

"Look here," said Abby, ignoring his usual jibe about her office—the cab of her truck. "It's this morning's *Denver Post*. Guess what the gold quote is today? Guess?" She rattled the paper out the window, teasing him.

"I haven't a notion, missy."

"Oh, come on, John, try." She was bubbling with excitement and he wouldn't even play her game.

"Eight hundred."

Abby shook her head admonishingly. "No, silly, but it *has* hit five hundred twenty-eight! Do you know what that means?"

"No, tell me," he replied sarcastically.

"It means, Mr. John Gibbs, that when those trucks get here in the next few days to pick up the ore, we'll be able to make at least four more payrolls."

"Still gotta haul it all to El Paso, missy. Takes a day or two truckin' it. The price could drop in the meantime."

"Not according to the experts, it won't. Here, read this." But she stopped herself, remembering how much John hated the papers, calling them "a bunch of yellow rag sheets'' he ''never had no use fer.'' ''Never mind,'' she was quick to say, ''just keep your fingers crossed.''

It had been over three weeks since Abby had officially opened the mine. Everything had gone amazingly well, too, considering that the men hadn't worked in a long time. ''The blastin' takes on a rhythm after a while,'' John had told her. ''Once the boys get into the swing of it.''

Well, the rhythm was there. And stockpiled alongside the road to the Nola Jane was enough ore to fill two trucks. What's more, Abby's payrolls had been less than she'd anticipated. Of course, she could have used twenty men instead of sixteen—well, seventeen, counting John whom she'd paid faithfully each and every week. She'd figured on $2,400 per day, but was running a little over $1,900. She hadn't paid herself, though, but she would. Oh, how she would!

Abby's pickup truck had served quite well as an office, actually, although she always did her tedious paperwork at home in the evening. It didn't leave much time for anything else, and she was terribly afraid the boys were suffering somehow, although, by the way they acted—happy and active—Abby would have sworn they were fine. Well, one of these days she'd have more time for them, when things calmed down. One of these days... She could hear her mother laughing at her.

And as for her social life? Well, she and Karen frequently cooked outside together in the warm summer evenings, but, except for an outing to Woodland Park for a movie two weeks ago, Abby had practically been a hermit.

She thought about Ty, unflaggingly and incurably. He seemed to be inside her head like a chronic illness, filling it no matter how hard she tried to get rid of him. There were dozens of images stored in her brain: Ty pounding a nail into her kitchen steps, resting on his haunches, his broad shoulders straining at the fabric of his shirt. Or Ty, steering his Jeep up to her mine, his hair catching the golden light, his strong forearms flexing as the wheel pulled against his hands. And there was Ty the night she'd gone to the Mother Lode, his dark eyes fixed on her relentlessly. And the fire. Ty with a kid under each arm; Ty, half naked, his smooth skin gleaming in the light, his flat belly, the sharp curve of his hip beneath his hastily pulled on jeans...

"Are you comin' to work or not?" asked John from the entrance to the Nola Jane. "Gotta make hay while the sun shines, missy." He cleared his throat and disappeared like a ghost into the dark hole.

The morning went smoothly and productively. They ate lunch outside, sitting on the rocks with the strong noon sun warming their shoulders pleasantly while Abby got better acquainted with her men. One o'clock saw them all standing and stretching, rested and ready for the long afternoon ahead. At 1:20 the accident happened.

Abby was on her way to watch the men blasting when the shouts reached her, echoing eerily along the black corridors and off the rock walls. She rushed along the tracks, half stumbling once, uncertain, afraid for her men. When she reached the crew they were all scurrying around, their headlamps making crisscrossing tunnels of light on soil-darkened faces and black rock.

"What happened?" Abby asked. "I heard shouts..." Then she saw Len Hughes, lying on the wet earthen floor, blood pumping from his thigh. Someone was tearing a cloth for a tourniquet, another was yelling for a stick or a rod with which to twist the rag. Abby crouched down on her knees beside Len and shined her light near his face. "It'll be okay, Len. Just lie there calmly and take it easy. We'll have you out soon."

Where had her words come from? She'd said what she had to, what was right, what Len needed to hear. And yet her eyes told her another story. He was bleeding profusely, the severed artery pumping blood all over. How much blood could a man lose before he . . . ? But no. She wouldn't think of that: Len was married, had two small children. He had to be okay.

Dick Jacobs worked feverishly on Len's leg, pulling the tourniquet tight, twisting it above the wound with the thin pipe they'd found. "Damn," he swore, his grimy face shining with oily sweat, "the bleeding's real bad. I don't know . . ."

Len was trying to sit up and Abby pressed him back down gently. "Lie still, Len. It's okay, lie still." Someone, John, she thought, handed her a cool wet bandanna, which she used to wipe the cold sweat from Len's brow and eyes. "There, it's okay. Take it easy."

"Soon as the bleeding's controlled," said Dick, "we'll get him out to the truck and down to Doc Clements." He turned the pipe another fraction of an inch; blood still welled out steadily from the leg, however, and Abby felt a chill crawl up her spine. Would the bleeding stop? She looked into Dick's eyes, aware that the question was written all over her face.

"It's bad, but it'll stop. Already starting to," Dick told her quietly.

Abby could hear the men behind her, mumbling, their voices low and angry sounding. John Gibbs was asking questions and she heard him say, "Damn jack leg was workin' fine this morning . . . Don't understand it."

Another voice interrupted. "It was the safety switch. I saw it with my own eyes. Len was up there on that scaffolding working the drill. He went to put it out of the hole and shut it off and it jammed. Spun him around off that planking like a top, it did, and six feet down he came, damn jack leg right on his leg, too. Cut him open like a knife."

Five of the men slowly and carefully lifted Len while Dick kept pressure on the tourniquet, alternately loosening it and tightening it. "Watch it there," said Dick in an angry voice. "Goldarn, I almost lost my hold on this thing."

Someone went ahead with the lantern. It was slow going down the dark, twisted shafts as Abby followed the crew, feeling her way, wiping the dripping water from the ceiling out of her eyes.

"I don't get it," she said to John in a whisper. "What exactly happened?"

"There's a safety switch on them drills, supposed to shut the things off automatically when you let go. Guess it didn't work, though, but it should've. Them things don't break like that."

"What are you saying?" asked Abby, bewildered. Things just broke sometimes, didn't they?

"I'm saying that we better be lookin' over that jack leg real careful like. Never heard of a switch going sour that way."

Abby wanted to press him further, but they were outside finally and there was some confusion as to who was going to drive Len into town and in what truck. As it turned out, they used Abby's pickup, cushioning Len in the rear between three of the crew and Dick Jacobs who, having been a medic in Vietnam, knew enough to keep loosening the tourniquet so that gangrene would not set into the leg.

"I'm driving," said Abby, pulling herself up into the cab.

"She'll shake him all over that road!" protested one of the men.

John put a restraining hand on the man's arm. "Hold up there. Missy'll do fine. That's her man lying in the back there. She'll do just fine."

But the road seemed bumpier than ever as Abby steered along the right-hand side, avoiding the washboard ruts and deep pits. She hoped to God she wasn't harming Len any further, but she knew she was doing the best she could. No one could have driven it any better, she kept telling herself.

Doc Clements, she remembered Karen telling her, was a semi-retired M.D. from Colorado Springs, who lived somewhere behind the sheriff's department on A Street. Abby hadn't needed him yet—the twins, so far, had only scraped and bruised themselves—but she'd asked Karen just in case.

His house was not difficult to find; of course, nothing in Cripple Creek was hard to locate. Outside the picket fence there was even a painted sign: Doc Clements—Please Knock. The men unloaded Len, who, in the bright light of day, looked as pallid as a daytime moon. Had her driving done him more damage?

"Take him into the back there," Doc was saying. "Easy does it, boys. Watch that step."

Doc was in his seventies, or so Abby surmised. He was stooped and bone thin; his bifocals were slipping off his nose. His brown-splotched hands shook, too, and Abby cowered silently.

The men stretched Len out carefully on a raised table in the back room; Dick stepped aside and let the doctor take over. "I'm headin' off to the sheriff's," he said to the other men. "We're gonna have Loring check out that drill, boys. I got this gut feelin'..."

"The sheriff?" asked Abby, following them to the front door of the doctor's house. "Will someone please tell me what's going on?"

"Yes, ma'am," piped up young Jeff McLaughlin. "You should know, I guess. We're thinkin' someone messed with the jack leg."

"You mean," said Abby, shielding her eyes from the sun, "someone might have tampered with it?"

"Yes, ma'am. There's been talk, you see, about that Wayne fella and his wanting the Nola Jane so bad..."

"But...he wouldn't resort to sabotage," said Abby uncertainly.

"Let the sheriff handle it, Miz McAlister," put in Dick, heading off down the street.

Doc Clements knew his stuff, Abby was soon to learn. He had Len sedated and the deep wound stitched cleanly within a half hour, and all without the benefit of a surgeon or an operating room. His wife told Abby that he used to make house calls in Colorado Springs and if tonsils needed taking out, he'd do it on the kitchen table. "Course," she said, "that was back in the thirties. Not everyone ran to a clinic or a hospital then. Cup of coffee while we wait?"

Rob Loring met Abby in front of Doc's. "I think I better follow you on up to the mine, Abby, and check this thing out before the gossip starts flyin' round here."

Her heart beat a little faster. "Rob, do you think the drill really might have been tampered with? I mean..."

"Now, we won't know that, will we, till I get on up there?"

Rob was meticulous and careful as he examined the jack-leg drill out in front of the mine. It seemed to take him forever, too, while Abby and the crew hovered over his shoulder. Finally he stood, pushed his Stetson hat back on his head with a steady finger and said, "The pin's been sheared, looks like. Can't say for certain, though, till we have this thing looked at by a welder."

"Told you so," began Jeff McLaughlin. "Wayne's figurin' on scaring Miz McAlister off. That no-good bum . . ."

"Now hold on there, son," began the sheriff, but Abby's attention was suddenly drawn away from the scene and onto the winding dirt road. There was a Jeep coming around the bend; she could hear it, an all-too-familiar sound. She felt a lump form in her throat and her chest constricted.

Before she collected her thoughts he was shutting off his engine and swinging out onto the ground. "I just heard," he said, striding straight to Abby's side. How could she have forgotten how tall he was, or how light his hair was in the sun? And were his eyes always so dark? *Oh Ty,* she cried silently, *why can't you let me be?* "Is Len okay?" he was asking, a look of grave concern creasing his forehead.

"He'll be all right," said Abby carefully, her voice shaky. "He lost a lot of blood, though, and he'll be off work for quite awhile."

Ty took his gaze away from her for a moment and met Rob Loring's eyes. "What's going on here?" he asked, puzzled.

No one spoke for a long moment. Finally Dick said, "Your boss is gettin' mighty anxious, I'd say."

"What're you driving at?" Ty turned around cautiously to face the man.

"I'm saying we think Wayne had this jack leg here tampered with."

Abby was holding her breath, looking from one man to the other, feeling the warm air crackle with hostility. "Dick," she said, taking a step in between the two big men, "I don't think we can jump to any conclusions."

"I think we should all settle down," put in Rob Loring hastily. "I mean that, men. I won't stand for any out-of-control talk, and that means in the bars, as well, boys, until we get this settled."

"Abby, can I talk to you?" Ty said meaningfully. "Alone."

She looked at him for a moment, and then nodded. "We can walk, if you want." Then she said to John, "You'd better take that jack leg into town and have it checked out for Rob."

"Don't you worry, now, missy. I'll take care of everything," replied John.

She and Ty headed up a sloping meadow on a deer trail. It was finally hot out. Abby walked a way, then stopped, sank down onto a boulder and wiped her brow. It was a beautiful spot, overlooking the whole valley, with a breathtaking view of the surrounding peaks, still dotted with snow in the strong July sun. "Oh, Ty," she said, sighing and looking up at him.

He put a hand on her arm. "I know. Accidents are terrible things. Guess I've seen my share."

She shaded her eyes with a hand and asked carefully, "What if it wasn't an accident?"

He squatted on his heels beside her, pushing the brim of his hat up and meeting her eyes. "You don't believe that stuff about Wayne bustin' your jack leg, do you?"

"I don't know. He's been pressuring me. He wants the Nola Jane."

"That doesn't mean he's going to try to scare you off, Abby."

"I don't know. My men think he did it," she said uncertainly.

"Abby, you don't think *I* had anything to do with it, do you?" Ty demanded, almost angrily.

She shook her head. "No."

He whistled in relief. "Now, look, I came up here to see if you needed any help. Can I do anything, call Len's family, whatever?"

She smiled wanly at him. "Thanks, but it's all taken care of."

"Well, then, what about you? Can I take you out for a drink tonight? You know, to relax."

"I can't. I'll have to work late now..."

"Please, Abby. I want to apologize for the other night after the fire. I was mean. I had no right to say..."

"Sure you did," she said, looking down at her knees.

"You know I'm crazy about you, Abby. Please let me help."

"Ty," she said softly, "you can't help. I have to do it myself."

He stood, pulling Abby up and holding her hands. "You don't have to be alone. Whatever you have to do you can do it with someone. Me."

He was standing close, so close, his breath fanning her hair, his eyes searching her face, his lips parted half expectantly. Abruptly, Abby couldn't breathe or think. She tried to pull her hands out of his but he only held them tighter. "Ty," she whispered.

His mouth was close, the grooves on either side deepening, a muscle working in his jaw. "Don't hurt us both, Abby."

She grew weak with longing and confusion. "I . . . I can't be the way you want me to be, Ty."

He pulled her to his chest and rubbed a hand up and down her back. She could feel the buttons of his shirt against her cheek and smell the man scent of his skin.

"I guess I'll have to wait awhile longer," he said. Then he held her out at arm's length. "You do try my patience, though, ma'am."

She laughed shakily and pushed the hair away from her forehead. "I really do have to get back."

He took her hand as they started down the path. "You sure you got everything under control here?"

"Everything but my baby-sitting schedule," she said ruefully. "I'll need to run home and tell Janet I'll be late. I hope she can stay. Darn, I wish I had a phone at the mine."

"Now, you just relax. I'll go on by and tell Janet. No, even better, I'll take care of the boys after work. Then Janet won't have to stay."

"Ty, you don't have to do that."

He winked at her. "Shucks, ma'am, my pleasure."

"OH, MR. HOLLINGER," said Janet when she saw him at Abby's door. "Mrs. McAlister isn't home yet."

"I know. She sent me to collect the two wild men."

"Oh, wow!" yelled Ben. Well, at least Ty thought it was Ben.

"Can we go fishing, Uncle Ty?" cried the other.

"Sure. Fishing. Why not?"

It took Ty several minutes to distinguish one boy from the other. He took them both by the arm and pulled them into the bathroom. "Where's your mom's nail polish?" he asked, frowning.

"I don't know," said Sean, confused.

Ty searched around the medicine chest. He finally found the polish. "Okay, guys, who wants to be pink and who wants to be red?"

"What for?" In unison.

"We're gonna paint a little lock of your hair—just a small piece—so I can tell you apart. I've been put on enough for one day, guys."

He locked up Abby's house, hid the key in her spot above the door, and made sure the front gate was closed so Barney couldn't escape the yard, although he suspected Abby wouldn't be too undone if Barney up and disappeared. Then it was off to his house to find the fishing poles.

The twins bounced around in the back of the open Jeep like corks on the river as Ty drove along what was known as Teller 1, an unpaved county road that led past Mount Pisgah toward some nationally acclaimed fossil beds and then climbed up through gently sloping grasslands, where white-faced cattle grazed in the afternoon sun. He loved this part of Colorado. There were more trees, it seemed, and the grass was greener and taller and maybe the sky just a little bluer than elsewhere.

He had just the spot in mind: a slow-moving stream that wound lazily down a meadow to meet the rushing river below. Now, most folks wouldn't have known about the rainbow trout in this one deep hole, but Ty did.

Pulling up on the shoulder of the road, Ty said, "Okay, troops, out we go. Time to dig us some fat, squishy worms." The boys loved the idea. Ty wished

Abby were along, although he'd never seen a woman yet who particularly liked to pull slimy worms out of holes.

Ty only owned two poles but that was okay. He would watch while the twins fished their hearts out. Then, too, he imagined they'd both be needing some help from time to time.

He was right. First Ben cried, "I got my bait stuck!" Then Sean hollered, "I lost the hook, Uncle Ty! Quick, the fish will leave!"

"The fish aren't going anywhere, unless, of course, you keep yellin' and scarin' them half to death."

"They can't hear," said Ben staunchly, and Ty had to explain all about fish and animals and how, when in the woods, a man had to keep silent in order to see all of God's critters.

"Just like the Ute Indians, boys. You gotta move around real soft and stay real, real quiet or you'll go hungry."

Fishing was not going too well. But then, it was their first time out, and Ty hadn't really expected the twins to catch anything. He checked his watch. Six-thirty. Heck, it didn't get dark till after nine. They had time.

It was seven when Sean screeched, "I got one! I got one! What do I do?"

And at seven-fifteen, after Ty had moved Ben's line into the eddy near the hole, the child called, "Uncle Ty! Quick! It's eating the pole!"

Evening, thought Ty as he boosted each boy back into the Jeep, evening was his favorite time of day in the mountains. Everything was so soft out; the white tree trunks of the cottonwoods and aspens were golden in the light. It was an easy time, when a man could settle back and rest a spell, when insects flitted through the patches of light and the mountains cast long shadows in the deep silent valleys. He pointed out a doe grazing with her fawn on the hillside above them and the boys were as quiet as mice—like Indians. He pointed to the sky and showed them a hawk rising on an ascending shaft of warm air, scouting out his dinner below.

He drove along in silence for a spell, pleased with the boys' behavior, pleased that he'd gotten out of town and relaxed for a bit. He looked at the dashboard. "Empty? But I . . ."

"Uncle Ty? What's wrong?"

"Ah . . . Well, I thought I filled the gas tank, fellas, but I guess I, ah, forgot."

"Are we out of gas, Uncle Ty?"

"In about thirty seconds, if I know this Jeep." Actually, it was closer to a minute, but who was counting?

They'd just passed by the fossil ruins and if Ty was correct, it would still be three and a half, maybe four miles back into town. Now, usually he carried a spare can of gas tied onto the rear bumper of the Jeep, but recently he'd been forgetting a lot of things, too many. It was amazing how muddled a man's head could get when he had romantic problems.

"We can hitchhike," said Sean, craning his neck up and down the winding dirt road.

"See any traffic, fellas?" asked Ty. "I'd say it's academic."

"What's academic?"

The kids were great sports, really, because Ty wasn't about to leave his poles and boots and spare jackets in the open Jeep. So, not only were they forced to walk, but they pitched in, carrying stuff—Ty, of course, bearing the brunt of the weight.

He worried about them, though. Could the youngsters make it? Those short little legs of theirs had him wondering.

"How we doing?" he asked after the first mile. They were fine so far, still caught up in the adventure aspect of things. "You guys are pretty good outdoorsmen for city kids," he teased and tousled their hair with his hand.

The hike was an inconvenience, but it did afford Ty a chance to really talk to the boys—without Mom around. And they were amazingly well-behaved, too, polite and curious. What a jerk Steve McAlister must have been to leave these two in the care of a single parent. Boys needed a man around, if for no other reason than to discipline them and teach them things like camping out and fishing. Then there were girls, of course, mused Ty as he ambled along. It wouldn't be so bad to have a little girl someday....

Often Ty checked his watch. It was getting late. He hoped when dusk gave way to night that the boys wouldn't be scared. It wasn't uncommon for a wolf to howl or a coyote to sing his mournful song under the canopy of stars.

"I see lights!" cried Sean. "Look!"

Indeed he had. Coming from the direction of Cripple Creek were a set of headlights that appeared to belong to a four-wheel-drive vehicle. "Guys, we might just be rescued yet."

It was Rob Loring, heading home to his ranch about eight miles farther along Teller 1. "Looks like you men could use a lift," he told them, helping the boys pile into the back of the Blazer with all of Ty's gear.

"Wow," breathed Ben, "can you put on the siren and lights and stuff?"

"You bet," said Rob, winking at Ty, "but we better turn them off before town, huh? Don't want to scare anyone."

"Like Abby," said Ty wryly, knowing darn good and well she was going to be frantic... "Oh, no!" He slapped his forehead. "Hell's bells, I forgot to leave her a note!" On went the siren and flashing lights.

"I wonder," said Ty as they pulled up in front of Abby's, "if there's any word on that jack leg yet."

"The welder said the safety mechanism was sheared clean off." Rob put his hands on the wheel and looked at Ty meaningfully.

As expected, Abby was out of her mind with worry and ran from the house to meet them. The only saving grace was that Janet had seen Ty drive off with the kids and the fishing poles in tow. "But I thought you'd had an accident or something!" Abby wept as she hugged the squirming boys.

"I'm real sorry, Abby," said Ty, "honest I am. Taking them fishing turned out great..." He held up the two trout. "But the rest of it..." Ty shrugged apologetically as he noted her swollen eyes and the damp Kleenex clutched in her hand.

"Mommy," said Ben, "did you feed Barney?" Then both boys were off and running.

Abby wiped at her smudged mascara, which only served to make the streaks worse, and turned to Ty. "I'm being silly," she said, drawing in a deep breath. "Acting like an overprotective mother."

"No, you're not," said Ty quietly. "Honest. The kids are all your responsibility and I know how hard it is on you. Go ahead and scream," he said, hiding a smile. "I'll understand."

The boys were out back, chasing the burro, their cries of delight reaching Ty where he stood alongside Abby, his hands in his pockets, his heart beginning a heavy pounding rhythm. What would she do if he pulled her into his arms and kissed her?

"Abby," he said, gazing up at the blanket of brilliant stars, "the boys were great on our little excursion. I can sure tell they've learned a lot this summer. About being trustworthy and independent and all that stuff. They're good kids."

"For other people they are," she said quietly, "but for me, well, it's hard raising them alone. I worry so much..."

"You don't have to be alone."

Abby said nothing. She merely ducked her head and looked down at her feet. If he was going to kiss her, now was the time.

He took his hands out of his pockets and turned toward her. "Shh," he whispered as if to calm a skittish animal, while he put both hands on either side of her face tenderly and drew her toward him. She came, willingly, and in the shaft of light spilling out from the living room, he could see the heavy rise and fall of her breasts beneath the cotton shirt. He sighed painfully, his need suddenly overpowering. "Abby," he said close to her mouth. He bent his head and touched his lips to hers with infinite care.

Dear God, how good she tasted, how warm and soft and round her body was pressed to his. He moved his hands down to her shoulders and then around her waist, pulling her closer yet, feeling her bosom against his chest, firm and soft all at once. Her lips parted beneath his, and he searched her mouth gently with his tongue, his need sending hot darts of pleasure shooting through his belly. He held her closer still, unable to get enough of her warmth, desperate now to culminate what must eventually be between them. And for a time there was no night sky, no cool breeze, no town, no roads, no houses, only the two of them.

"Mommy! I'm hungry!"

Abby jerked away in shock, stunned, as shattered as Ty. "Oh, God," she said.

"Yeah," he managed to utter, his heart racing a mile a minute, his legs ready to fold on him.

"Oh, Ty..."

"I know...I know."

"Mommy!" came another yell from the kitchen.

"I have to...go, Ty. I..."

"Don't say anything, please, Abby. This has been too special to spoil. I'm afraid we'll argue or something." She nodded. "I better go. Do you want me to go?" God, he was brain dead, and he was fumbling over his words, uncertain, weak with his longing.

"You better...go, that is. The kids..."

"They'll be in bed soon."

"I...I'm not sure, Ty. I need time."

"You were sure a minute ago... No, sorry, I only meant..."

"I know. It's okay."

"I'll, ah, go..." So why were his feet glued to the ground? She'd said she wasn't ready, but her body told a different story.

"Good night, Ty."

"Ah...good night, Abby."

She left him standing there. What else could she do? He must have stood there for a long time until he realized he was all alone, drenched in frustrated perspiration, his shirt wet and clinging while the cold night air made goose bumps rise on his flesh. He put his hands in his pockets again and headed toward the street, to his dark, empty house and to Gertrude, the cat, the only company he'd have that night.

CHAPTER TWELVE

JOHN GIBBS STALKED OUT of the mine entrance, waving his arms. "He's done it now," he shouted to Abby. "Wayne's blasted right into the Nola Jane!"

Abby was in her "office" paying some bills. "What do you mean?"

"I mean, missy, that there's boundaries underground just like above, and you don't go trespassing on somebody else's property!"

"And Wayne's on *our* property?"

"His crew just blasted a hole through to our north crosscut, right where we've been followin' that vein! And I checked my figures and I'll tell you, missy, I ain't ever been *that* far off my figgerin'! He's twenty yards inside the Nola Jane's north boundary."

"John, are you absolutely positive?"

"I'll show you." He unrolled a chart that he'd been carrying in the pocket of his faded overalls, weighed the corners down with rocks and creaked to his knees on the ground. "See here?" His blunt finger pointed to a clearly marked shaft running north. "And there? That's our boundary, surveyed to these figures. And there—" he pointed again "—that's where Wayne's crew just blasted through. An' I rechecked my survey lines, let me tell you. I couldn't believe my old eyes! But there's more. He's not only on our territory, he's also been minin' our vein!"

"What?"

"Well, there's this apex law says any vein on your property you follow that's unbroken, even if it goes onto another man's property, it's your vein. Ya got the right to mine it."

"Do you mean that he's been following the same vein we've been following?" asked Abby, trying to sort out all the facts.

"Sure has." John looked mad enough to spit. "But from the wrong end!"

"Do you think he's doing this deliberately," asked Abby again, "or is it a mistake?"

"Well, missy, if it's a mistake it's a whoppin' big one and I know darn well Ty Hollinger's a better miner than to make such a blasted dumb one." Gibbs pushed himself to his feet, rolled his chart up and paced. "We can't do a whole lot. Go to the law. That's Rob Loring. But apex law's real hard to prove and you'd spend a bundle on lawyers, and Wayne could hang ya up in court for years."

"There must be something we can do."

"Sure. In the old days you'd go in there blazin', and shoot the tar out of Wayne's crew. That'd show 'em."

"This isn't the old days, John. What can we do?"

"Go to Wayne and warn him off." Gibbs looked her up and down doubtfully. "Course, he might laugh. A girl like you, missy."

"I'm not a girl, John, I'm a grown woman. I know my rights. You just give me that chart and show me all those lines and numbers and I'll go face Wayne." Abby stamped her foot. "He can't do this to me. It's not fair!"

"Fair!" John gave a short laugh. "Fair's who's got the most money, the most men, the most power."

"You know what the men are saying about Len's accident, don't you? They all think the jack leg was tampered with. They think Wayne did it or had somebody do it. And the welder in town said the safety pin had been sheared off. John, do you think Wayne is really capable of trying to put me out of business?"

Gibbs looked down, frowning. "Could be. He's a tough fella. Been workin' for a year with no competition."

"Well, he's got competition now," said Abby.

Her truck rattled as if it were going to fall apart going down the dirt road. She was driving too fast, she knew, angry and nervous and keyed up. She had to face Kevin Wayne down. What was she going to say? Phrases kept forming in her mind, but they dissolved as fast as they appeared. She gave up, trusting to inspiration when she was actually face to face with him.

Oh, Lord, would Ty be there? Would she be able to go through with this ordeal if he was? She clenched her teeth and yanked the truck around a tight curve, raising a rooster tail of dust behind her. She'd go through with it because she had to, Ty or no Ty.

She turned onto the highway. Ty had been wonderful that night, that awful night of the fire. She had to admit it. And he'd been wonderful again when Len had been hurt. The boys adored him and asked for Uncle Ty all the time.

It was Abby who kept pushing him away. She was the intolerant one, the distrustful and cruel one, keeping Ty at an arm's length, insulting him, closing her door in his face. She was thankless, mean, rude. And still he forgave her every time; he was unfailingly nice, kind, helpful. Could it all be a pose? Honest, lovable, adorable Ty, pretending?

So, then, if he wasn't pretending to be as wonderful as he seemed, if he really was wonderful, then what was Abby afraid of?

Nothing... She wasn't afraid of anything. Ty might very well be Kevin Wayne's confidant, his henchman. She couldn't afford to trust him. Especially now, with this new development.

The Golden Slipper was a much more official looking mine than the Nola Jane. There was the hoist house, trucks lined up, piles of ore, men bustling around. There was even a real office, a little trailer, and it had "Wayne Consolidated Mining" stenciled on its side.

Abby parked her truck, took the rolled-up chart and walked toward the trailer. She didn't allow herself to think; she was too rattled. What if he wasn't there? She'd wait.

But Kevin Wayne was there, sitting on his folding chair behind a desk made of a sheet of plywood. He rose instantly when he saw Abby at the open door and smiled a particularly charming smile. "Mrs. McAlister, so good to see you. Decided to sell the Nola Jane, eh? Good, good."

"No, Mr. Wayne, that's not why I'm here at all," Abby said, afraid her voice was shaking. "In fact, there's something I'd like to show you." She unrolled the chart on his desk. "My foreman tells me that one of your crews is in violation of my boundary line right here." She pointed. "And that's well inside my line, so there shouldn't have been any mistake."

"Ridiculous," said Wayne smoothly. "That old coot you call a mine foreman was senile before I was born."

"Insults won't cover up your illegal activities, Mr. Wayne. John Gibbs is in full possession of his faculties. And so am I."

"Illegal activities! Mrs. McAlister, I defy you to prove that." Wayne leaned back and waved a hand negligently. "That chicken scratching means nothing."

"You've been mining my vein, too," said Abby staunchly. "And I truly think you tampered with the jack leg that nearly killed one of my men the other day." She thrust her face closer to Wayne. "Did you, Mr. Wayne?"

"Preposterous," he said calmly. "I'm a businessman, not a thug."

"I'll take you to court over your violation of my boundary," said Abby.

"Go on. You'll be broke and running home with your tail between your legs before it gets on the docket," he said coldly.

"We'll see about that. Don't underestimate me, Mr. Wayne. Right now I'm going to the courthouse to file charges against you."

He waved his hand at her. "Go on. You're wasting my time. It'll take you years to prove I did anything. Which I didn't, by the way. Don't blame your failures on me, Mrs. McAlister."

"I haven't failed yet," said Abby coolly, turning and leaving.

She drove quickly away from the Golden Slipper, turned into a driveway a mile down the road and sat there, shaking. What a dreadful man; his eyes shone with evil like one of the villains in the Saturday cartoons the twins watched. He was out to get her; now she was absolutely convinced of that. He'd sabotaged the jack leg and deliberately blasted into her mine. What would he do next? What awful thing? It was terrifying, wondering always when you were going to be attacked in some new, insidious way.

When her hands stopped shaking, Abby put the truck back in gear and drove slowly into town. She was going to the sheriff, at least to find out how to start proceedings against Wayne.

After she left the sheriff's office, the question hit her: just how aware was Ty of Wayne's activities? How deep was he into the scheme?

There had been those first days, when he'd tried so hard to discourage her. Okay. She could forgive him that; she might have been wrong about Wayne putting him up to it. Then there was the jack-leg accident. Ty, she recalled clearly, had never denied Wayne's involvement. Of course, she couldn't picture Ty actually cutting that pin, but had he heard talk of it around the Golden Slipper?

But regarding this boundary dispute—Ty was the engineer. He did the surveying, he was a graduate of one of the top mining schools in the country. Heck, he'd even bragged to her about his education. He must have known where his men were blasting; he must have thrown those survey lines himself. Abby's heart sank to the floorboards and she choked back tears. Then suddenly, at the next corner, she spun around the curve, knowing what she had to do.

He hadn't been at the mine office. She knew he often worked at home in the mornings. Stepping on the gas, she chugged up the hill. Yes, his Jeep was there!

She pulled up behind his Jeep and swung out of the truck. Marching up the walk, her thoughts flip-flopped and she told herself he'd be shocked, he'd be furious, he would offer to help her against Wayne.

He'd phone his boss and quit his job on the spot!

The door was open. She stepped in, calling, "Ty! You home?" No answer. She walked through the living room. He had to be there. "Ty?"

He was on the phone in the kitchen. He raised his eyebrows when he saw her, cupped his hand over the receiver and mouthed, "Just a minute."

Abby stalked around impatiently. *Holy Toledo, I come to have it out with the man and he's on the phone!* She looked at a few pictures Ty had on a table. Family stuff. Sisters and their husbands and lots of kids. A big family. A warm, loving family, Ty had told her, despite being poor. His orange Broncos hat rested on the back of the couch. Who in heck were the Broncos? Some football team, she supposed, fingering it.

There were some charts open on a table. Abby looked at them, but the lines meant nothing to her. *Come on, Ty, finish it up!*

She couldn't help hearing his side of the conversation. "Sure, Sheila, any time." Ty nodded and listened for a long time and then raised an apologetic eyebrow at Abby. "Yes, Sheila." More listening. "It's never locked. Come right on in if I'm not home." Then he turned away. "Yes, Sheila, I got that bill. But I'm only..." More listening, but this time Abby could tell he was getting impatient.

He finally hung up. "Sorry," he said, "but that was important."

"Who's Sheila?" Abby blurted out.

"My ex-wife," said Ty. "She wants the china."

"Oh," said Abby in a small voice.

There was a strained silence for a moment too long before Ty said, "I went to see Len yesterday. He'll be home in a few days."

"Uh, yes, I know. He's doing pretty well," Abby replied.

Another silence.

"Did you...uh...want something, Abby?" Ty asked carefully.

She was acting like a kid in the principal's office. "Actually, I wanted to ask you something," she finally managed.

"Shoot," he said, smiling.

She cleared her throat. "Ty, did you know Wayne was following my vein and going over my north boundary line?"

He didn't say anything right away, but his face seemed to turn grim and stiff. He wasn't shocked, Abby realized painfully, not even surprised. "Do you have any proof of this?" he asked.

She nodded, feeling her throat constrict. He knew. "John Gibbs checked the survey lines when one of Wayne's crews blasted through this morning. On Nola Jane territory."

"Damn." Ty turned from her and stuck his hands in his pockets, hunching his shoulders.

"I went to Wayne and told him..." Abby began.

"You what?" Ty spun around.

"I just talked to your boss, Ty, and he was very nasty. He told me to go ahead and take him to court, and I'm going to." Abby paused, feeling her heart sink even lower. "I just...well, I thought I should tell you."

Ty was quiet for a time. Abby felt terribly uncomfortable facing him in the awkward silence. "Well," she finally said, turning to go, "I guess I'll go on down and talk to the sheriff."

"I suppose you think it's all my doing."

She stood still and hung her head, unable to answer him.

"Isn't that why you came here?"

"I don't know why I came," Abby flared. "It was a waste of my time."

"Abby, I swear I didn't know Wayne had a crew blasting there. I warned him a month ago..."

"You're the engineer. And you're a pretty lousy one if you don't know where your crews are blasting!"

Shocked silence followed. "That was a real low blow, Abby," Ty said in a taut voice.

"What you and your pal, Wayne, are doing is even lower," she said in a whisper.

"Well, why don't you just get your friend, the sheriff, to put me in jail?"

"Maybe I will. You and your boss both. And Sheila can come visit you there!" Then she marched out and slammed the door behind her.

That night Abby had promised to take Karen and Sheriff Rob out for hamburgers at the Mother Lode. She wasn't in any mood for socializing but she'd set the date up the week before, insisting on treating them because they'd both helped her clean up the awful mess left by the fire. She had to go through with it. And besides, Janet was counting on the extra baby-sitting money.

Sean and Benny were outside playing with Barney—as usual. Abby had decided that the little burro was better than television for keeping the boys occupied. He followed them around like a puppy dog and, to tell the truth, he wasn't much larger than a big dog. He had an endearing way of sticking his bristly soft nose into a person's pockets when looking for cornflakes. And he was cheaper than a dog; Abby didn't even have to buy special food for him. Actually, come to think of it, he was cheaper than a lawn mower too.

She finished the boys' dinner dishes, straightened up the kitchen, put some toys away and then went into her bedroom to get dressed. She'd had to launder every single washable item in the house, as everything had reeked of tarry smoke. Thank heavens she had that old washer. She couldn't imagine a hundred trips to the laundromat; when would she have found time, anyway?

She decided to wear a new pair of white jeans she'd treated herself to now that she was slim and trim. Yes, her white jeans and a blue and white striped shirt and her navy-blue sweater. She'd learned not to venture from the house in the evening without a sweater or a jacket, not at ten thousand feet. Even in July it got downright cold the minute the sun set.

"I'm here, Mrs. McAlister!" called Janet as she walked in. Nobody locked doors or knocked in Cripple Creek.

"Oh, good. Is your mom ready?"

"Sure is. Dolled up for the big night."

"Big night? In the Mother Lode?" asked Abby, dubious.

"It's a big night getting Rob away from the baseball game," Janet said.

Rob drove them downtown. The door of the saloon was open; a few men even stood outside with their beers. They all tipped their hats politely. "Howdy, Miz McAlister, Miz Lockley, Rob."

Rob stopped to chat with one of the men for a minute. "Get us a table, hon," he told Karen. "I'll be along directly."

Karen looked heavenward. "Oh, sure. Once he gets to talking, it's a cold day in hell before he quits," she said ruefully to Abby.

The two ladies found a table in the back. The bar was filled with people and smoke and music, as usual. Abby couldn't help remembering the last time she'd been in the Mother Lode. What a scene that had been. But it had worked, and now her mine was going and the weekly trucks were coming to take her ore to El Paso, and everything was fine.

Well, except for Kevin Wayne—and Ty.

They ordered beers. Barb delivered them, plus one for the still-absent Rob.

The jukebox was playing "Ramblin' Rose" and Karen sang along in snatches. She had a terrific voice, Abby decided, tapping her foot and taking in the atmosphere. It certainly was different from the bars in Newark! Here, everyone knew each other. All the day's gossip was exchanged, business deals made, problems discussed, election issues decided.

"Oh, here he comes at last," said Karen. Sure enough, there was big Rob forging his way through the crowd.

"Say," he said, grinning widely, "look who I found walking down the street!" He stood aside, ushering the man forward.

Abby swallowed, feeling the blood drain from her face. Her heart gave a terrible jump and her stomach knotted.

"Well, hello stranger," Karen was saying. "Take a load off."

"Don't mind if I do. Hi, Abby," he said, tipping his orange cap.

"Hello, Ty."

Karen was looking at her oddly as Ty pulled a chair up and seated himself. Karen knew she and Ty had been having some problems, but after Len's accident she'd told Karen they had—sort of—made up. Until this morning.

They all ordered hamburgers, French fries and more beer. The men talked easily and Ty didn't seem the least bit uncomfortable. How did he do it? Abby nervously drank beer until she had to excuse herself and go to the ladies' room. That was embarrassing enough but, in order to get there, she had to squeeze by Ty's chair and her thigh brushed his shoulder.

When she returned she had to squeeze by him again, touching him in that dreadfully intimate manner. The spot on her leg burned as if he had branded her, and she felt herself flush with chagrin and shame that a casual touch could disconcert her so badly. Ty turned and looked up at her, as if feeling her reaction, his dark brows drawing together in a bar of annoyance. She switched her eyes away and sat down.

Karen and Rob were so studiously nice after that that Abby was sure Ty must have told them the whole story of that morning.

Rob Loring, of course, knew about Abby's problem, because she'd spoken to him of filing charges that day, but he avoided the subject with scrupulous care. Obviously he didn't think Ty was some kind of criminal. Or was that just small-town courtesy? After all, people had to live together here—they had to get along.

"Nice weather we've been having," Rob offered.

"Real nice summer. There's going to be a frost soon, though," said Ty.

"Isn't Janet expecting us back pretty soon?" Abby asked.

"Heck, no. She's probably on the phone, gabbing with that boyfriend of hers," said Karen, dashing Abby's escape plan.

"I think that was a good idea, gettin' Janet to sit for the boys," Ty said to Abby. "She's a nice girl."

"Nice!" remarked Karen. "At home she's pretty hard to handle at times. Teenagers! But her workin' this summer has really been great. She's saving for a horse, she says, and she's been so darn busy she can't get into trouble. She doesn't even have time to bellyache about how strict I am anymore. It's been a treat."

"I don't know what I would have done without her," said Abby, terribly aware of Ty's gaze on her, of his dark eyes caressing her skin. She felt her flesh crawl and tried desperately to ignore it. "The boys love her. She's awfully good with them, too. They really listen to her."

"You ever get that stovepipe cleaned out?" asked Ty.

Abby looked down. "Yes, but it was almost cleaned by the time the sweep got to it."

"I'll bet," said Rob.

"Most excitement this town's seen since old Gold Dust got out of the nursing home and shot up the town with blanks," said Karen.

"The fire was awful," said Abby, cringing.

"Coulda been a lot worse."

"I still feel as if I smell of smoke. I've washed everything, but still . . ." Abby said.

"You don't smell like smoke," Ty commented. "You smell sweet, like roses."

Rob and Karen looked away. Abby blushed and stared at her hamburger, which sat half eaten on her plate, all cold and congealed, with catsup oozing out of it.

The silence stretched as thin as a high-tension wire and Abby felt like screaming. Finally Karen said, "Hey, Rob, how about taking a turn around the floor?"

Rob looked bemused.

"You know," urged Karen, "let's dance."

"But I don't . . ."

Karen had him on the floor doing a two-step before he could finish. "Poor Rob," said Ty, smiling, pushing his food around his plate with his fork.

"Um," replied Abby.

"Didn't mean to embarrass you," Ty offered. "Sometimes my mouth gets away from me."

"I wasn't embarrassed," lied Abby quickly, and then fell quiet. Ty picked up a French fry and turned it around and around with his fingers, studying it before eating it bite by slow bite, chewing pensively, swallowing, chewing some more. Abby tried her hamburger but could barely get it past the lump in her throat. If only the song would end and Karen and Rob would sit back down.

"Good fries," said Ty.

"Um."

"How's the burger?"

"Fine."

"I'd say the weather was nice but you'd probably just say um, wouldn't you?"

"I don't have much to say, I guess."

"Are you mad I sat down?"

Abby eyed him thoughtfully. "Yes. This isn't easy for me."

"Me, neither. So let's get out of here and walk or something. We could talk."

"I don't think . . ."

"Phew!" exclaimed Karen. "I think dancing on a full stomach is a bad idea." She laughed, swung her heavy brown hair off her shoulder and sat down cheerfully. "Rob loves dancing, don't you?" she teased.

"Oh, sure."

Ty turned to Abby, his expression sad and concerned. "Would you like to dance? I should have asked . . ."

"No. Thank you, though."

At last the meal was over. Rob had to get up early, thank goodness, so he offered to drive them home. "Unless you want to stay," he said.

"Oh, no, really, I have to get up early, too, you know. I'm awfully tired," Abby hastened to explain.

"I think I'll stay awhile," said Ty, leaning back in his chair. "I sure did enjoy the evenin', though. Night, Abby."

Abby escaped outside into the cool air, drew in a deep, shuddering breath, and sagged against the building as she waited for Rob and Karen. Oh, she was glad that was over. Never again, she swore. Next time Ty pulled a trick like that she'd get suddenly ill—or something.

Karen broached the subject in the car. "Guess that wasn't a brilliant idea, Rob, bringin' Ty along. What's goin' on between you two?"

"Nothing."

"Come on, Abby. I was afraid to breathe too hard for fear I'd set the atomic bomb off."

"We had a little argument, that's all."

"A little argument. Oh, I see."

"Don't worry, Karen, they'll sort things out," said Rob. "Leave Abby alone."

Fervently, silently, Abby thanked Rob for his gentlemanly tact.

"Well, I'm sure glad we don't have little arguments, Rob," said Karen.

"No, we used to have real big ones, didn't we, hon?"

"We have had our ups and downs. For a while there, I wasn't sure we were going to make it." Then Karen winked. "But I guess true love conquers all."

Rob blushed.

Abby crossed to her own backyard under a black velvet sky that was studded with diamonds. The air was clear and fragrant. Barney trotted out to nose her pockets and she patted his shaggy back. Silence pressed in on her and she was glad for the burro's company.

She wished she had a man to go home with, as Karen did, a loving man like Rob. Oh, how she envied the two of them. Sometimes the loneliness became unbearable, like now, and Abby dreamed futile daydreams in which she was coming home to Ty and he was smiling, greeting her with a hug and a kiss and warm, welcoming love. Well, it wouldn't be Ty, and it certainly wouldn't be soon. But maybe one of these days . . .

Janet was gone, the twins were asleep, the house was dark and quiet. Abby lay in bed and thought about Ty, about their quarrel. Maybe she should have listened to him more closely. What had he said? Something about warning Wayne a month ago. Warning him about trespassing on Nola Jane property? Maybe Ty really had warned his boss and Wayne had gone ahead anyway, without telling Ty.

"Oh, blast it all!" she whispered, sitting up and turning on her light. She was too upset to sleep. She reached for the diary, angry with herself. The entry she turned to was dated November 2, 1894, and Abby could tell immediately that her great-grandmother had been upset.

Dear Diary,

What shall I do? Randy did not believe me when I told him that Rausch was trying to lure my men away with promises of higher wages. And that isn't all. I'm sure Rausch sent his men to set fire to my store of shoring lumber. The police said it was an accident. Accident! We had a terrible argument and I cried myself to sleep.

My Randy. He is such a beautiful man, so gentle and kindhearted. We talk of books we have both read and he tells me of his childhood and his two dear sisters whom I would so love to meet.

But he must believe me when I tell him about his unscrupulous employer and he will not!

I am in anguish. What shall I do?

Abby put the diary down. It had only made her own confusion worse. She knew exactly how Nola Jane felt, knew every nuance of the agonized self-questioning. Nola Jane's situation and her own were uncannily similar. How could you love a man who worked for the enemy?

CHAPTER THIRTEEN

"IT'S A CONSPIRACY," Abby complained to John. "Everything's falling apart around me."

"It's only the switch on the jack leg, missy, and it can't cost too much to have her fixed."

"I'm not made of money, John," replied Abby as she trudged back up the shaft, her crew parting silently and respectfully to let her past. Outside, the sun was blazing in the midafternoon sky. Usually, when she left the dark, cool mine and breathed in fresh air, Abby felt renewed and peaceful, but not this August day.

She settled herself on the open tailgate of her pickup, her legs dangling, and pushed her hair off the back of her neck. Her hair had grown past her shoulders, her bangs were in her eyes, and she couldn't even afford a haircut. Swell.

Money. I need more money.

Always, it circled back to that. If Abby had just another three or four hundred dollars in the bank, she could cope.

She took a long, cool drink of water from her thermos and sighed. Now the jack leg, because it had never been fixed properly in the first place, needed a new part—an eighty-dollar one at that. And the last truckload of ore that had reached El Paso had been of a poorer grade than the previous ones, yielding her less return. And the price of gold had leveled off, as well.

True, it had hit five hundred fifty on the world market, but it could drop off any day.

"You okay?" came John's voice from behind, and Abby jumped.

"You scared me, John. You're always sneaking around." She could have bitten her tongue off. What was the matter with her? "I'm sorry. Really I am. I guess I'm just down lately."

His faded blue eyes fixed on her keenly. "Money again, missy?"

Abby nodded. "What else?" She tried to smile. "If it isn't one thing, it's another. This morning that antique washing machine of mine conked out. Do you know how much it costs to do laundry at the laundromat?"

"I wouldn't be knowin'."

"Too much. And the, ah, person who fixed my machine in the first place isn't, ah, available."

John rubbed at the gray stubble on his chin. "Ty Hollinger? He fixed it?"

"Ah . . . yes."

"Ain't seen him around much, missy. You have a fight with him?"

Abby narrowed her eyes at John. He didn't miss much, did he? "Not that it's any of your business, John," she said loftily, "but I don't make it a habit to hang around with Kevin Wayne's employees."

"Humph," replied John, heading back into the Nola Jane.

As the afternoon waned, the sun reached toward Mount Pisgah, and the shadows grew longer across the smooth green valley. Abby entered the mine and worked alongside the men loading ore until her muscles told her it was quitting time.

"You sure put in a hard day today," said Dick.

"Guess I needed to." Abby gave him a weary shrug. "Sometimes physical work takes my mind off things."

"Miz McAlister," he began hesitantly, "is everything okay here at the mine?"

"It's fine. I'm making ends meet, anyhow." Abby noticed that he seemed to breathe a sigh of relief. "How's Len doing?" she asked as they put their tools back inside the mine opening.

"He'll be back to work Wednesday. Leastways, that's what Doc Clements thinks."

"Good. Well, see you in the morning, Dick."

"Bye, Miz McAlister." He paused alongside his truck. "By the way, I got a feelin' this week's ore load'll be a lot richer than the last."

"Oh, really?"

"Yep. Thing is, the vein's gettin' wider as we dynamite, and though I ain't no assayer, it's lookin' richer, too."

"I hope you're right, Dick."

"Me too, Miz McAlister. Things keep going along good, maybe you'll be able to put some more men on."

"I'll keep my fingers crossed that the vein keeps up, not to mention the price of gold." She smiled and waved goodbye, thinking all the time that her men were dyed-in-the-wool optimists, each and every one of them.

THE DRIVE DOWN THE MOUNTAINSIDE and into Cripple Creek seemed to take longer than usual that afternoon. Of course, it was because Abby was tired. She needed a rest—and not just sleep, either. Her days had taken on an awful monotony and she seemed to be weighed down with worry too much lately. Was her life always going to be like this, work and more work, never really going under but never really making it, either?

It's better than flagging cars in Newark, she told herself and managed a smile.

The kids and Janet were nowhere to be seen that afternoon, so Abby left them a note and headed to the grocery store and the laundromat, along the way passing Ty's Jeep parked in front of the Mother Lode.

Was that all he did? Work, then stop off for a cold one every evening?

It was six-thirty by the time she returned home. The kids would be hungry and Janet, no doubt, dying to be relieved. But what was Abby to do, let all the errands go and start living like a complete slob? It was bad enough that she traipsed around town in her soiled work clothes with dirt on her neck. Maybe this weekend she'd take the kids to Colorado Springs, to shop for new school shoes and a dress for herself. Sure, that would be fun—a good outing for the family.

"Hi!" called Abby, lugging in the groceries. "I'm home!"

No answer. Now where were those kids?

She put the groceries away, caught up on some correspondence, primarily writing the promised postcard to Mrs. Howell, and started her weekly epistle to her mother.

By seven she noticed Barney was missing, as well, and she was beginning to worry. She walked next door to Karen's. "Do you know where they went?"

"Walking, I think. Janet called me at the shop around, let's see, three or so, and said she was taking them for ice cream and a hike."

Both women looked at each other with worried expressions. "Maybe you should call Rob or something," suggested Abby, trying to keep the gnawing fear out of her voice.

"I could," replied Karen. "It is kind of weird, them disappearing for all this time."

"Well, it wouldn't hurt to notify Rob."

Karen picked up the phone and dialed.

By eight o'clock they still weren't back. Rob put a call out on the police radio band, assuring Abby and Karen it was just routine.

"Everyone round here listens in. Maybe someone saw the kids," he told them.

Abby sank down onto Karen's couch and wrung her hands. "I don't see how they could get lost around here," she said to no one in particular. "I mean, there's a vantage point of town from every hill. How could they get lost?"

The front door banged open just then and they all started. "I heard on the radio at the Mother Lode," said Ty, out of breath, striding over to Abby. "Any word yet?"

She saw him exchange a grim glance with Rob Loring over her head, but he smiled encouragingly at her.

"We haven't a clue," she said, feeling, suddenly, like crying. Why did Ty always have to be there when she needed someone? Why *this* man?

John took the first call about the kids over the radio in his Blazer. He came rushing back into the house. "Miz Thompson down at the depot saw the kids, all right, but that was around four, she thinks."

"The train depot?" asked Ty.

"Yeah, up near Bob Womack's cabin. She said she noticed them because they had the burro along, walking behind them like a puppy dog."

Suddenly Abby drew in a breath of panic. "The mine shafts! It's full of old exposed mine shafts up there! Why would those stupid kids go near that area!"

"Now, calm down, there, Abby," said Ty, sinking down onto the couch next to her. "I'm sure they just hiked along the railroad tracks and probably went too far."

"Let's get the lanterns out," said Karen, and Rob nodded.

By nine it was quite dark out, as the summer evenings were growing shorter. Rob and Karen had taken off on foot along with several volunteers and headed southeast from the train depot. Abby and Ty, who had hooked to his belt a portable two-way radio, had started out along the tracks heading southwest. There was no road so they were all on foot, although a few of the townspeople had shown up at the depot in their four-wheel-drive vehicles and were going to check the many dirt roads that crisscrossed the hillsides.

"I'm scared," said Abby as she walked alongside Ty past Bob Womack's cabin.

"And you're freezing," he said gently, stopping for a moment while he handed her the lantern and took off his leather jacket. "Here, put this on."

"But *you'll* freeze, then."

"No, I won't. Come on, I'm used to Colorado nights. Come on." He helped Abby into the jacket, and she felt the strength and the assurance of his hands as they closed momentarily over her shoulders.

"And don't be afraid," he said, taking the lantern out of her hands and giving her a big, comforting smile. "There're plenty of old mines around these parts, but the kids know better than to monkey around in them."

"Kids," said Abby, looking up into his eyes, "may know what's right and what's wrong, but they don't always use their common sense."

They stayed near the tracks, assuming that if the three children had come this way they would have stayed on them also. Of course, it was all guesswork, but there was no other way to proceed. Full night fell over the wide expanse of valley and the lights of Cripple Creek could be seen below, more distant now. Overhead, a brilliant canopy of stars and a half-moon lit the way. There were little animal sounds all around them, coming from the undergrowth alongside the railroad tracks, and somewhere in the shadowed night a coyote howled lingeringly.

"Oh, God, Ty," Abby said, stumbling over the tracks, her heart torn with worry. "We'll never find them! Oh, God . . ."

He put down the lantern and took her by the arms, holding her tightly. "Don't even think that, Abigail McAlister. Not for even a minute. We *will* find them. Have you got that?" His voice was purposefully stern and deep, commanding yet sympathetic.

Abby took a breath and tried to calm herself. He was right. Panicking would get them nowhere. "I know we'll find them," she said quietly. "I know we will." Ty dropped his hold on her arms and put his hand on the back of her head, hesitantly and cautiously, pressing her forehead against his chest for a moment. Abby felt a surge of hope. She didn't have to go it alone, not tonight. Ty was there in the darkness with her. If only he could always be there, and not just in the moments of crisis. If only there was no Kevin Wayne and no ugly past between them.

Rob's call came over the handset at 9:50. "Seen anything?" The sheriff's voice crackled.

Ty took the radio off his belt and pressed the call button. "Nothing. We're just below the Holy Ghost mine. Where're you?"

"Below the Molly Kathleen now. We're going to circle back soon."

Ty pressed the button again. "We're going ahead. Keep in touch."

"Roger."

"We'll never find them," whispered Abby. "And it's so cold out . . ."

"Sh. We *will* find them. And it's not even below fifty degrees. We're lucky it's summer. Come on. We're bound to locate them soon. And look," said Ty, carefully turning her around toward the direction of town. "See the lanterns and car lights on the hillsides? Those folks are all searching, Abby. We'll find them."

It *was* reassuring to see the bobbing lights in the distance, to know that half the town had turned out to search for the children. They were a good lot, and in spite of Abby's frantic worry, she could not fail to appreciate the concern of the people.

"Come on. Let's keep going. Maybe they're around this next bend."

Bend after bend passed, but there was still no sign of them. And Abby knew she was running out of steam; she'd worked long and hard that day already and now this, combined with the surges of adrenaline coursing through her body, was draining her dry. Yet she knew she'd keep on going, and going, for days if necessary, to find her boys. *God, let them be safe, please!*

Ten-thirty came and fled. Abby's feet ached and her head pounded and her heart felt like lead in her chest from the unending fear. *Where were the kids?* "Someone should have found them by now, Ty," she said, sinking down onto the tracks and putting her face in her hands. "I'm sorry," she began as she wept, "but I'm so damn worried. . . ."

He came to rest on his haunches beside her, a reassuring presence in the silvery half glow of the moon. "It's okay, Abby. Cry. It'll do you good."

"Oh, damn," she managed, letting the tears of exhaustion and strain finally come freely, "oh, damn it all!" Then suddenly she looked directly into Ty's shadowed gaze. "If I'd been a better mother," she said, sobbing, "if I'd been home where I belonged . . ."

"Bull," he said softly. "Those kids have the best mom in the world. You're strong and you're tough and you get things done. You're a mom *and* dad to them."

"Big deal." She wept unashamedly. "But where was I when they took off walking!"

It must have been a minute later that Abby felt Ty's hand tighten on her shoulder. "Quiet," he said. "Be still, Abby."

Her head jerked up.

"Hear it?"

"What?" she whispered, hope springing into her heart.

"That. That scraping sound."

"An animal?"

"No. Sh, listen." A few seconds later, he whispered, "Below us."

Abby heard it, too, a kind of scraping, like something rubbing on wood. It could have been a night creature, of course, but Ty obviously didn't seem to think so.

"Here," he said, coming to his feet in one fluid motion, "hold the lantern while I go on down the hillside."

"I'm coming, too!" cried Abby. "Don't leave me!"

"Okay, okay. But be real careful. This rock is loose as all get out. Hang onto my arm. There, okay."

Earth slid out from under their boots as Abby held onto Ty's shirtsleeve and followed him down the gravelly railroad grade and across a pile of rock that sloped steadily down into a gully. Then suddenly Ty stopped and Abby came up short against his back. "What?" she asked fiercely. "What is it?"

"See that over there?" He pointed toward a deeply shadowed spot in between two boulders. Something was standing in there—a deer? Abby's hand clutched Ty's arm. "Come on," he said. "I think that's Barney."

"Oh, God," breathed Abby, "oh, God."

It was Barney, all right, and when he saw the two figures hurrying toward him he let out a long whinny and honked, pawing at the old timber pile he stood on—that was the sound they'd heard, Barney's pawing. What if they hadn't stopped on the tracks up there?

"It's a shaft, I think," said Ty as he approached Barney carefully, his hand out in friendship.

"Ty, you don't think the kids are . . ." began Abby, but the lump in her throat stopped her from finishing.

"I don't know. Barney could've wandered off."

It was a dangerous spot, no two ways about it. The lip of the abandoned mine shaft fell steadily away into a black abyss. "Sean? Ben?" cried Abby with a catch in her voice. "Kids?"

"Careful." Ty gently pushed her away from the gaping hole, and then fell to his knees, cupping his hands and calling, "Kids, can you hear me? It's Ty and Abby. Kids?"

A small whimpering sound—afraid and alone—came from beneath them. Abby let out a strangled cry and lurched forward again, only to be stopped by Ty's firm hand. "For Pete's sake, Abby, that's all we need, you fallin' in there, too!" She backed off reluctantly. "I'm going down," said Ty. "Here, take the radio. Tell Rob we're just below the trestle bridge. He can get to it from the highway. Tell him to look for the lantern."

"But *you'll* need it, Ty."

He pulled a flashlight from his back pocket and smiled at her. "Don't worry. The kids are probably only dazed. They'll be okay." But all Abby could think was the worst. While Ty lowered himself, hanging onto loose rock, losing his footing, slipping and catching himself, then sliding again, Abby used the radio.

"We'll be there in ten minutes," said Rob. "I'll bring along the rope. Wait... Karen wants to know if they're okay."

Abby pressed the button. "I don't know. We heard a crying sound, though. Oh, Rob, please hurry!"

"Roger." And he was off the air.

She could only hear Ty now, making his way down the steeply sloping hole. It was like descending into hell, Abby thought involuntarily. And her boys were in that hell! "Ty," she called, crouching next to the lip of the mine, "Ty!"

"I'm all right." His voice echoed back from the darkness. "I've got Janet here...can you hear me? Abby?"

"Yes! I can hear you! Janet...but where're the boys! Ty!"

"Here too... I think they're okay."

He thinks, her mind screamed. *He thinks they're okay!*

"Abby," came Ty's voice, "did you reach Rob?"

"He's on his way. With a rope," she called shakily. "Ty, the kids. Are the kids talking?"

"A little. All three are real scared. I think Janet's ankle might be broken. The boys are cold and dazed."

They're alive! They're going to make it! Abby's heart sang a tune of relief as she sat above waiting, desperate to hold the boys in her arms, joyously, anxiously, scanning the darkness for Rob and Karen as she held the lantern aloft to guide them.

A rope, the light from two extra lanterns and two strong men to help, and Abby soon had both her boys safely in her arms. They were shaken and terrified, probably suffering from exposure, Rob suggested. "We better get these three on down to Doc's pronto." The boys were carried by Karen and Abby. The men took Janet, as her ankle was painfully swollen and the path to where the sheriff's Blazer was parked below was narrow and rocky. Barney tagged along behind and Rob was thoughtful enough to radio for a pickup truck to haul the hungry hero of the hour back to Abby's yard.

"I'm personally buying that burro a Milky Way," said Karen, laughing and crying at the same time.

The story came out once they were all piled in the Blazer. Janet was groggy but coherent, the nasty bump on her head evidently not too serious. "We were walking, Mom," she said, her head resting on Karen's sturdy shoulder. "Then Ben got curious about the shaft and he got too close and the next thing I knew—oh, Mom!" she broke off, sobbing. "We called out for help forever! No one came. No one!"

"What I'd like to know," said Ty in an easy, relieved voice, "is how, if Ben was the one who fell in, you all got down there. Havin' a party or something?"

Janet tried a laugh, but it came out as a wail. "I don't know. First I tried to get him. Then I slipped and Sean came falling in, too."

"Mommy," said Sean, his face buried in Abby's lap, "I was just looking in . . . honest. Oh, Mommy . . ."

"It's okay, honey, I promise."

"Well, there's a lesson here, guys," said Ty. "Anybody know what it is?"

"We shouldn't have gone walking so far," said Ben in a muffled tone.

"We should have told someone where we went," put in Janet.

"Right on both counts. But the main thing," added Ty, "and I think Rob'll agree with me here, is that when one fell in the hole you should have gotten help instead of trying to save him yourself. Know what I mean, guys?"

There was silence and then, "Uh-huh," from all of them.

Ty was let off to pick up his Jeep where he'd left it at the depot and Abby rode up to Doc's in the Blazer. She wanted desperately to thank Ty, to tell him all those things she should have before. Would he follow them to Doc Clements'?

Janet had a badly sprained ankle, a knot on her head and various bruises and scrapes. The boys were suffering from mild exposure, a few not too serious bumps, and exhaustion. Over and over Janet kept saying, "I'm so sorry, Mrs. McAlister. I'm so sorry."

And then Abby felt him there, standing behind her in the room, his comforting presence filling the close space. And she felt, too, his hand come to rest on the small of her back, warm and gentle, moving ever so slightly against her shirt beneath the leather jacket she still wore.

"I wanna go home," complained Benny, yawning after Doc had poked and prodded him everywhere. "Where's Barney?"

"I'll drive you home," said Ty quietly at her ear. "Okay?"

She merely nodded, too tired suddenly to think.

"Say there—" Doc squinted his eyes at Ty and scrutinized him "—you got a few scratches there yourself, young man. You should get those cleaned up."

"I'm fine," Ty assured the doctor but Abby turned to study him in the light. He *was* cut up; his forearms and one cheek were badly scratched from his descent into the mine shaft. She wanted to reach out and touch his face, to soothe him as she would the boys. But that would never do. Ty was a grown man—and not even *her* man, at that.

"Just watch for infection, then," said Doc and turned away, shrugging.

It struck Abby, as they were all nestled together in Ty's Jeep for the three-block ride, that she was sick and tired of battling her emotions, tired of denying her desire for Ty Hollinger.

So what if he was on the other side of the fence? It hadn't yet, not for a moment, changed the fact that she wanted him so terribly. There it was, wrenched from her finally, the naked truth. Not nice or pretty, but honest. She hugged the kids to her breast and glanced over at him through the cool darkness. His hair was mussed, blowing slightly, and his shadowed profile looked strong and handsome. As he steered, she saw his hands and goose bumps rose on her flesh, remembering those big, roughened hands that had held her to him. She'd give anything to have those hands on her flesh right then. She needed Ty, she needed the comfort he could give.

Abby tore her eyes away and sighed. She was dreaming. She'd alienated him completely. Ty couldn't possibly be interested in her that way anymore, not after all the accusations she'd thrown in his face. He couldn't possibly want her now. Or could he?

CHAPTER FOURTEEN

"THANK GOD THEY'RE ALL RIGHT," said Abby as she stood next to the bunk beds and watched the twins sleeping. "I don't know what I would have done if..."

"Sh." Ty put a protective arm around Abby's shoulder and she could feel the warmth of his body seeping into her. "Come on," he whispered. "I could use a drink. How 'bout you?"

She nodded, obediently following Ty into the kitchen with his arm still around her shoulders. "I haven't got anything much to drink," she admitted. "Entertaining hasn't exactly been a top priority since I moved here."

"Beer?"

She shook her head. "Maybe some cooking sherry I packed and brought along. Check under the sink."

"Logical spot." He pressed Abby down onto a kitchen chair while he crouched over and searched through the clutter beneath her sink. She watched him distractedly, feeling as if her brain and body had become detached somehow. Weariness from the aftermath of the search settled into her limbs. There was another time Ty had rummaged around under there—a time when they'd just met each other. Now Abby felt as if she'd known him forever, and at the same time she barely knew him at all.

She glanced idly at the back of his shirt, which was stretched across his shoulders tautly as he stooped and searched for the sherry. "You sure it's under here?" came his muffled voice.

"I thought it was."

"Um..."

She'd studied his back and his neck and his forearms dozens of times and never once really touched him.

Abby's hands clenched in her lap as her thoughts continued involuntarily. And he had lovely long legs, well-shaped and muscular. She could almost feel them up against hers—almost.

"Aha!" he called. "Got it." He pulled himself out from under the sink and stood, his tall form seeming to fill Abby's kitchen all of a sudden. "Glasses?"

"Oh... up in that cupboard. Over there. No, on the left." As he reached up, the lean line of his stomach under the shirt was displayed. She clenched her fists a little harder.

"Sherry it is," said Ty, striding over to the table with bottle and glasses clinking negligently. Then he turned his chair around backward, plunked himself down with his knees spread and opened the bottle. He put it to his nose. "Holy cow! *This* is booze?"

"Cooking booze. I admit it's kind of awful stuff to drink."

"Yeah, well, beggars can't be choosers." He smiled at her charmingly and poured, handing Abby a glass and clinking his to hers. "Cheers."

"Cheers." She took a swallow, sputtered, then took another. "It's awful."

"It's like drinking honey or something."

"But with a kick." She managed a tentative smile. "You know, we ought to clean out those scratches on your face, Ty."

"I'm fine."

"But Doc said..."

"Ah...come on, Abby, forget it." And she could have sworn he blushed.

Cleaning out Ty's scrapes with cotton and peroxide was almost as bad as tending to the boys' abrasions. He wiggled and squirmed and yelled ouch a few times as Abby dabbed away, paying absolutely no attention whatsoever to his objections. Anyway, it was pleasant doing something for him for a change. She took her time, holding his head still and then tilting it to one side and the other, studying the long straight line of his shapely nose and the deep grooves along the sides of his mouth. His chin was firm and square. She could see where he'd shaved that morning: that nick on his neck, the whiskers growing in above his upper lip and on his cheeks. The cotton was sticking to the whiskers and Abby plucked it away carefully.

"Enjoying yourself?" asked Ty sarcastically, embarrassed still.

"As a matter of fact," she began, "it's about time *I* did something for *you*."

He was silent for a breath of time, his dark eyes looking up into her golden ones, imprisoning them. She began to feel a slow pounding of her blood and was filled with a strange excitement. "It's time we talked," said Ty in almost a whisper. "Can we do that, Abby?"

She nodded, putting the cap back on the peroxide and hiding her expression from him. He handed her the sherry then, and she sat back down facing him, putting a little distance between them, her senses abruptly keen. "So?" she said to break the brittle silence. "What are we going to talk about, Ty?" She tried to laugh but nothing came.

"We're going to discuss us. It's time, Abigail McAlister, that we have a few things out and clear the air."

"Okay." She began to swirl the sherry around in the glass, her gaze transfixed by the amber liquid that clung to the sides and made long streaks back into the bowl.

"I like you," he began, "a lot. And I think maybe you like me, too. Boy," he breathed, "this ain't easy." But he continued, "The point is, Abby, I'd like to know if I'm wastin' my time with you. This obsession you've got with the Nola Jane and my workin' for Kevin Wayne... well, as far as I'm concerned, my job's got nothing to do with *us*." He reached over and took her chin in his hand, carefully tipping her face up to meet his. "You listenin' or playing with your drink?"

"I'm listening, Ty, really I am. I just don't know what to say."

"That's okay. Just let me get this stuff off my chest, as long as I'm on a roll here. I guess I realized how much I felt for you the other day when Sheila called. I mean, I felt nothing for her. It was amazing. I wasn't hurt anymore or angry or even attracted. I was married to her for four years and she's a complete stranger to me."

"Oh, Ty," began Abby, sighing.

"Well, what about Steve, what about *your* ex-husband?"

"What about him?"

Abby felt as if the kitchen wall were closing in on her, and there was suddenly a catch in her throat. She couldn't breathe.

"I shouldn't have asked," said Ty quickly, reaching over to clutch her hand in his. "That was a stupid question. None of my damn business..."

"But it's an honest question," replied Abby, clearing her throat, fighting for control. "It's just that I haven't really thought of Steve in terms of... love. I mean, he's the father of my children...."

"Who hasn't seen them in months," put in Ty cautiously, "or sent you a lousy cent to help support them."

"I... did love Steve," said Abby slowly.

"But do you now?"

Time hung suspended between them like a drop of water ready to fall. She started to say something but hesitated, uncertain, her heart contracting with anxiety.

"No," Abby finally got out, seeing Ty's body sag with relief.

"So, that's taken care of," he said, resting his chin on his hands in satisfaction.

"But Ty," Abby said, "it doesn't make any difference."

"What are you talking about? Don't we really like each other... more than like? And now there's nothing stoppin' us from gettin' to know each other better, is there?"

She looked away. "It's not so easy, Ty. I can't just let myself go like that. I have two boys to raise and I don't spend enough time with them as it is and I have the mine to worry about. And the future. Who knows what will happen?" She stared at him, begging understanding, feeling sad and confused. "Frankly, I don't think I can handle another relationship. I don't have the time or the energy or... or anything."

"That's a real cop-out, if I ever heard one. Listen, Abby, I *love* you and no way am I lettin' you slide away from me like that!"

"Oh, Ty," she said again, sorrowfully, realizing he'd just said he loved her.

"Now, you just pay attention. If you're still worried about your damn mine, I'll tell you this. I warned Wayne about getting too close to your boundary a month ago. In the morning I'll confront him about it again. It's against the law and I'll back you up a hundred percent. Okay?"

"You will?"

"Yep. It'll probably mean my job, Abby, but I'll do that for you, I swear, if it makes you believe I'm on your side. No job means that much to me."

"You'd really do that, Ty?"

He nodded emphatically. "You bet your bottom dollar."

"But if he fired you, what would you do?" He'd said he loved her!

"Oh, I can manage for a time. I could help you out."

"I can't ask you . . . I can't afford to pay you . . ."

"I think, Abby, that you're too all-fired hung up on the almighty dollar and I wish it wouldn't enter into your calculations anymore. At least, not concernin' us," he added firmly.

"But I have to, Ty. My kids. What about their future?" she asked, her emotions in a turmoil. He was going to quit his job over her; he loved her! Her thoughts whirled, unsettled, finding no safe haven.

Ty rose and pulled her up from the chair and held her hands. "I'll take care of you and your kids if you want me to, Abby. I'd consider it a great pleasure." Then he added, "And an honor."

Dazed, her eyes searched his face. "Are you asking me to . . . ?"

"Sure am." He smiled, a lazy curve to his mouth. "What do you say?"

"Oh, God," she whispered. "I don't know. It's too soon. I need to think."

"We got time, Abby," he said gently, pulling her close, so close that his lips rested on her forehead like the touch of a feather.

Abby's arms went around his back, slowly and tentatively, and her head came to rest on his chest. She could hear the heavy rhythm of his heart where it beat beneath her ear and goose bumps raised on her flesh.

He felt so good to her, so right, as if she'd always belonged in the protection of his arms. Her blood was coursing through her veins, quickening, and there was an unaccountable ringing in her ears while she caught her breath.

This is it, Abby knew. *Either he leaves right this instant or he stays the night.*

Who was going to make the first move?

Neither Abby nor Ty did move, however, for a very long time. She simply stayed in his arms, undecided, realizing that her desire to know Ty fully would soon be out of control. He stroked her back gently, his fingers moving up and down, down across her bra strap beneath the thin fabric of her shirt, and up once more. His scent was tantalizing, Abby realized, like sage, sweet and natural and clean. He smelled so good to her, so beautiful, and she felt tears press behind her eyelids, tears of wonder and joy.

It was finally Ty who moved back a step and caught her gaze. "I'm not made of iron," he whispered, his eyes moving over her ardently, like a hot wind, fanning her with its intensity. "Do you want me to go, Abby?"

Her mouth formed the word no, but not a sound came from her constricted throat.

"And do you trust me? Do you know that I'd never hurt you?"

"I know that now... I'm so sorry for all the things I said and..."

"Sh." He put his finger on her lips and smiled, and her heart gave a great leap, like a bird set free. Then his mouth replaced his finger, gliding across her lips, silky and hot, lovely, so lovely that she gasped gently and sagged against him, needing more, much more.

Ty led the way into her bedroom, holding her hand tightly in his, snapping off lights as they went. Abby followed him, willing and certain of what she wanted.

With only the light from the bathroom spilling in to illuminate them, Ty unfastened the buttons on his shirt. Then slowly, with a gentle touch, he undid hers and slipped it off her shoulders, dropping it heedlessly to the floor. His warm, callused hands moved over her shoulders and his lips followed, kissing and nibbling, igniting a fire deep in her belly, until she moaned and pressed herself against him, dragging his shirt off until it, too, joined the mounting heap of clothing on the floor. Naked, finally, they collapsed on the bed together as one entity, kissing and touching, almost lazily, as if they had the freedom of time on their side at last.

Ty, she was learning, was a practiced lover, a considerate lover. Like everything else he did, he caressed her slowly and easily; there was no rush, no frantic clasping of body to body, no hurried, painful entry. No man had ever touched Abby so thoughtfully, so skillfully. But then she'd sensed this side of Ty, she'd considered it and imagined it and ached for it. And still, at moments, as his hands trailed burning paths on her flesh, she believed she was only dreaming.

When his mouth wasn't exploring her neck or the swell of a breast, he'd kiss her softly, tracing the smooth warmth of her cheek across her lips to the other cheek, his tongue light on her skin, sending rippling shivers fluttering down her side to her hip until Abby squirmed against him and laughed gently and pleasurably.

She watched him in the semi-darkness through heavy-lidded eyes and then, with a slim finger, touched the long corded muscles in his neck and caressed his ear-lobe. There was time, so much time, finally, for them to savor each other, and Abby was taking as much as she pleased, feasting on the moments, reveling in them.

The heat in her body built, his warmth surrounding her like a potent, mellowing drug, and she became acutely aware of each nuance of touch and of the steadily growing beat of their hearts. Reality receded. There were only his thighs and hers, molding together as he finally penetrated her. And then they were stomach to stomach, chest to chest, her body delighting in his masculine form, his muscle and bone and uncompromising strength. She arched up to meet him, her movements rhythmic and unhurried, and then she subsided, only to press upward again, and again, as pure instinct joined an equally primitive physical need.

Sweat-slicked and gasping, Abby reached a climax and held onto Ty's shoulders as arrow after arrow of sensation passed through her. And then she felt him quake above her and he, too, was clinging, grasping, breathing out his fulfillment into her ear until they both lay together silently, replete.

Abby must have dozed because the next thing she knew she was half awake, staring up into his eyes.

"What're you doing?" she whispered, aware that he was lying on his side, head propped on a hand, wide awake.

"I'm looking at you, ma'am," he replied softly, a corner of his mouth lifting playfully.

"Aren't you sleepy?"

"Nope." He looked so adorable to her suddenly, lazily propped up, his hair all tousled, his eyes dark and warm, soft, like the rich luxury of sable fur.

"Well, then," said Abby, reaching up to trace his lip with a finger, "you must be tired, at least."

"A little. But nice tired."

"Um," said Abby, "me, too. The difference is, I have to get up and go to work. Early."

"You can sleep in. You're allowed. Especially after the ordeal you went through."

"Maybe." She could catch an extra hour. The crew would understand, wouldn't they? And the twins sure could use the rest . . .

"And if we did sleep in," said Ty, a rakish tilt to his mouth, "we'd have time to . . . you know."

"What?" As if she didn't know.

"This." His head came down and his mouth covered hers in a kiss filled with need and male power, and a sudden explosion of fire shot through her body.

Later she fell asleep in the crook of his arm, a smile still on her lips. Her bedroom, which had previously seemed lonely and strange at times, was for once the most welcome, secure place in the world.

It was dawn when Abby stirred, realizing that the other side of the bed was empty. She half opened her eyes and saw Ty dressing in the mother-of-pearl luminescence, his tall, lanky form bent over, glimmering palely, as he found his pants on the floor. Already she missed him, his warmth and strength, his deliberately soft touch. And yet she didn't speak, reluctant to break the fragile, secret moments that she could steal watching him, knowing that he was unaware of the innocent encroachment. He buttoned his fly and then glanced over to see if he'd disturbed her. She closed her eyes. Then he pulled on his shirt and fastened it, tucking it in, but leaving the tail flapping carelessly out in the back. He picked up his boots and tiptoed to the door, giving Abby one last, long look before disappearing.

She followed him in her thoughts. He was crossing the living room, pulling on his socks and boots. Then she heard the front door snick open and shut and the sound of his walking through the grass. The gate opening and closing. Oh, yes, and Ty's Jeep—it was still parked out front. Amazingly Abby heard its tires rolling soundlessly on the gravel road and she smiled, knowing that he hadn't wanted to awaken the whole neighborhood.

As quiet as a mouse, she thought, moments before she heard his whistling as it split the silent dawn.

CHAPTER FIFTEEN

"HE ACTUALLY *FIRED* YOU!" gasped Abby, spinning around where she stood at her kitchen sink.

"What'd you expect Wayne would do when I laid it on the line? Give me a raise?"

"But Ty..." She wiped her hands on a towel and crossed the room to him.

"I warned you he would. Did you think I was kiddin'?"

"No, but you didn't have to go at it so deliberately, Ty. I mean... I told you I trusted you. Oh, your job..." A wave of guilt swept Abby. If she'd believed in Ty, if she'd trusted him in the first place and kept her nose out of his business, none of this would have happened.

"Hey," said Ty, brushing her bangs aside with a gentle finger, "don't look so down. It's no big deal. There're other jobs around, lady. Wayne's not the only trout in the stream."

"You mean fish in the sea," she said distractedly.

"If I was from New Jersey maybe I'd mean that."

Abby sighed and looked up into his dark, dancing eyes. "Nothing bothers you, does it?"

"Not much. *You* bother me, though, Abigail McAlister. A whole lot." He put his hands at the sides of her head, and he bent to kiss her, sending her feelings of guilt flying, replacing them with tiny little stabs of pleasure in her stomach.

For a long time they stood in the middle of the room while water boiled over onto the stove, tasting each other's lips, mouth moving against mouth, lingeringly. She could feel his hands trailing a delicious path up her back beneath her cotton shirt, his fingers kneading her shoulders, the back of her neck. He felt so good....

"Mommy!" came a small voice from the yard. "When's dinner going to be ready? I'm hungry!"

Reluctantly, Ty stepped aside and took her hands in his and laughed abruptly, his head tipping back until all Abby could see was his Adam's apple and the long cords of muscle stretched taut. "What's so funny?" she asked, perplexed.

"I thought these interruptions only happened in the movies, ma'am," he said, his lazy Western drawl accentuated.

"Oh, they're real," explained Abby, "too real."

And then, as Ty was pulling her up against him playfully, and Abby was ducking her head and laughing, the phone rang.

Abby picked up the receiver irritably. "Yes? This is Abby."

"Kevin Wayne here." Abby felt as if he'd struck her with an automobile. "I think," he said crisply, "it's time you sat down with your pencil and paper and did some figuring, Mrs. McAlister. I'll give you twenty-five thousand for the Nola Jane. That's my top offer and—" he paused for effect "—my last offer."

"Hold on a minute," said Abby, cupping her hand over the receiver and motioning to Ty. "It's Wayne," she whispered, seeing the frown glide across Ty's features. "He's making me another offer. Twenty-five thousand! It's a lot, Ty."

Ty's answer was angry and instantaneous. "Tell him to go to the devil."

Abby stood there for a long moment, her gaze locked with Ty's. Then she removed her hand and brought the phone back to her ear. "Thank you very much, Mr. Wayne, but I'm not interested. Goodbye." She hung up and let out a long breath. Then she giggled. "I don't believe I just did that! I can't believe I just said that and hung up on him!"

"Well, I don't think it's funny. I think the man has a hell of a nerve calling you like that after the stuff he's been pulling."

"Oh, he has nerve all right. He tunneled into my mine and told me to go ahead and file suit. Now that's nerve."

"I'm beginning to think he's dumb."

"I'm beginning to think he's desperate," said Abby pensively, her laughter gone.

THE SUMMER BEGAN to slip away, the mid-August nights growing shorter and cooler. The Nola Jane mine was just holding its own, and Abby's personal bills were stacking up. She wrote herself a check for eight hundred dollars and stuck it in the bank, wondering if the next check from El Paso would cover her. If not, what was she going to do? And then there was Ty—and his still being out of work.

She began the familiar conversation over dinner at her house one night. "Any luck today?" she asked casually.

"I always feel lucky," said Ty, grinning at her between forkfuls of spaghetti.

"You know what I mean. Are there any leads on a job?"

He shook his head. "Something'll turn up. Always does. And in the meanwhile, I could be helping you out at the Nola Jane."

"You know I can't pay you and I worry that you're running low on money. I mean, what're you living on, Ty? I know I shouldn't ask, but..."

"Oh, I always have a little tucked away for a rainy day. I'm doin' just fine."

"Still..."

"Quit worrying, Abby. If I'm not bothered, why should you be? Afraid of getting too involved with a loafer?"

"You're not a loafer, Ty."

"But you *are* scared of getting involved, you may as well admit it. Seems like I've been hinting around, trying to make an honest woman out of you for weeks, and you do a pretty good job of avoidin' the subject."

"I'm not avoiding anything, Ty," said Abby firmly, knowing, nevertheless, that he'd hit the nail on the head.

"Then let's make some plans." He rolled his coffee mug between his hands and studied her face quietly.

"We will," said Abby, "but later. As soon as I'm really on my feet."

"What you mean is," replied Ty slowly and deliberately, "as soon as you're rich. Which'll be never. This isn't 1895, Abby."

"Let's not talk about money. We always argue." But it didn't work, and they did quarrel, and Abby went to bed that night alone and wretched.

If only she had a job for Ty. A paying job, that was. She could always give in and let him help out, but she couldn't possibly stretch her payroll any thinner. And besides, if Ty were helping her, he couldn't be out job hunting. What, she wondered for the hundredth time, was going to happen when Ty's nest egg ran out and he had to leave Cripple Creek? An educated mining engineer couldn't just afford to sit around forever. And there were jobs elsewhere. She'd read in the *Denver Post* the other day that the Amax mine up in Leadville was hiring. Oh, God, what if Ty *did* have to leave? What had Nola Jane done in this situation? How had she handled the problem of Randy's employment?

Think positively, Abby told herself. She could always strike it rich at the Nola Jane. And then Ty could have any job he wanted. Why, he and John could even run the mine for her while Abby spent more time with Sean and Ben. Wouldn't that be perfect?

ABBY SIGHED AND PUSHED HERSELF UP in bed. She took up Nola Jane's diary, trying to get Ty and all of her problems out of her head. *Let's see,* Abby thought, *I left off where Nola and Randy had just had a terrible fight.*

Dear Diary,

Everything will be all right now. Randy has agreed, with reservations, to work for me instead of George Rausch. Thank heavens I can afford to pay him as much as Rausch did. I must keep my head cool. I must be a hard-hearted businesswoman where he is concerned. Randy could not bear any favoritism.

Does he see through my ploy? Do I dare tell myself that Randy looks at me sometimes with a certain affection?

He is with me every day now and, if he is not, I find an excuse to call on him at the mine or leave a message for him to see me. I am insatiable. I cannot think properly when he is near me. I am falling in love. I never felt this way about Mike. I didn't realize the strength and depth of feelings buried within me. But I know now. Dear Diary, I am aching with my need to know Randy completely. Am I a wanton woman? It was different with Mike. I never knew...

If only, mused Abby, she could be as certain of her own happy ending as she was of her great-grandmother's. Then, maybe, she could give herself to Ty unreservedly. She turned a page in the diary, carefully, the faded old paper feeling as if it might crumble in her hand. The next entry was dated February 5, 1895.

I have managed to buy back the forty-nine percent of the Nola Jane that Lil owned. It stretched my resources badly, but I felt the need. I thanked Lil, shook her hand proudly and left the Bon Ton a better woman for having known Lily Francis.

I am, however, having a difficult time keeping my feelings from my beloved Randy. He must know how I feel. Yet he is a gentleman, always, and never presumes any familiarity.

Other matters. Randy reports a promising vein. I could use a touch of luck, as I can barely afford to pay the men this month, after having regained my shares from Lil. Mama says she told me so, that no woman can run a gold mine. Oh, God, she must be wrong, or nothing makes any sense.

Abby smiled at Nola's fervor to have everything make

sense. She turned a page and found an entry dated March 2, 1895.

> We have struck it rich! The mother lode! I have never seen anything more lovely than that dark vein! Randy and I are going out on the town in celebration. My heart is beating so rapidly I feel it may burst. I am not going to wear black! A year is gone by and that part of my life is over. I shall wear my dark red taffeta with the ruching on the bodice and the lace at the neckline. It is a decorous dress, fitting the occasion. And it flatters my dark hair and eyes. Randy laughed and told me to wear the black cloak he first met me in. I shall never live down that episode. I suppose he'll tell it to our grandchildren!

The next entry was dated mid-March.

> Hello again, Diary. I am remiss in not keeping my journal but so much has happened in the past two weeks. Randy and I are in love with each other! I, Nola Jane Mann, widow, have the most gentle and dear lover in the whole world. I feel that all my senses have been awakened at last. The flowers smell sweeter, the rain more fresh. I am so in love, Diary.

Abby turned the diary over onto her stomach and smiled. So that was how Nola Jane had made it in Cripple Creek. But was Abby fashioned of the same stern stuff as her great-grandmother? Was hard work enough, or would she need a big dose of luck, as well? And then, of course, there was Ty. Just how much did

Abby love him? Enough to overcome her reluctance and fear of involvement? Could she risk her future and that of her sons as well?

Abby slept alone that night, and the following one, as well. Ty did stop by to take the boys off Janet's hands and drive them up to his old fishing spot on the third day after their quarrel. Abby got home from the mine and found his note: "Hope you don't mind but I thought the kids could use an outing. We've gone fishing up the Teller 1 road. Be back around six. How about a pizza with the boys at the café? Love, Ty."

Love, Ty. Her heart sang. She looked at the wall clock. Five forty-five. No time to bathe, but she could manage to scrub her face and hands and do something with a washcloth. *Love, Ty.* Well, then he wasn't *that* mad at her. The past three days had been awful, as she went around wondering, fearing that it was all over between them. Relief streamed through her as she cleaned up and changed into a light green summer sweater and a khaki skirt.

And I don't even have to cook dinner.

Sean burned the roof of his mouth on his first bit of pizza and cried. Benny laughed at him. Ty frowned and said, "If you guys can't behave in public then you'll stay home next time."

But that led to an outburst from Sean. "I don't want to stay home when Janet's boyfriend is there. I don't like him."

Abby reflected for a moment. "Does Janet ignore you when he's there?" she asked carefully.

"She kisses him," put in Ben, making a scornful face, and Ty rolled his eyes heavenward.

"I'll speak to her," said Abby, wondering if that was *all* Janet and her friend were doing in the house.

The boys went to bed at eight-thirty, their tummies swollen with pizza and ice-cream sundaes. And then Abby confessed her need to take a real bath. "Do you mind? I'm pretty beat tonight. I'd like to relax."

Ty shook his head and strode to the door. "I'm going to change the oil filter on the Jeep anyway. Maybe I'll come back later, if that's okay?" His voice was hesitant; he obviously wasn't sure if they had truly made up.

"Do come back," said Abby, smiling.

"See you later, then." He winked at her endearingly and was gone.

The bathroom was soon steamed up as the tub filled. Abby poured bath oil into the water and pulled off her clothes, padding naked into the bedroom to hang them up. She was closing the bathroom door, anticipating the relaxing warmth of the tub, when suddenly there was a hand behind her holding open the door. Abby gasped, but it was only Ty. Still, she wanted to reach for a towel; she was embarrassed and felt caught in the act. "What're you doing?" she asked breathlessly.

"I finished changing the oil," he said, his gaze never leaving hers. Somehow, as she stood rooted to the spot, watching his eyes darken to the color of coal, Abby felt weak and terribly uncertain. She and Steve never... "Come on," he said quietly, "climb into the tub. I'll wash your back."

"Ty...I think..." But her lips closed over her words and she couldn't think at all.

Acutely aware of Ty watching her step into the bath, Abby felt her skin flush all over, and was glad that the hot water would hide her turmoil from him. Standing there above her, Ty looked somehow taller and sturdier; his shoulders under his dark blue shirt seemed broader. He stooped, his eyes fixed on her, and picked up the bar of soap.

"Ty, don't you think..." began Abby once more, but he silenced her with a sun-browned finger to her lips before lightly tracing them, a fingernail lingering on a corner. He rolled up his sleeves, dipped his hands into the steamy water and made a lather with the soap. Abby was still sitting up, unsure, her heart beating madly against her ribs. He began at her shoulders and smoothed the soap down her back and beneath the water all the way to her buttocks. Then he moved up again, and relathered his hands.

"Feel good?"

"Um," sighed Abby, her eyes closing a little as a heat was borne in her veins, like the kindling of a fire. He soaped her neck, pressing her head forward gently, then proceeded along her collarbone and lower, to the swell of her breasts. *Oh, yes,* thought Abby, her nipples hardening to his caresses. There was a singing in her ears, a lazy ringing, like a string of bells, as his fingers closed over her breasts and moved down along the round swell of her stomach.

"Lie back," he said. "That's it." And Abby obeyed him, her eyes now fully closed, her lips parted as his hands moved leisurely over her body. Her thighs, her calves, even her feet tingled with the gift of his touch. "If there was room," whispered Ty, "I'd climb in there with you." Abby laughed lightly, imagining them together in the old narrow tub, splashing, trying to position their bodies to make love. "Out now," he said finally. "I can't take too much more of this." Neither could she.

While Abby stood in front of the mirror, Ty toweled her dry, slowly, patiently, whispering into her damp hair, sending waves of pleasure along her spine. He turned her so that her back rested against his chest and she could feel the heat of his desire from behind. In the partly steamed-up mirror, she discerned their reflections, her hair water-darkened and lying in strands on her neck and shoulders, the swell of her breasts, rising and falling unsteadily above the terry-cloth towel. And Ty, above her, all lean and hard and very male, his eyes passion dark, his lips parted slightly. The sight of them standing there so close in her bathroom, the memory of his soap-slick hands caressing her flesh, left her weak with need.

Clinging together, they made their way into the bedroom, which was shadowed in deep purple now in the last light of day. With anxious fingers, Abby undid the buttons of his shirt and then his belt. Shortly his clothes were lying scattered at their feet and he was easing her down onto the bed. Abby drew in a sharp breath as his lips closed over a nipple, and he drew the peak into his warm mouth. She was half on the bed and half off, Ty poised above her, positioning her to meet him. And then, with few preliminaries, he was moving down a little and his body pressed upward and he was inside her, deep within her, and she clung onto him, crying out softly into the night.

Abby slept soundly for several hours before she stirred, aware of their bodies still entwined, Ty's leg thrown over hers, his arm warm and tickly across her breasts. She stared up silently into the dark and held on to the moment, to the muscled feel of his body next to hers, to the rightness of their union. And then her lips curved up into an impish smile. Maybe she should awaken him....

It didn't take much nudging to rouse Ty. He moved and kissed her lips and then her temple. Slowly he pulled her to him, and for a time they lay tasting the night sweetness of their lips, languidly enjoying the sensations, purring together like contented felines. Abby could feel his arousal, however, and was struck by a fleeting moment of guilt; they both needed their sleep. But then he was propping himself up on his elbows and cupping her head with his hands and kissing away her objections. His body glided over hers, he held her hips with his hands, and she rose once again to meet his thrusts, until both lay trembling in the aftermath, the sheets kicked off, the cold morning air washing over their bodies, calming and soothing them.

"That was mean of me," whispered Abby.

"No, it wasn't." He laughed softly against her neck. "You can be mean to me that way any old time you want, ma'am. I'm game."

"But we can't do this every night."

"Oh? And why not? The kids are asleep... I'm always gone by dawn."

Abby sighed. "I was thinking about work. I'll be exhausted."

He propped himself up on an elbow and studied her through the darkness. "Sometimes a person needs to let go, Abby. It can't be all work and no play."

Abby's languid mood vanished. "We don't think very much alike, do we." It was not a question. Nevertheless, Abby tried to keep a slight edge of irritation out of her voice.

"I'll bet you're thinking about your bank account right now, aren't you?" He sounded as if he were teasing, but was he?

"I am not," protested Abby, pulling the sheet up.

"Are you telling me that you never think about money?"

"Why are you trying to start an argument, Ty?"

"I'm not. I'm only thinking about us."

"Well, I am, too. But our future together depends on a lot of things."

"Mainly money."

"What if it does?" chimed in Abby abruptly. "Money...or let's be fair, and call it security. Whatever, it means a great deal to me."

"No kidding." Now his voice was sarcastic and scratchy. *Oh, no,* thought Abby. *Here we go again.* "When I was a kid," said Ty, stirring around restlessly, "love was what mattered. My folks didn't have a cent to their names most of the time, but I'm a pretty happy man. And so are my sisters and their families."

"What about your divorce?" threw in Abby. "You can't tell me everything in your life has been sweetness and light."

"I made a mistake. I picked the wrong mate. But I wasn't...I'm not afraid to go at it again. I know what I'm looking for now. Do you?"

"To be honest, Ty, no, I don't." There. It was said. "I'm not sure I can risk so much again. If I had—" she paused "—if I had enough security, I wouldn't feel so afraid."

"That's a cop-out."

"It's the truth."

Ty swung his legs over the side of the bed and came to his feet. She could see him searching for his clothes in the shadows. Oh, she cried inwardly, why did it always have to end this way?

"You know," he said, pulling up his trousers with hurried, irate jerks, "all that glitters, Abigail McAlister, is not your damned gold!"

CHAPTER SIXTEEN

ABBY KNEW SHE WAS GOING to be late getting to the mine that Friday. It was payday, and she had to write the checks at home that morning, not to mention dashing off to the laundromat and the grocery store. But there was another chore hanging over her head, a very unpleasant one: she had to speak to Janet about that boyfriend of hers.

Janet arrived at eleven and Abby took a deep breath before launching in.

"Can you sit down a minute, Janet? I want to have a talk with you."

It was harder than Abby thought, though, because Janet was still a teenager and the girl's feelings were easily hurt. At first Janet was horrified, saying, "I wouldn't let Hank kiss me in front of the boys, honest, Mrs. McAlister." But then it got down to, "Well, maybe he did, but only once, and I told him he couldn't." And finally she said, "Listen, I just don't know what to do with him, Mrs. McAlister. I mean, he doesn't work or anything in the summer, and I'm real busy, you know." She twisted her hands in her lap, and Abby thought she was going to cry, but somehow she managed not to. Eventually, she blurted out, "I think I'm going to break up with him. When school starts again, you know."

"I see," said Abby carefully.

"He's not as cool as I thought, Mrs. McAlister, and I don't know, I guess I've kind of grown up this summer and, well, he hasn't. You know."

"Yes," replied Abby, hiding a smile, "I do know exactly what you mean."

"I should probably talk to Mom about it, shouldn't I?"

"I think your mom would be very happy if you did," said Abby, and then she let the subject drop. It was plain that Janet was indeed growing up.

When Abby did finally get up to the mine late that afternoon, the men were already emerging from the mine entrance, talking and laughing and trading jokes, their work week over, a rousing, rowdy Friday night in the old mining town awaiting them. Abby handed out the checks, thanking each man personally, as she did every week.

Len Hughes was the last man to leave. "Miz McAlister, that last winze we blasted is looking better and better. Gibbs'll tell you about it."

"Good. We could use some better ore. How's the leg doing?"

"Pretty good. It's still a little weak, but better every day."

"I sure am glad to hear that, Len. You go on and have a good weekend now." *Listen to me,* Abby thought, *I sound like a Westerner!*

They all drove off, leaving dust sifting back onto the road. Abby looked after them with a smile; they were her men, good men, and she wanted this new vein to pan out for them, too. John Gibbs had taken some samples from the vein to the assayer last week. The preliminary report had been excellent, but she was still waiting for the final word. This could be it, she told herself, but she held back from celebrating, held herself strictly in check. No sense getting her hopes up only to have them dashed.

"Hey there, missy," came John Gibbs' voice from the entrance, "I got me a bad problem in that new winze we're blastin' out. I just ain't sure of the kinda rock we're dealin' with and I can't figger the shoring loads for it."

Abby was mildly surprised. She'd never heard John Gibbs admit to a problem yet, much less one as elementary as calculating shoring loads. What was going on here?

"What do you mean, John?" she asked, puzzled. "You could figure shoring loads for the devil himself."

He shook his head lugubriously. "This here is a kinda rock I ain't never dealt with, I tell you. Wouldn't want to make any mistakes, now would I, missy?"

"No, of course not. So what do you plan on doing?"

"Well, now." John pushed his hard hat back so that strands of grizzled hair stuck out over his eyes. "I got me an idea yesterday. I phoned up that minin' engineer."

"Who?"

"That there friend of yers, Ty Hollinger."

"Ty?"

"Sure enough, seein' as he's not workin' no more. He said he'd be glad to help me and he's coming over right about now to take a look see."

His plan struck Abby like a thunderbolt. "Gosh darn it, John! You cooked this whole thing up..."

"Don't quite follow you there, missy. I got this problem in the new winze and I needed help."

"Problem! You have a problem, all right! Me. I'm your problem!"

"What's the matter? You don't think this Ty fella's any good at his job?" John asked serenely.

"Of course he's good at his job! It's just that I don't need a...a matchmaker, John. I wish you'd stay out of this."

"Do you now, missy?" He squinted, scrutinizing her closely, looking for all the world like a wise old scarecrow.

Then, of course, she heard the sound of Ty's Jeep crawling up the road. Boy, John had set things up perfectly. They were there all alone, face-to-face. But what did John think would happen? Would all their problems blow away with the wind?

"Abby," Ty said as he swung out of his Jeep. He sounded surprised. Obviously, John hadn't mentioned she'd still be there at that hour.

"Hello, Ty." She would try to act perfectly cool, perfectly natural and unaffected. This was no time for recriminations or confessions or anything of the sort.

"How've you been?" he asked carefully, having apparently decided to behave in a civilized manner, as well.

"Fine, thanks. And you?"

"Pretty good."

"Did you find a job yet?" This charade of civility was ludicrous.

"Had an offer to go to Alaska I'm still considerin'."

Abby's heart hit the ground. Alaska. Oh, my God, Alaska. "Oh." If only he wasn't so tall and straight and uncompromisingly handsome. If only his dark eyes didn't hold her and search out all her secrets. He'd had a haircut since last week, she noticed, and he wore a shirt she hadn't seen before, a red and blue checked one that clung to his torso and made her remember the whipcord strong feel of his chest and stomach.

"Well," Abby finally said, "I guess I'll be getting home. It's nice of you to help John out." Alaska.

"Hey, missy, not so fast," said Gibbs. "You come with us. I want you to see this vein."

"But, really, I don't know anything about veins, John." Boy, wasn't there any way to get out of this?

"You better take a look at this here ore. It's a beauty. I wouldn't be surprised if it assayed out at ten, fifteen dollars an ounce."

"It's that good, John?" asked Ty doubtfully.

"Bet my bottom dollar on it."

"And it's the same one Wayne's been followin'?"

"Well, sorta an offshoot of that one. The vein splits, see, and this one goes down and to the west of the other one." John cackled. "I think Mr. Wayne's missin' the real mother lode!"

"I hope so," muttered Abby darkly.

"Now, missy, you come on along and see this for yerself. This is gonna be your salvation, this here vein, and you should witness it with yer own two eyes."

"Okay, John, but it won't take long, will it? I promised Janet I wouldn't be late."

"Just long enough fer Ty to take a good look and tell me how far apart to set the shoring."

They grabbed some hard hats, snapped their lamps on and entered the dark, echoing shaft, their lights sending spears of brightness bouncing off the dripping walls, the shoring logs, the empty ore cars and ladders to other levels of the Nola Jane. Abby had learned some of the main crosscuts and winzes, but the one John was leading them to was new and she hadn't had time to visit it yet.

down ladders, around bends. The cool darkness never varied and Abby wondered how far they'd come; it seemed miles but, of course, it couldn't have been that far.

"See?" John pointed to a pile of rubble and a small opening. "That's where Wayne's crew blasted in. You see, Ty? Must be twenty, thirty yards inside our boundary."

"Sure seems to be. Course, I'd need my equipment..."

"Take my word fer it, boy, that's Nola Jane territory." John waved them on. "Now, it ain't far. See this vein, Ty?" And John tilted his head back so that they could see the dark, meandering thread of rock above.

"Six inches wide, if it's an inch," said Ty admiringly.

"Yep."

Abby wasn't exactly frightened in the mine, but she wasn't very comfortable, not the way Ty and John were. She hated the close, dank feel of the air, but the mine fascinated her despite her discomfort. Out of the somber bowels of the dripping granite came gold, that ancient metal that men had craved since the dawn of time. It seemed magic to Abby.

She wished this particular trip were over. Ty's closeness became more disturbing by the minute; he seemed to always be a step behind her, reaching out to take her elbow while she climbed down a ladder or over a pile of rock. Alaska. He must be joking! He wouldn't leave just like that. Or would he? The thought was like having a pail of ice water thrown in her face. *Don't take the job, Ty. Don't do it.*

Abby's mind was racing while John talked to Ty who listened, nodding, and took out a pad and pencil from his shirt pocket and scribbled notes.

"This is just ordinary granite," he told John. "Can't see your problem, actually. You can shore every thirty, forty feet, as usual."

"Well now, I thought this rock looked funny," John said. "Must be these old eyes of mine."

Ty looked at him oddly, but Abby knew what the old-timer had tried. He was as transparent as glass.

"Can we go now?" Abby asked.

"Sure, soon as ya take a good gander at this vein," John said. "See how it's all purple there? That means it's fluoride. It's a good indicator of gold ore. And the dark streak. See it?"

"Yes, there," Abby said, peering up. "That's it, isn't it?"

"Yep. That's rich ore, missy." John shuffled his feet. "As a matter of fact, it's the richest ore anybody's come across in this valley since the gold rush. I got the assay report back, missy."

"How good is it, Gibbs?" asked Ty.

"So good that Miz McAlister here needs to hire another crew so we can get it out faster."

"I can't afford to hire another crew, John," said Abby.

"Ya can now, missy. I tell ya, I need more men but we're all gonna be so goldanged busy I don't know how I'm gonna run this here operation anymore. Not by myself."

Abby pondered his statement in silence. Ty was curiously untalkative, too. She couldn't help giving Ty a sidelong glance, though. John's motives must be as obvious to Ty as they were to her; he wanted her to hire Ty to help him run the mine.

Well, maybe she could afford to now, if the vein really was rich. She tried to stifle her mounting excitement, but a sneaky joy tickled her insides, bubbling a little, percolating through her veins. Gold. Nola Jane's gold.

They made their way back through the maze of drifts and crosscuts to the original part of the mine, which looked more familiar to Abby. She recognized that stack of lumber and around the next turn she could see the light of the opening, a big round blossom of brilliance.

John stopped to check some wiring. "I'll be right there," he said. "I thought this darned switch didn't work so well today."

So Abby followed Ty, anxious to be out in the fresh air again, confused about the bomb Gibbs had just dropped on her head, wanting to be alone to sort out her thoughts. She wanted to be away from the mine and Ty, whose presence upset her and launched her all over again into the unending round of regret and longing and self-doubt and loneliness. And now—new hope.

The welcome light from the outside world reflected off the rough, black, glistening walls as they neared the entrance. Ty stopped and turned to Abby in the darkness; his light swung in berserk beams, dancing off the walls.

"Abby," he started to say, "I . . ." But he never finished.

Just then the whole world tilted crazily, flared and went dark, and a terrible pressure beat at Abby's ears, a concussion so powerful that it did not register as noise. Dust rose in a choking shroud, filling the air. She was aware only of movement and awful, ripping noises around her and dust in her nose and eyes and throat. She couldn't breathe, she couldn't see, she couldn't think.

Then there was utter silence and dust sifting down onto her and Abby was on the hard rock floor, stunned, deafened, horribly confused. Only a slim knife blade of light poked aslant through the thick dust, and Abby realized that it came from the carbide lamp on her own hard hat.

"Missy!" She heard the word faintly through the ringing in her ears. "Missy!"

John Gibb's figure stumbled toward her, his light stabbing through the dense air frantically.

"Here." But no sound came from her lips as she licked them, tasting grit, and tried again. "John, here."

"Missy, the Lord be praised! What in tarnation happened? Are you hurt?"

Abby sat up and tried moving the various parts of her body. "No, I'm okay, I think." Then it struck her. "Ty, oh, my God, he was closer to the entrance! Ty!" It was a scream by then, a cry that echoed off the walls of the mine. She scrambled up, not even aware of her bruises and cuts.

"Hold it. Take it easy, missy. I see him." John bent over, his funnel of light swinging down. She could see a man's legs, so covered by dirt that she could have missed them. "I gotta get this timber off him." John cursed under his breath and heaved at a big log that had collapsed into the passageway.

"Can I help?" gasped Abby.

"Here, push, but be careful it doesn't settle onto him. Goddamn, we gotta get this offa him."

They struggled, two shadows in an immensity of blackness, their lights cutting the dark into segments.

The log moved slightly; the rumble and scrape of falling rocks clattered around them. "Push," said John, and Abby braced herself and pushed until the veins stood out on her neck.

"It's movin'. A little more," urged John.

But did either of them—a woman and an old man—have any more to give? They pulled some rocks away and tried again. Abby avoided thinking about anything but the effort of moving the timber. Her mind wanted desperately to ask *what if?* But she wouldn't let it.

They attacked the timber from a different angle and it shifted again. "Okay! I got it," grunted Gibbs. "If I hold it like this can you pull him out?"

Abby stepped back, breathing hard, and took hold of Ty's jeans. Then she dragged at them. Yes! He was moving; she dug her heels in and pulled and he came free just as a jumble of rocks collapsed under the log.

"He out?" gasped John.

"Yes, he's out," cried Abby, and John let go of the log, stepping nimbly out of the way as it fell.

She knelt down by Ty's side and trained her light on his face. It was gray with dust, his eyes closed, a raw scrape on his forehead. "Ty," she whimpered, brushing at the dirt. Was he breathing?

John kneeled on the other side of Ty, put a finger on the pulse at his neck and said, "He's alive, missy."

She closed her eyes and swayed, so relieved that she felt consciousness recede.

"Missy!" John's cry brought her back abruptly.

"Oh, John . . . I'm sorry . . ."

"Okay now. He's alive, but I can't tell if he's hurt bad or not. Ya watch him. I'm goin' to see if we can get outta here. I'll be back right away."

And then Abby was alone, crouched on the cold, wet floor, holding Ty's head on her lap. Unaccountably, her thoughts were all concentrated on getting the dirt off his face, and somehow it mattered terribly. She was brushing at his eyes—how horrible to have grit in your eyes—when he stirred.

"Ty?" she whispered.

He groaned and she drew in her breath. He was in pain. How bad were his injuries? "Ty? My darling, please, wake up."

He moved again and his eyes opened, blinked, opened again. "Abby?" he mouthed.

"Oh, Ty! Where does it hurt?"

"Um." He licked at his dirt-encrusted lips. Oh, that awful grit!

"Ty, darling. Oh, please..."

"What...?"

"There was, I don't know, some kind of explosion. John's looking to see if we can get out."

"Explosion?"

She pushed his hair back and smoothed some dirt off his face. "I don't know what really happened. It was awful. A timber fell on you but John and I got you out."

"You okay?"

She gave a high-pitched laugh, near hysteria. "Me? I'm fine. Don't worry about me. How are you?

"Hurts to breathe. Right side."

"Don't talk. You'll be fine," she said fiercely.

"Missy?" she heard, and John's light swung along the wall toward her.

"Here, John. He's awake."

"Good, good."

"His chest hurts."

"Don't doubt it. That darn log was on it."

"Can we get out?" Abby asked.

"Not a raindrop's chance in hell," said John. "That hole's filled in with five feet of rock now. The whole thing went. Now, I'd like to know who in tarnation blew up this mine!"

"John, what do we do?" asked Abby.

"Don't worry about that for a minute, missy. I'm more concerned with Ty here." John kneeled down and shone his light on Ty. "How bad are ya?"

"Don't know. Hard to breathe."

"Probably got some busted ribs. You hang in there, boy."

Ty tried to raise himself on an elbow but sank back, grimacing. "What you going to do, John?" he wheezed.

"I'm gonna go on back to where Wayne's crew blasted that hole and get out through the Golden Slipper. That's the closest way. There are others, too, but they're farther from town. Then I'll get a ride, maybe walk, to the nearest phone and call up a rescue party."

"How long will that take, John?" asked Abby. "Ty needs . . ."

"Well, now, it's near a mile to the hole, then maybe four out to the entrance. I'll have to climb out of the Golden Slipper, seein' as no one's in the hoist shack now. Then walk out to the road. Five, six hours."

"Oh, no. That's a long time. What about Ty?"

"He'll make it, missy, a young fella like him. There's not much else we can do. We can't carry him out all those miles and ladders and stuff. You got a better idea?"

"No."

"You know your way in the Golden Slipper? I can tell you . . ." said Ty with effort.

"Sonny, save yer breath. I knew that mine before ya was born. I can find my way in the dark, and I may have to if this battery runs out." He slapped the lamp on his hard hat. Then he pulled down the straps of his overalls and unbuttoned his shirt. "Here, missy, you take this. It ain't much but I don't need it and you two'll get a mite chilly sittin' here and waitin'."

"Oh, John, you're sure you'll be okay?" asked Abby.

"Darn, woman! Sure, I'll be okay. You watch that fella of yers there and don't worry none over me."

"Hurry, please."

"I'll hurry, missy, and I'll get you two outta here by morning. Then I'm gonna find the no-good scum who blew my mine up!" John turned, taking his beam of light with him, and moved away down the inky corridor of rock until Abby couldn't hear even the faint echo of his footsteps.

She was alone with Ty, crouched in the maw of a black beast, swallowed alive. Panic clutched at her with sharp talons and she fought it off. She had her light. Ty's was lost somewhere under the fallen rubble, but hers was bright. She was unhurt, and John would get them out; she only had to wait a few hours. Only a few quick hours . . .

She looked down at Ty. His eyes were closed and his breathing was labored, his face etched in lines of pain. *Oh, hurry, John!*

"He gone?" Ty asked weakly.

"Yes. He said a few hours, Ty. You can hang on, can't you?"

"Sure, I can. I'm okay."

Abby felt in her pocket for a handkerchief. She was sure she had one...She found it, a crumpled ball in one pocket, which she had to squirm to reach. She spat on one corner and tried to wipe at the dirt on Ty's face, but she only made muddy streaks.

Time passed. She grew chilly and cramped from sitting so still with Ty's head in her lap, but she was afraid to move. She kept a hand on his chest to assure herself that he was breathing. She'd wrapped John's shirt around Ty but it wasn't enough; she could feel his hands and they were like bricks of ice. Could he be in shock? People died of shock, she knew.

He moved once in a while, obviously in pain. "Abby," he said.

"I'm here. Ty, darling, I won't leave you. You're going to be fine."

"Sure am," he said, trying to smile.

More time ticked by, but far too slowly. Abby began to shiver. She looked at her watch in the light of her lamp; it was 7:24. She still had hours to wait, hours and minutes and seconds, and Ty's breath was gasping away with each one of them.

At 8:10, Ty coughed. It must have hurt him terribly. *Hurry, John.* She bent her head to whisper encouragement to him when she saw a dark stain on his lips. Blood. He coughed again, grimacing in pain. Abby wiped his lips with her dirty handkerchief and stared at the red spots on it. Blood... His lung could be punctured. She closed her eyes and fought terror while her body shivered in great quivering spasms as the cold seeped into her bones.

At 9:47, Abby considered the fact the battery of her carbide lamp might wear down and leave her in pitch darkness. No light! She debated whether to turn her lamp off now and conserve the battery, but she tried it and the blackness smote her like a living creature.

Ty was restless, half conscious. He coughed occasionally and Abby found herself waiting for those awful wracking sounds. Waiting and waiting . . .

Around ten-thirty, Ty seemed to rouse. "Abby?" he asked clearly.

"I'm here."

"I can taste blood in my mouth," he said.

"You must have cut your lip."

"Sure," he said. "I love you, Abby. You'll remember that, won't you?"

Good Lord, he thought he was dying! Abby's heart froze, but her voice sounded normal. "Of course I will, Ty. You can tell me every day. And I'll tell you every day how much I love you."

"Took you long enough to figure it out," he said with a ghost of his old humor.

She squeezed his hand and thought: *If he dies I can't go on. He can't die.* "John'll be back soon, Ty."

"Yeah, the old coot." Then he coughed and gasped for breath and Abby felt so helpless, so horribly frightened and alone. *John, hurry!*

Her light started dimming at 11:40. Why hadn't someone recharged it properly? The batteries were supposed to be recharged every night! John had told that to everyone over and over. But then she remembered: this one had been used all day, and now it had been on for hours longer, and it was going out. Her heart thudded with panic; she felt as if she were going blind. Yet, strangely enough, she had stopped shivering. She was cold, though, cold to her bones, and so very tired.

Oh, my God, what if something happened to John? She thought suddenly: what if he'd fallen or gotten hurt or had a heart attack? What if no one came for them? What if Ty died in her arms and no one ever found her and she was buried alive in this mine, in Nola Jane's mine? *Nola Jane, how do I get out of this one? What do I do now?*

Her circle of light narrowed, and then it dimmed some more. Ty moved restlessly, mumbling. She was thankful, at least, that he was unaware of the long, slow crawl of frigid hours that had passed, that still must pass.

Then her mind meandered sluggishly back to the explosion. Someone must have set it off. Who? Why?

Wayne came up repeatedly as the most likely suspect. Kevin Wayne. Had he done it himself? Did he mean to trap them in the mine?

The last time Abby saw her watch it said twelve-fifteen. Shortly after that, the carbide lamp dimmed, flickered, gave off its characteristic warning whistle, flared once and went out. Then there was only the icy, echoing darkness around her, the weakening rasp of Ty's breathing and the endless night ahead.

CHAPTER SEVENTEEN

THE SOUND OF CRUMBLING ROCK and a thin, sharp spear of light partially roused Abby from her state of numbness. And then there was another spear and another, arrows of brilliance that blinded her. She closed her eyes against the intrusion.

"So cold, so cold," Abby whispered against Ty's frigid cheek. And then she subsided, passing back across that fine edge of consciousness into insensibility once again.

She was dreaming, not unpleasantly. There were voices echoing somewhere in her head and too many lights pressing on her eyelids. But then she sensed warmth, too, and that was nice. Dreaming, she felt herself rising on her own accord—but, no, she was being lifted, and there were many hands supporting her. Warm, gentle hands. And then the light was too dazzling to stand and she needed to turn her head away, but everywhere she twisted there was only more light.

"No," Abby moaned, feeling herself being set down. A hand at her jaw, was keeping her head still. "Ty..."

"Mrs. McAlister. Wake up, Mrs. McAlister. Come on, now, Abby wake up." The hand gripped her jaw more forcefully. It was starting to hurt. "Come on, now. It's Doc. Wake up."

"Don't," she protested through dry lips. "You're hurting me."

"Good. Now open your eyes. You're all right, only a little shock and cold. Try to wake up."

Abby saw him finally with blurred vision. It was Doc, all right. Then she couldn't still be dreaming, and there *were* blankets around her, wonderfully warm blankets! "You found us," she said. "Oh, my God, you found us!"

"Lie there and take it easy," said Doc. "I'll be right back."

Abby could hear him issuing orders, and as awareness slowly seeped back she saw dozens of men hurrying around. She focused on a stretcher; John was leaning over it alongside Doc.

"Ty!" Abby cried, rising to a sitting position, panic coursing through her. "Ty!"

"Take it easy." It was Rob Loring, pressing her down onto the blankets. "You've had quite a shock. And you need to thaw out there, lady. Just take it easy."

Abby obeyed reluctantly. "Is Ty... is he..."

"He's pretty banged up. Doc thinks he'll be all right if we can get him to the hospital. We've radioed for a chopper from Colorado Springs."

"Oh, my God!" Tears sprang into her eyes. "Rob..."

"I know. I know. Now don't worry. You're going along, too."

"But I... I can't. The kids..."

"Karen has them, and they know you're okay by now. You need to be gone over thoroughly, Abby, and Doc doesn't have the facilities."

"I'll be with... Ty?" she asked, afraid, so afraid to leave the children but scared, also, to let Ty be taken from her.

Rob stroked her head. "It's all right now, Abby. I'm sure Ty is going to make it." A moment later, he asked. "Hear that?"

Abby shook her head, confused.

"It's the helicopter. They're landing below us in a clearing. It's all set." Rob pressed a button on his radio and spoke into it for a minute. "Okay now, Abby, we're going to put you in the front of the Blazer. Ty's in the back already. Okay?"

"Okay," she said weakly, still weaving in and out of her dazed state, her brain sluggish from the endless hours of bone-chilling cold.

A funny thing happened then; Abby began shivering. Her body shook, her teeth chattered. She didn't even feel cold anymore, but her body wouldn't stop.

"It's normal," said Rob, "when you start warming up. Just relax and it'll go away."

Rob lifted her and she found she could walk, but her legs felt numb, as if she'd slept on them. She crossed the space between where she'd been lying and the Blazer, and saw the stretcher in the back and Ty, his white, stricken face peering out from a mountain of blankets. *He's dead,* she thought, horrified. *He's dead and they aren't telling me!*

"He's not dead," said Rob, and she realized she'd spoken aloud. "Here, let me help you up. That's it. Now keep the blanket around you. There." Finally, they began to move. Rob drove and John Gibbs called out to her from behind the Blazer as they pulled away from the mine.

"You do like the doctors say!" came his old, wheezing voice. She turned in her seat and watched his figure grow smaller and smaller, until the Blazer rounded a bend and he was gone.

"He saved us," she whispered. "John did it." Shivering, she pulled the blanket around her.

"You bet he did," replied Rob, his capable hands steering carefully as the paramedic in the back held the stretcher steady. Abby kept turning to look at Ty, to reassure herself that he was still alive. But he looked so pale and silent, she finally trained her eyes out the front window.

"I wish I could see Sean and Ben," said Abby as they neared the clearing where the helicopter had landed.

Rob turned momentarily and gave her a glance. "Tell you what. I'll drive Karen and the boys to the hospital this afternoon. Okay?"

"Would you, Rob? Would you?"

"Of course. Now settle back and take it easy. You'll be in the Springs within fifteen minutes. Everything's all right."

"And you'll go get the twins?"

"I promise." He smiled, pulling up alongside the chopper.

Abby must have dozed part of the way to Colorado Springs. She remembered the dark, massive hump of Pike's Peak to their left, and alongside her the stretcher and Ty. There was color in his cheeks now, wasn't there? Occasionally, while the helicopter's rotors beat at the thin air and her body shivered along with the vibration, she opened her eyes to sunlight, brilliant, beautiful sunlight all around her. She'd drift, half asleep, half awake, as if her brain were working in some kind of thick, clinging bog. Sean and Ben appeared in the mist of her mind's eye, but then they disappeared, and the whole world seemed to tip. Suddenly they were motionless, only the chopping sound of the rotors keeping Abby in touch with reality.

She knew she really was coming around when the doctor in emergency looked down her throat with one of those Popsicle sticks and she gagged and pushed his hand away. No wonder Sean and Ben always objected to the doctor!

"I'm all right," insisted Abby, "but can you please go see how Mr. Hollinger is?" Of course, everyone in emergency was efficient but patronizing, and Abby was unable to learn a thing about Ty.

"Is he your husband?" asked a nurse. But when Abby replied that he wasn't, the woman said, "Well, I'm afraid I cannot give out that information, Mrs. McAlister."

Abby was taken to a room, the blankets still wrapped warmly around her; the doctor's diagnosis was hypothermia. His instructions were for Abby to have a night's rest in the hospital.

"Please, can you get someone to find out about Mr. Hollinger?" begged Abby as she was settled into her bed. "That's Mr. Tyson Hollinger. Please." And then she had to squirm and fret until finally, an hour and a half later, a nurse poked her head in the door. "He's going to be fine, Mrs. McAlister. He's in room 303, down the hall, to the left."

"Thanks." Abby beamed. "Thank you very, very much!"

She was quite unsteady on her feet, but nevertheless Abby peered out of the door, checked the hallway and, holding the scanty hospital gown together in the back, sneaked down to room 303. Pushing open the door gingerly, Abby found him, an oxygen tube in his nose, some sort of other tube in his side. What had they done to him?

The room was semidark, the curtains drawn. Abby crossed the cold floor to his bed and rested her hand on his. Why all these tubes?

"Ty," she whispered, "can you hear me? Ty?"

His eyes opened slowly, drowsily. He'd been drugged or...or maybe he was still out of it. Oh, dear. "Abby." He licked his lips. "Hi."

"Hi, sport," she said, smiling, her heart heaving a sigh of relief. "How do you feel?"

"Godawful." He circled his lips again with his tongue. "Water? Can I have some water?"

"I don't know," confessed Abby. "I sneaked in and I don't know any more than you. Maybe you better not."

He swore softly, his eyelids threatening to close. "Wanna climb in with me?" His words were slurred, too; he'd definitely been given something.

"Bad idea. They'd kick us both out."

"You okay?"

"I'm perfect."

"Honest?"

She nodded slowly, sinking down into the chair just in time for the nurse to catch her. "You shouldn't be in here," admonished the woman. "I take it you belong in bed yourself." She eyed Abby's attire. "Come on. What room are you in?"

"I don't know the number," said Abby, rising against her will, allowing herself to be led to the door. "I'll be back later," she said over her shoulder. "I promise."

Shortly, Ty's nurse had Abby tucked into her own bed. "Now, try to stay put, Mrs. McAlister. You don't want any complications to spring up."

"All right," said Abby, "but can you tell me something about Mr. Hollinger's condition? I mean, it's like it's top secret or something."

The woman shrugged. "A lung collapsed. Broken rib, I believe. They're simply draining out the fluid now."

"The tubes?"

"Standard procedure. He'll be fine, I'm sure. Now you get some rest."

Amazingly, Abby did doze off, and awoke to find Rob and Karen standing over her. On the other side of Abby's bed were the twins, their eyes as round as saucers. And John Gibbs stood off to one side, stiff and uncomfortable-looking.

"You okay, Mommy?" asked Sean tentatively.

She gave them each a big, long hug. "Mommy is just fine, babies. They're keeping me overnight, though. You know how careful doctors like to be."

"Mommy," asked Benny in a sad voice, "do we have to go back to Newark now?"

Abby was touched. "No, honey, we're staying. Cripple Creek is home now."

"Boy, am I glad. It's the neatest place in the whole world."

A broad smile split Abby's face. It *was* the best place in the world. Leave it to the kids to recognize the simple truth. She'd been so worried about the twins, but they were just fine.

"And how's Ty doing?" Karen asked.

Abby told them all she knew before Karen started to usher the boys out and head to the cafeteria. Hospital regulations stated that no one under age twelve was allowed in the rooms, Karen told her at the door.

"I'll see you two little imps tomorrow at home," promised Abby, giving them a big smile and blowing them each a kiss. "And thanks, Karen. I don't know what I would have done..."

"Forget it. I'm just happy you're okay... That filthy scum Wayne..." But Rob silenced her, explaining that he and John had a lot to tell Abby and that he'd meet Karen and the boys in the cafeteria.

John approached her bed gingerly. "Well, missy, yer lookin' fit as a fiddle, considerin'." He rubbed at the gray bristles on his chin.

Abby pushed herself up. "John, you saved our lives. I can never thank you enough. You're a hero." She took his wrinkled hand in hers and squeezed it.

"Aw, gee, missy, anyone would've done the same."

She shook her head. "No one else could have done it. No one else knows the mines like you do."

"She's right, Gibbs," said Rob. "The town owes you a vote of thanks."

"Get outta here," said John, and Abby saw a blush rise from his neck.

"Abby, a few things happened after you and Ty were flown out," began Rob. "I'd like to explain it all to you."

"It was Wayne, wasn't it?" guessed Abby. "I thought..."

"To be honest with you," said Rob, "we might never have proved who set off that dynamite, but the culprit marched himself into my office just after you were flown here."

"You mean...Kevin Wayne confessed!" gasped Abby, taken aback.

Rob shook his head. "Not exactly. It was Herb Lacouter, an employee of Wayne's who actually planted and set off the charge. He confessed he sheared the pin on the jack leg, too."

"Wayne paid him, then," surmised Abby.

"Exactly. Herb's got six kids, and another on the way. Guess he needed the money."

"But . . . attempted murder?" Abby shuddered.

"Herb claimed that was why he turned himself in. He was only supposed to frighten you off, Abby, not harm anyone. I suppose Wayne thought you'd go broke trying to reopen. At any rate, Herb swears he thought everyone had left for the weekend . . ."

"Baloney! Our cars were there. Ty's and mine."

"He claims he saw them, but figured they were two old clunkers left there over the weekend."

"Do you believe him?"

"He was frightened, all right. I tend to think he's telling the truth, Abby, but that's for a court of law to decide, not us."

"And Wayne?" asked Abby.

"Oh, he'll be charged with complicity. They'll both be punished."

Abby sighed. "It doesn't seem like enough. I mean, we could've been killed, Rob."

"I know. I'm bettin' the Teller County D.A. will ask for an attempted murder charge. It'll be up to Wayne's lawyers to prove otherwise."

"Good. I hope he rots in jail. He deserves it. You should see Ty. He's all hooked up to tubes and drugged . . . It's terrible."

"There's more," said Rob. "The phone's been ringing off the hook, Karen told me. Every TV station in the state wants interviews, and they want to film the mine. I guess they sort of like the idea of a lady mine owner." He turned to John then. "And they want to interview the hero of the hour, too."

"Hero, my tail!" growled John, but Abby could see he was flattered.

"Well, John, no one'll call you daft anymore, will they?" commented Abby. "You might get more job offers than you can handle."

"I ain't leavin' you, missy, don't worry. Now that we hit the mother lode, you need me more than ever."

That remark sobered Abby. Her mine. Blown to smithereens, shut down. Just when they'd hit it rich. She could have cried. "Oh, my poor mine. How'll I ever get it going again?" she moaned.

Rob smiled as if he were party to a state secret. "Well, Abby, the town's got this idea. You see, the old mining towns always look after their own, and you're one of our own now."

"But, Rob, I just moved here."

"I guess it's not how long you've lived in Cripple Creek, but what you give to the town. Anyhow, everyone is organizing to go on up to the Nola Jane and open her up again. Wilt Jenkins even donated his bulldozer..."

Abby felt tears sting her eyes. "Oh, Rob..."

He shrugged. "You'd do the same."

"But how can I ever repay them all?"

"You strike it rich and keep that mine going, Abby. You brought some pride back into this town."

Abby was allowed by Ty's doctor to sit with him that night for an hour. She wished it could have been all night, but then Ty did need his rest in order to make a complete recovery. Still, she hated the thought of leaving him, and held on to each minute in his room as if it were precious, as if it might be their last together.

He dozed on and off; the effects of the painkilling injection given him had still not worn off. While he was awake they talked quietly, relieved, even laughing sometimes to think how warm it was in the hospital room and how cold it had been that horrible night. Then when he slept, Abby grew worried and tense: was he really all right? She'd watch his chest rise and fall and rise and fall until she had to blink and rub her eyes. She kept his hand in hers, though, savoring the warmth, vowing that she'd never let either of them be cold again. Never.

He awakened once, and smiled at her. "You still here?"

"My room is boring," she said lightly.

"Tell me what happened again, Abby. I'm so damn confused you'd think I got kicked by a mule."

She told him everything that Rob had told her, and how John Gibbs had saved them, and how the town was going to reopen the mine.

"That old coot," said Ty wonderingly.

"He wants you to help him run the mine, Ty," Abby said.

"Yeah, I do recall him hinting around . . ."

"And *I* want you to help him, too. Full wages. I guess I'll be able to afford you now."

"Abby, you always could afford me. Love comes free."

She smiled and glowed all over and held his hand until he dozed off again.

The light in the room began to fade slowly, the purple shadows sneaking out of the corners. Abby rubbed her arms, ridiculously afraid of the inevitable dark, and snapped on the reading lamp beside Ty's bed. She was just settling back to watch over him when it struck her like a jolt of electricity: until Rob had mentioned the Nola Jane, she hadn't given the mine a single thought.

Not once. All she'd cared about was Ty, his welfare, what he'd been through for her.

"Wow," Abby whispered wonderingly. How had that happened? And, too, she'd forgotten all about the explosion and Kevin Wayne. Nothing had mattered, nothing but Ty.

"Now there's a thoughtful face," commented Ty quietly.

"You're awake."

"What were you thinking about, Abby?" He tried to move but subsided. "Man, oh, man, does that smart!"

Abby jerked to her feet, alarmed. "Are you all right? Should I ring for the nurse?"

He waved a hand at her. "No. They'll just tell you to leave."

"You're right."

"So what were you thinkin' in that pretty little head of yours?"

"Oh...nothing," replied Abby, looking down at her silly hospital slippers.

"Come on."

"Well... I don't want you to get a swelled head, Ty Hollinger, but I was thinking how grateful I am that you're alive."

"Me, too." He laughed lightly. "And was that all?

"You into mind reading or something?"

"With you I am. Well?"

"Oh, darn. I was thinking that the mine important as our health. You know, yo kids'." She shrugged airily, as if dismis

"So security comes in other packag

Abby thought a minute, and th squarely. "I'll regret saying this a h

I just know I will...But you were right that morning when you stormed out of my house. All that glitters is not my gold."

"Well, good for you!"

"But," she was quick to add, "it's still right up there on the top of my list."

"Well, that's okay, now that you've found that rich vein. You won't have to worry anymore."

"Ty, you know I'll always worry," confessed Abby. "I know there's gold in the Nola Jane, but it won't make me rich. You know that, Ty. Comfortable, maybe, but not rich."

"Things could be worse," Ty said dryly.

"You know, my mother told me that Nola Jane and Randy lost their money when all the mines closed down. They moved to New York and Randy worked as an engineer on the tunnels under the Hudson River. But they were happy."

"See? Life goes on."

"Will you remind me of that once in a while? When I start worrying again?"

Ty gave her a crooked grin. "Well, ma'am, does that mean I can make an honest woman of you so we can get started on having that little girl?"

"What little girl?"

"The one who'll inherit the Nola Jane," he said f-factly.

al," said Abby teasingly, "on one condi-

my blasted washing machine."

GIFTS FROM THE HEART

MAIL-IN-OFFER

OFFER CERTIFICATE

I have enclosed the required number of proofs of purchase from any specially marked "Gifts From The Heart" Harlequin romance book, plus cash register receipts and a check or money order payable to Harlequin Gifts From The Heart Offer, to cover postage and handling.

002

CHECK ONE	ITEM	# OF PROOFS OF PURCHASE	POSTAGE & HANDLING FEE
	01 Brass Picture Frame	2	$ 1.00
	02 Heart-Shaped Candle Holders with Candles	3	$ 1.00
	03 Heart-Shaped Keepsake Box	4	$ 1.00
	04 Gold-Plated Heart Pendant	5	$ 1.00
	05 Collectors' Doll Limited quantities available	12	$ 2.75

NAME ______________________________

STREET ADDRESS ____________________

CITY ______________ STATE ________

Mail this certificate, designated number of proofs c
back page) and check or money order for postage
Gifts From The Heart, P.O. Box 4814
Reidsville, N. Carolina 27322-4814

NOTE THIS IMPORTANT OFFER'S TER

Requests must be postmarked by May 31, 1988. Only proofs of purc marked "Gifts From The Heart" Harlequin books will be accepted. T cash register receipts and a check or money order to cover postage a accompany your request and may not be reproduced in any manner. prohibited, taxed or restricted by law. LIMIT ONE REQUEST PER NA ORGANIZATION OR ADDRESS. Please allow up to 8 weeks after re shipment. Offer only good in the U.S.A. Hurry—Limited quantitie available. Collectors' dolls will be mailed to first 15,000 qualifyi submitters will receive 12 free previously unpublished Harlequi handling refund.